KEYS

To Living from the Inside Out

By:

Elfie H.M. Leddy

 www.trafford.com

North America & international
toll-free: 1 888 232 4444 (USA & Canada)
phone: 250 383 6864 ✦ fax: 812 355 4082

Table of Contents

Acknowledgements

I thank everyone who is in my life to abuse me, trigger me, challenge me, manipulate me, criticize & judge me, believe in me, uplift me, nourish me, and accept & love me. You have caused me to look within myself to explore & find the treasure & potential of my authentic identity.

Some of you know who you are & many of you precious souls have no idea what important mirrors & helpmates you were during our interactions in my journey of self-awareness.

A special thanks to Katrice Balmer for giving me permission to use her introductory poem, Homecoming to reflect the content & intention of Keys. My heart-felt thanks also to Michael West of MousePad Publishing. I value his intuitive ability to produce my vision of the book cover & accurately duplicate the models.

I also extend my heart-felt thanks to Kolina Logan & Katrice Balmer, for the arduous task of proofing my manuscript. Their diligent & articulate dedication to this task was invaluable, as was the feedback from my dear soul sister, Aimee Johnston, who courageously applied the material in the first few chapters of KEYS & found it works!

On a deep soul-level, this book could not have come into existence without meeting 'The Evergreens' through deep-trance medium & special friend, Michael Blake-Read. Their gentle but powerful support gave me both the courage and nourishment to heal my wounded being, confirming that we are always guided by kindred souls. With great joy & deep respect, I thank them for touching my soul and irrevocably changing my life.

Please accept my deep appreciation of you all!

I dedicate this book to all who have mustered the courage to begin this most fascinating & fulfilling journey of exploring your own consciousness & expanding your awareness. Remember, you are always guided by divine grace in action!

Homecoming...

Many moons have come and gone since my feet first
touched this shore
Many lifetimes too have passed since I felt the wind and
more.
The guidance that first spurred me on is Oh, so very
present,
And in my Heart I truly know that this is Heaven sent,
Assisting me and guiding me to look both long and deep,
Unearthing all those parts of me that have been so fast
asleep.

The flickering of the eyelids as I slowly start to waken,
The breathing starts to quicken as I realize I'm shaken
Right to the center of my Soul because I surely know,
This Life of mine is at the point where it is set to grow.
The Purpose that I started with has made its presence
known,
'Tis now I see, it carries me, much closer to my Home...

... From the heart and soul of Katrice Balmer"

Chapter 1

The Framework of Reality

"Energy is the universal frequency upon which all consciousness rides."

BEFORE you can understand how your mind works, or what role your mind, biological body, and spiritual identity play in this physical experience, you need to know what kind of reality this is. A framework defines how everything works within any reality. The dictionary defines framework as *'the structure'*, and just as the structure of the branches of a tree determines its overall shape, this reality's framework defines the nature of experience within it.

Everything in existence, including you, consists of energy - electromagnetic energy pulsing on various frequencies. From our perception, the universe looks like an empty void dotted with what appear to be lifeless planets. In fact, the universe is teeming with life – creative consciousness energy in a constant state of self-expression, interaction, and transformation. This consciousness experiences itself as fully on their frequencies within our universe as we do on ours. Attuned only to the frequencies that pulse on the same or on a lower energy vibration than your own, you are generally unaware of the frequencies that pulse at a higher and faster rate than you do. It is much like turning a dial to the band-wave of a particular radio station. You can only tune into other frequencies when you raise the vibration of your own consciousness to match those frequencies. This includes your own higher frequency spiritual identity.

Energy is the universal frequency upon which all consciousness rides regardless of its form. Energy is neutral, so it is consciousness that directs what form energy will take within the framework of each reality. Despite the diversity of consciousness in existence, it all came from, and stays connected to the originating energy source of all consciousness in existence. Although each type of consciousness experiences its own kind of creative expression, certain alignments do exist. There is a universal energy synchronicity between them although each operates on its own frequency. This synchronicity allows them to exist in the same space in inter-dependent relationships or to share this space without being aware of each other.

In this reality, human consciousness interacts on a cooperative inter-dependent level with earth and animal consciousness. As the physical backdrop for our life-games, Earth consciousness sustains both the physical environment and all forms of life residing on its surface. It also provides the raw materials with which human consciousness transforms thought projections into physical manifestations.

Your beliefs about this physical environment begin to develop the moment you are born. As a sentient being, you begin to accept collective root assumptions about reality as being true; assumptions that help maintain the appearance of constancy within this reality. The solar system's electromagnetic fields that surround this planet help maintain the cyclic activity and atmospheric conditions necessary to support the self-actualization processes of all consciousness within this reality. Yet, there is cause and effect connectivity between your individual creative experiences and the environment that can change both As a sentient biological-energy being you are influenced by this cause and effect activity whether you are aware of it or not. The dictionary defines 'sentient' as, *'responsive to or conscious of sense impressions'* and as *'finely sensitive in perception or feeling'*. Environmental fluctuations like the waxing and waning of the moon, tidal movements, and weather patterns influence both your state of mind and feelings as reflected by your changing emotions.

Your sensory perception of how your environment appears to you is uniquely your own. You can be one of six individuals watching the same sunset yet each of you will experience and describe this shared event in your own way. Your individual sensory responses will both support and alter the essence of what you collectively see to some degree. It may seem a moot point now, but perception is important when you want to change the kind of life experiences you have.

The frequency pulsation each kind of energy consciousness emits influences its shape and form in your environment. The slower the frequency pulsation, the denser an object will appear in this reality. For example, a rock has consciousness but since its energy vibrates at a much slower and lower frequency rate than your own, it appears solid and unmoving to you. A rock is no more solid than you are and experiences its own consciousness as fully on its frequency as you do on yours. You may think other kinds of consciousness are unaware of your existence but on an energy level, you are all aware of each other's presence and consciousness to varying degrees. Once you raise your own frequency, you can begin to change the nature of your interactions with these other forms of consciousness to varying degrees.

There is, in fact, nothing solid or constant about your physical environment outside of your belief that it is solid and constant. Mass consciousness supports the illusion of solidity of what is actually an energy holographic projection, continually created and reformed. Although the energy that produces this illusion originates from outside this reality, *mass consciousness within this reality supports the root assumptions that maintain its apparent constancy.* Your root assumptions duplicate these energy constructs so seamlessly your environment appears stable and unchanged to you. You continue to see what you expect to see not because it actually exists in that form, but because the energy of your *beliefs* maintains this illusion of constancy. On a larger scale, universal consciousness supports its solar and atmospheric framework, earth consciousness supports the environment's framework, and spiritual energy-entities support the framework of their biological sentient counterparts – you and me. Although they maintain their own integrity on their own frequency, these varied kinds of consciousness groupings help maintain the root assumptions human consciousness energizes within our existing reality.

Earth consciousness also mirrors the overall state or condition of human consciousness. It reflects either a balanced interactive synergy or imbalance in itself and/or with the natural environment. The harsher climatic environment experienced by prehistoric man was actually in perfect alignment with the lower frequency consciousness of the human and animal species at that time. A substantial energy shift in one results in a ripple effect that changes all other consciousness to some degree. As human consciousness evolved so did earth consciousness. The physical environment became more hospitable as humanity began to cultivate the earth and form interactive communities. When humanity worked with its natural environment by maintaining a balanced level of consumption, this synergy sustained both. However, when we began to manipulate and thoughtlessly destroy the natural environment, the resulting imbalance triggered earth consciousness to seek realignment of itself and its human inhabitants.

Many resulting climatic fluctuations not only help maintain the planet's essential environmental balances but also reflect harmony or imbalances of human consciousness in various geographic or cultural locations. Natural disasters often shift mindsets and create an opportunity for human consciousness to realign itself. Many people who have experienced earthquakes, volcanic eruptions, floods or other natural disasters say these events changed their lives by shifting their priorities, for a while at least.

The Integrity of Form

The density of any object results from the rate of oscillation of its energy particles. *Form constructs*, or what we consider solid objects in our physical environment, are no exception. Collectively we perceive these form constructs in a similar fashion, and doing so, reinforce the integrity of their form. This applies to everything in your environment, even those things that undergo a transformation, like a caterpillar turning into a butterfly or a small seed growing into edible fruit. When a caterpillar goes through its metamorphosis, the consciousness within its blueprint for existence ensures the emergence of a butterfly or moth, not a rose or mouse. Liquid transforms into vapor, then disappears, then appears as rain outside your cousin's window in Idaho or crystallized snow in the French Alps. Solid rock-like minerals can be ground to dust and with the application of intense heat or through chemical processes to create molten liquids easily transformed and molded into new kinds of materialistic form-constructs.

Although universal consciousness maintains the overall framework of this reality, our collective root assumptions support the stability of objects within our physical environment. These root assumptions ensure that all our form constructs, like the couch we sit on, maintain their form. Viewed under a microscope these form constructs are not actually solid. They are all comprised of subatomic energy particles in a constant state of chaotic activity within a void of space. Yet, to us the couch not only looks and feels solid, but thankfully also supports our body when we sit on it. The energy behind our belief that the couch is solid prevents us from falling through it. Despite all this re-creation of matter taking place, when you plan a vacation to Hawaii the islands will be in the same location as they were when your friends visited last month. A cup left on the kitchen counter will stay where you left it unless someone moves it. It will not have changed into an apple, book, or cat while you are out of the room. Your root assumptions *maintain a stability of form in the collective perception of your environment* even though each of you perceives and describes these conditions and form constructs in your own unique way. Despite these root assumptions, the physical environment is a holographic illusion, an illusion each of you can change.

Your physical body also maintains its form within a common genetic blueprint. If you are born with dark skin, your skin will remain so and not turn white halfway through your life, or vice versa. Rest assured you will not awake one morning, reach for your alarm clock and find your arm has turned into a bird's claw. A pregnant woman does not have to worry that she will birth a hedgehog instead of a human baby since her genetic blueprint is faithful to the framework of human DNA in spite of the potential dormant variables within that blueprint.

Your body is an excellent example of consciousness synchronicity at work within a complex biological framework. Comprised of countless individual cells that can be broken down to even smaller increments of subatomic particles, each cell knows its function in relation to its specific purpose as well as its cooperative functions with other cells. The consciousness of these individual cells ensures that when old cells die, new cells imprinted with their specific function automatically replace them. Outside of an imbalance called dis-ease (where the trilogy of your spiritual, mental & emotional self are not in balance), there is no confusion of purpose despite all this chaotic activity on a subatomic level as you move through the various developmental phases of your physical life. However, your beliefs about these developmental phases determines how you experience them and at what rate your aging processes take place.

This same kind of co-operative consciousness ensures that the form constructs within your environment do not compromise each other unless that is your intention. When you lean against a wall, you do not fall through the wall or merge with it. In actuality, with some frequency adjustments in your own consciousness, you could. The fun begins when you realize you can manipulate your reality and intentionally alter the relationship between yourself and these form constructs should you choose to.

When this happens spontaneously, you may think your imagination is playing tricks on you. As a shared event, you view such phenomenon with fearful and self-doubting awe and do not credit it as visual proof of energy manipulation. Experts of all kinds within the scientific community immediately attempt to explain away these events using the limited perception of their existing knowledge and beliefs about reality. I find such skepticism a hoot, considering the intention of science is to observe, examine, and experiment in order to expand our understanding of ourselves in relation to, and within our physical environment.

The Conscious You/The Subconscious You

Just for a moment, imagine that as a Spiritual energy-being you chose this physical experience and agreed to operate within the framework of this three-dimensional reality. Hence, you squeezed a portion of your multi-dimensional self into the confines of a physical body in order to experience yourself through that body's senses. You decide on an overall story line, choose your desired historical and ethnic environment, and gather your supporting cast. Then a portion of your higher frequency consciousness identity jumps into the biological form to play the leading role in your own personal Broadway hit called "Life on Planet Earth as (who you are now)'.

The point of focus on your outer reality while you are having this physical experience is your conscious view of this reality – or consciousness. The unseen inner portion of yourself still connected to your higher frequency spiritual self is your subconscious. The problem is, once you take up residence in a physical body you become enraptured and distracted by the extraordinary sensory feedback both it and your environment provide. You lose yourself within this rich sensory physical experience and forget all about your spiritual identity and intentions for being here. Your spiritual agenda sinks into your subconscious, beneath the surface of your conscious view of reality. Entrenched in the beliefs formed by this conscious focus, you begin to use only your outer five senses to interpret your physical experience.

It is because you keep forgetting why you are here that one corporeal or physical experience often leads to another and another, creating a cycle of physical experiences called reincarnation. Only this unique 3-dimensional reality enables you to project your thoughts outward as holographic manifestations and experience them first through physical sensation, then again through your conscious interpretation of these sensations. It is a wondrous experiment in projecting your inner consciousness into your outer reality. That is the prime reason physical *'earth lives'* are so coveted by spiritual beings and why the higher frequency aspect of your identity wants to come back time and time again.

In spite of forgetting why you are here, you are still connected to your spiritual identity through your inner consciousness, or subconscious. Imbedded within your psyche is the *curiosity* inherited from the consciousness of the Original Creator and its need for *stimulation* - the impetus behind your own consciousness' desire to learn more about itself. As a child, you expressed this innate curiosity and need for stimulation naturally, until conscious life programming compromised this innate trust in the spiritually creative portion of yourself - your imagination. When imagination, the *'imaging tool of creation'*, is stifled, the conscious connection to your spiritual identity weakens and you stop using this extra sensory resource. You forget the magical entities and creatures that played with you as a child are as 'real' as your parents and friends are now. You also forget you can wish your desires into reality.

Once an adult, you largely mistrusted your imagination unless you became an artist or work in a creative field. No longer stimulated by your inner imaging senses, you live only through your outer five senses and the conscious stimuli provided by your outer environment. This limited focus results in a repetitive cycle of similar kinds of experiences based on the beliefs formed by your individual life programming. You believe your conscious beliefs about reality *are* reality, when in fact they are not.

The Concept of Time

The concept of Time is unique to the framework of this particular reality. Once you leave the electromagnetic and gravitational grids surrounding Planet Earth and move into outer space there is no such thing as time, as we know it. Although a kind of time does exist outside of this reality, it is more an awareness of cause and effect resulting from the interaction between negative and positive electromagnetic energy. As difficult as this may be to grasp, it is a crucial key when you want to make changes within this reality. To your higher frequency consciousness (or Self as I shall call it, since it is still you), there exists only an ever-present NOW consisting of diverse experiences layered one upon each other in the same 'space' but on different frequencies. What prevents awareness of other frequency aspects of your much more expansive identity is your conscious focus. Like a radio dial, your conscious focus is set exclusively to the band wave of radio station Earth, in the year of, in the drama of whatever role you have chosen for yourself now.

Time creates a specific point of focus as you project, experience, and view the conscious manifestations of your inner thoughts. Time organizes events in such a way that you can evaluate both your thoughts and their holographic manifestation individually and progressively instead of simultaneously. If there were no time, you would experience every possible and probable result of each of your thoughts all at once. You would be aware of your past, present and future all at once. You would be aware of all of your other physical existences as well as the aspects of you operating on higher frequencies in other dimensions and realities.

Yikes! Under such sensory onslaught, it would seem impossible to maintain what you consider your conscious identity. You would not know who or where you are or where 'here' is without a point of reference like time. In fact, based on humanity's overall level of consciousness, if you could do so right now your existing mental and nervous systems could not handle it. You would short-circuit and implode or go insane under the deluge of so much information. Nevertheless, humanity is on the threshold of raising its consciousness in preparation for just such an expanded awareness of itself. This process involves remembering and becoming attuned to the different frequency aspects of your greater identity. Until this occurs, your mind uses time to organize your experiences so you can perceive your creative manifestations individually and consecutively. This progressive view is much like observing the individual frames of a motion picture filmstrip. Memory looks back to what you have already created and experienced on a sensory level and your thoughts move forward to envision future intentions and their desired or probable outcomes. However, the present, what you call your NOW is always your conscious point of awareness, focus, and creative action. Your NOW is the subjective point of focus from where you experience everything – past, present, and future.

Time itself was intentionally altered in this reality to control humanity. Prior to the implementation of the Gregorian calendar in the 1300s, biological man functioned on the same frequency wavelength as cosmic and earth energy. This symbiotic cycle operated on a 13 month, 28 day moon cycle calendar year. The artifacts of ancient cultures across the globe attest to this, as do repeated references to the 13th planet and the 13th astrological sign. Then, synergy with a central cosmic pulse kept human consciousness connected to its spiritual origins. The Gregorian calendar altered this biological resonance with the cosmos, physical environment, and our inner consciousness so those who used the power of this cosmic resonance could more easily control humanity.

Scientific research into the possibility that time can be manipulated has been going on for much longer than supposed. Although the discovery of what he called 'radiant energy' by the Russian scientist Nickola Tesla was suppressed in the 1950s, the Russians alone have been working on this technology for over seventy years. Their research confirmed the empty void of space was not empty at all. Rather it is seething with unlimited free energy. Based on the Russian premise of a unified energy field theory, they called this technology 'Energetics'. In North American free-energy research circles, it is referred to as Scalar Longitudinal Electromagnetic (EM) Waves Energy or *Scalar Energy* in short. Recently, scientists have dubbed it the *'time domain'*. They discovered time is actually a kind of compressed energy that exists outside of our 3-D reality but can be engineered to provide and manipulate energy within this 3-D reality. What is required is a simple mechanical or natural dipole to draw and collect this energy from the universe into a given location point within this reality.

Based on a variety of previous experiments, one of the most dramatic uses of Scalar Energy holds the potential to heal all disease in a completely non-invasive way. Diseased cells are not destroyed or altered when pumped with the frequency of this time energy as they are with existing medical intervention techniques. Instead, they are time-reversed back to when they were in healthy condition. Financed by the French Government in the 1960s and 1970s, experiments on lab animals and unsanctioned volunteer human participants resulted in an almost 100% success rate in reversing cancers, leukemia and many other chronic and fatal diseases.

Another dramatic use for Scalar Energy is in the production of free energy. Nickola Tesla said, *"Electric power is everywhere present in unlimited quantities and can drive the world's machinery without the need of coal, oil, gas, or any other of the common fuels."* He believed the successful engineering of these longitudinal electromagnetic (EM) waves using a dipole would enable everyone to generate their own energy without any environmental pollution. You purchase a generator or dipole, after which you can produce whatever energy you require at no cost. A Motionless Electric Generator (MEG), the first free-energy generator received its patent several years ago and was scheduled for production in the U.S. in 2004. Like many other radical but inexpensive alternate fossil fuel energy sources, the MEG has quietly slipped into oblivion.

The untapped potential within this vacuum of universal energy in space can change our world and reality. It all depends on how our Scientists and Governments intend to use it. The same technology can also be used for mass mind control, weather manipulation and weapons of destruction that make our existing nuclear weapons look like firecrackers. I feel weather manipulation and mind control experiments using this Scalar Energy have been going on since its discovery. Unexplained weather patterns, like the more recent movement of Katrina that devastated New Orleans deserve deeper scrutiny. Was Katrina and other global disasters a natural or orchestrated event? What also comes to mind is if the senseless and random acts of violence that were suddenly perpetuated by youngsters several years ago possibly a result of mind manipulation? I find it strange that they all had only a rather befuddled memory of what they did, as if something temporarily took over their minds.

Because your biological body is comprised of electromagnetic energy, you are already accessing this universal Scalar energy to some degree. The positive and negative polarities within your body make it your very own biological dipole. Each of you already manipulates time to some degree without knowing it. Think of when time seems to stand still and the hands on the clock barely seem to move versus when time flies. The variation in the time-duration of your physical experiences is a direct result of the focus and energy you project into any given event. Some of you are unaware that you have become quite adept at manipulating time and your reality in other ways as well.

Due to the frequency adjustments necessary for an essential shift in human consciousness, time is 'speeding up' to help raise humanity's frequency to a higher fourth dimensional reality. In such a reality your thoughts, which ride on energy frequency waves, would boomerang back to you and manifest almost instantly - all of them! Just imagine for a moment what it would be like to have every thought or idea you have racing through your mind now appear in your life as a real event or circumstance? You are already manifesting your thoughts without knowing it. Only you experience them in a kind of time-delay fashion that has been part of the framework of this reality throughout most of our known history. The rigid time orientation of this framework has already begun to change. Once you understand how thought and energy create your reality, how your mental systems use your own sensory data to create both your self-image and reality, you can begin to direct the process. You can then change your self-image and reality, *the latter being the by-product of the former,* not the other way around.

Your physical body is an extraordinary and extremely valuable vessel, for it houses both your outer and inner consciousness. Both provide you with a multitude of senses through which you perceive and interpret your reality. The mental mechanisms within your brain automatically process the sensory information it receives from both these sources. Your five outer senses of taste, touch, sight, hearing, and smell act as conscious interpretive tools, whereas your more expansive inner senses act as your spiritual interpretive tools. Your brain interprets and responds to all these energy frequencies in a specific manner. In turn, these sensory energy vibrations produce direct or indirect effects on other objects, persons, things, and events in your conscious physical environment. Operating only from your conscious perceptions, you miss the spiritual intention of why you create certain life circumstances for yourself. In order to direct your mental processes and utilize all the sensory resources you have at your disposal, you need to understand how your mind actually works to process all this sensory data.

Chapter 2

How Your Mind Works

"You create your outer reality by what your self-image believes."

YOUR mind processes everything you experience through both your outer and inner senses. Operating like a cosmic computer, its function is to record and categorize all sensory data. Although you view your world primarily from your conscious perspective, *your perception is the eye of your subconscious.* Perception is defined in the dictionary as, *"observable, discernable, impression, and intellection"*, among other things. Perception is the means through which your spiritual essence, or *Soul,* looks at what you create and experience in your conscious reality in order to learn more about itself.

All your actions are motivated by two primary needs: *survival* - to maintain your physical body's safety and biological needs, and *stimulation* - to feed your spiritual curiosity and need for creative expression so it can expand its awareness of itself by what it experiences in this 3-D reality. The automatic mechanisms of your brain, *your mental systems,* ensure you meet these two needs. From the moment you are born, this cosmic computer, your brain, automatically records everything in a vast generic storage compartment. It does so objectively - without exception and without judgment. It also records the physical sensations associated with each event as well as your thoughts of how you feel about these sensations. Your subconscious, or Soul, then views your outer reality *through* all this stored data.

Your mind is a wondrous mechanism! As a baby, you did little more than respond to your environment on a primal sensory level. Your perception of the world was based on the physical sensations you felt when your needs were or were not being met. Your mind records all sensory data relating to what you experienced in your immediate environment and from this forms your perception of the world. Once you learned to communicate through language, your mind's ability to assimilate this new kind of data automatically expanded. It refined its own processing system when you began to absorb a new kind of information - second-hand information. This second-hand information is the conscious beliefs of others or your *life programming*.

Model #1.

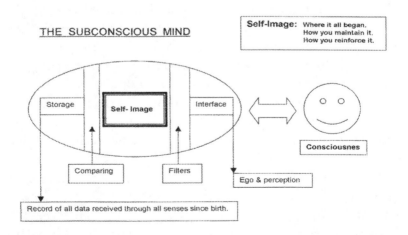

To understand the origins of your existing perception, you need to know how your mind actually manages and stores data.

Everything that comes in through all your senses goes through a process of *comparison* to everything your mind has recorded since the moment of your birth. Your subconscious views all this data with neutrality and without Judgment and compares it to everything previously recorded in your generic mental storage compartment. This sorting and comparing of related information is an automatic device, a mechanism of the brain that is always active - awake or asleep. Your thoughts are no exception. Your thoughts, *the impetus behind consciousness* that ensures your need for survival and stimulation is met are also recorded.

As this generic storage compartment accumulates more and more data, this comparing process automatically links similarities together. It takes similar data and files these related blocks of information into separate data banks or subject files. For Example: your mind automatically records your first dog experience in your generic storage compartment. Once you have a second dog experience, you now have two experiences with similar subject matter. Your mind creates a 'DOG' file and moves both dog-related experiences from the generic storage compartment into that subject file. All subsequent dog experiences throughout your life will be stored in this dog-related file. Simply put, the objective conclusions your mental systems reach throughout your life results from what is predominant in each of these subject files.

It is a neutral process of 'the more of'. What you have the most of in your mental data files forms your beliefs. Arising from this automatic process of comparison, these conclusions or beliefs create your inner *self-image*. This inner self-image in turn creates your conscious perception of yourself, based on everything you have experienced since birth. This automatic process either maintains or modifies this self-image as new data accumulates. Without this ongoing process of comparison, there would be no possibility for change. Your identity and conscious perception would result entirely from your earliest childhood experiences and stay that way throughout your whole life.

Your brain further refines how it references the growing volume of data your mind records. To streamline the comparison process, it forms a self-image for each of these separate data files, based on the 'more of' stored in each file. Thus, you have a self-image for your physical body, relationships, travel, family, physical pleasure, career, dogs, and all other subjects relating to your life experience. These self-images are either maintained or modified based on what these files contain as you move through the developmental stages of your life. As an adult, you can see now how you can be successful financially yet unsuccessful in relationship or inept at the most basic mechanical skills while extremely creative artistically. It all depends on the predominant information each of your mental data banks contains.

The consensus of all your self-images results in your overall identity, despite the contradictions and diversity of self-images in your various subject files. However, the files that hold the greatest amount of information and are most frequently accessed, form the foundation of your operating data banks. These are the files you access the most and therefore largely determine your basic view of yourself and perception of reality.

Your brain also records and compares the feeling-sensations attached to all the experiences recorded in your mental storage files. Utilizing a sophisticated method of cross-referencing, these feeling sensations are sorted into sub-files, each containing similar kinds of feeling sensations. You will have a variety of sub-file containing feelings like fear, shame, guilt, joy, satisfaction, awkwardness and so on. Cross-referenced with your experiences files, these sensation files influence your self-image as much as your experience subject files. Your sensory files may contain vastly unrelated experiences connected only by a similar feeling sensation. You will see how important this is when you want to change or expand your beliefs.

While your consciousness is engaged in your life experiences, your higher frequency spiritual self, or Soul, continues its own adventures of self-discovery in other historic periods as well as on other frequencies. As part of your greater identity, these kinds of experiences are recorded in your generic mental compartment. This is where all your metaphysical, defined in the dictionary as meaning: *'situated behind or beyond the physical'*, experiences are stored. Your mind processes the information in these generic files the same way as data received through your five senses. If these kinds of experiences do not get conscious validation, this data still stays in storage in related subject files. When you begin to consciously utilize these files, this data can inject new points of comparison that result in new conclusions about yourself and your reality. *These dormant files are your most powerful resource* as they connect you to your Soul identity. They are the key to your search for a meaningful life, and the means through which you can change your self-image and entire physical experience.

Interaction between your subconscious (where all these conclusions are recorded, sorted, and stored) and your conscious self (what you experience in your outer reality) takes place at the *Interface.* If this mental interface had a physical location, it would be located in the middle of your forehead between, and slightly above the eyebrows. This area has often been referred to as 'The Third Eye', or, the eye of your subconscious or Soul. The interface is the point of perception where information comes in through your senses and your description in the form of sensation, goes back out for your interpretation. Like the lens of your spiritual camera, it is from here that you view and communicate with both your conscious outer reality and subjective inner spiritual reality.

Another mechanism is all-ways active at this point of interface, your conscious *filters.* These filters ensure your survival and maintain your conscious self-image. Activated automatically, a filtering system for every self-image within each data bank protects your identity while you are having that particular kind of experience. Operating from your interface, this filtering system acts like a private security system managed by your conscious Ego. The dictionary defines Ego in part as, *'one of the three divisions of the psyche that serves as the organized conscious mediator between the person and reality'.* Your Ego uses this filtering system to protect your self-image/s by allowing in only what your beliefs allow. These filters create blocks, much like computer firewalls, to keep out any information that is not in alignment with the existing self-images in your operating data banks. You can see how this automatic protective filtering mechanism can be problematic. Since these filters are just the point between sensation, perception and description, they protect an identity based on a foundation of beliefs formed not only by you own past experiences but also by second-hand information (the beliefs of others). This second-hand information or life programming forms 80% of your *'core beliefs'* about yourself and reality.

Given that, situations repeat themselves because you have established core beliefs about all your experiences, and that your filters only allow in data that is in alignment with these beliefs, your mind creates an *emotional association* with the experiences that formed these core beliefs. Your brain draws an objective conclusion and establishes an automatic sensation reaction to these types of experiences called your reaction tapes. It is like an objective process of concluding that, *"this situation is similar to other experiences that have been,* for example, *fearful, so this situation is most likely fearful as well'.*

These programs and tapes represent your *automatic emotional reactions* to everything you experience. This means your emotions are a result of a series of automatic pre-decisions by your mind so your mental systems do not need to reach a new conclusion every time you have a new experience similar to something you have experienced before. Allowing these mental processes to run without any conscious participation on your part, perpetuates your existing beliefs, self-image, and reactions towards all future experiences. Although these automatic systems enable your mind to process an ever-expanding flow of new data efficiently, it is easy to assume these automatic reactions are the only legitimate responses to new events and circumstances.

Your interface is indeed a hotpot of activity. Like a cosmic control center for both your outer and inner consciousness, this is where everything happens. It is at this point of perception where all your life programs, automatic reaction tapes, and filtering blocks reside. Your Ego, as the gatekeeper of your conscious perception, supervises this automatic protective filtering system. If your filters block new information it still gets recorded and filed by itself, with similar data or in your generic storage compartment. Ego will just not allow it into your operating data banks if it butts-up against your existing self-image. New information cannot alter your operating data banks and conscious self-image unless it can slip by these protective filters. This automatic method of processing and comparing data is neither good nor bad. It is just how your mind works. It can work for or against you, to expand your perception of your experiences or limit it. You can avoid your filters consciously to some degree, but more quickly and effectively by bypassing your outer consciousness and inserting new information directly into your subconscious.

Your existing beliefs and the emotional sensation tapes associated with these beliefs creates your overall *personality*. Your personality determines how you interface, *'the face I put on between you and me'* when you communicate and interact with others in the outer world. It is here that information goes in then back out again creating consciousness and your conscious *identity*. The efficiency of these mental processes creates its own paradox. Ask yourself, *"Do you reap what you sow, or, do you sow what you reap?"* The key to changing the kind of experiences you have is to *choose a response* in every situation rather than to allow your mind to run a preset automatic reaction triggered by similar past experiences.

These conditioning programs and automatic reactions are self-perpetuating until they are changed. For Example: Let us say that as a toddler you encountered your first dog, a German Shepherd dog. I am using the dog example because it spells 'GOD' backwards. This German Shepherd may have appeared massive to you as a small toddler but since he was friendly, the experience is recorded as a pleasant dog experience in your generic mental compartment. The next dog you encounter may also have appeared pleasant at first but may have growled a warning when you pulled his ear. He may then have nipped you because you poked an exploratory finger into his eye. Your brain records this from your point of view only, based on the sensation you felt during this dog encounter. When your mind records the second dog experience it sees a similarity in subject matter to the first dog experience and automatically creates a 'DOG' subject file folder within your generic storage compartment. Both dog encounters are now stored in this dog subject file. If the nip the second dog gave you hurt and scared you, your brain records the emotional reaction of fear and pain and files it in a 'fear' and 'pain' sensation folder where every other fearful and painful experience you have had up to this point is stored.

As a toddler, you did not know your finger in the dog's eye hurt him and that is why he nipped you. Your mind does not record the reason why the dog nipped you only your experience and the sensations you felt. What your dog file contains becomes the point of reference for all subsequent dog experiences. Another dog may subsequently scare you by knocking you over in his enthusiasm to greet and play with you. Your mind will only record the experience and that you felt scared. It will also record any other data relating to dog you absorb through your senses, like second-hand information relating to any recorded subject.

Second-hand information, like what you hear others say, affects your subject file associations as much as your own physical experiences and your feeling reactions do. You may have heard people talk about how German Shepherds are vicious or dangerous and observed your parents recoil from them in fear. Based on information relating to their fears, beliefs or experiences, your 'dog' file can quickly log all kinds of negative second-hand information that reinforces a belief that you should be wary of, or terrified of dogs, particularly German Shepherd dogs. Only new information, like understanding the dog bit you because you hurt him, having a greater number of pleasant dog interactions or expanding invalid second-hand information will modify your existing beliefs. Until then, your mind will automatically trigger the predominant programmed reaction based on the 'more of' stored in your dog file. The same process applies to every other subject filed in your mental storage compartment.

As you gather a diversity of dog encounters, your mind refines its processes and generates a variety of sub-files in your overall dog file containing experiences with different types of dogs. Your resulting beliefs may range from a love of small dogs to distrust and wariness of all large dogs and a continued fear of German Shepherd dogs. As an adult, you may have forgotten your earliest childhood experiences and still feel that moment of fear when you see a German Shepherd dog. It all depends on the 'more of' in your data banks. All this data and the subsequent conclusions your mental systems reach forms your beliefs, conscious self-image, and personality. Coupled with your automatic emotional reactions, whatever is predominant in your operating data banks determines how you interact in your outer reality until you start participating in these mental processes.

Mental Software

Your Mind works like a cosmic super computer that is always plugged into the power outlet of the cosmic energy source of all consciousness called God, Prime Creator, All That Is or whatever you choose to call the originating energy force responsible for our very existence. Your mind utilizes two distinct programs – *Windows Self-Image* – the conscious programming that creates your life-view through your outer perceptions, and *Inner Windows* – your subconscious containing the resources associated with your more expansive identity. Inner Windows represents the largely hidden, intuitive, and spiritual aspect of what you really are – a divine spark of the God-source. Inner Windows connects you to the Cosmic Energy Database that sustains your very existence. However, you need to activate this cosmic database so it can influence your Windows Self-Image. To activate it you need to first acknowledge its existence.

The wonder of this celestial system is that it is tailor-made to your personal specifications, whoever you are. Your birth into this reality turns on a biological mental program that continually updates itself on an interactive basis. The hardware runs as long as you live and the software is both self-sustaining and self-upgrading for the duration of your physical life and beyond. Your server is your inner consciousness, a consciousness that was, and is, eternal. Once you activate this program this mental software can access any information you require or desire. Any discomforting power surges you may experience are a result of your Inner Windows prompting your Outer Windows to expand its database so you can expand your conscious awareness of yourself. You can view any Spam, like the unverified truths that others continually send you at leisure and then integrate or delete this data as you wish. The only virus that can infiltrate the system is that of dis-ease, which you create yourself. Changing your mind' eliminates these kinds of viruses.

You do not have to be computer literate to understand the workings of your mental and spiritual software programs. You only have to be willing to embrace the fundamentals of how your own mental systems create your reality – then participate! Your willingness to open, explore and utilize the unlimited windows available is the key to enhancing, expanding or changing the very essence of your physical experience. Most of humanity operates only through the Windows Self-Image program. This conscious program utilizes your five senses to move data in and out of your operating data banks like a worn tape, continually perpetuating the same beliefs and experiences. Many of you sit in front of your computer games or surf the net for information and human interaction. Once you participate, your own life-experience is a much grander game of discovery. It is a game of trial and error experimentation, of side stepping programmed roadblocks, or tricking your own filters into allowing new information into your operating data banks to enhance your personal reality.

Both these software programs have an important function, just as your very existence has a specific self-designed purpose. Your Windows Self-Image protects your physical survival, the Inner Windows ensures your spiritual need for stimulation, and creativity are realized. Physical survival is not the all-consuming issue it once was, particularly in the western world. Your real identity and greater consciousness is what you now seek to expand in order to survive the existing shift in consciousness. The Inner Windows program is where you find the extended senses you will need to do so. This connection to a vast sensory resource enables you to access even more windows of self-expression in order to expand your perception of yourself.

Conscious living is a result of using both programs simultaneously as originally intended. Your life programming and ensuing beliefs has created a separation of the two and buried your inner resources deep within your subconscious. Your willingness to participate via faith in the process is your password to access these inner resources and circumvent the firewalls protecting your conscious beliefs. If you want to understand your own identity, do a diagnostic of your Windows Self-Image program to see what kind of data your mental files actually contain. You do this by '*feeling your thoughts and thinking about what you are feeling*'.

Exercise #1.

1. Take one day this week to stop and explore three thoughts that go through your mind, within three different situations or circumstances.

2. Without judgment, write down what one thought was, and how it made you feel. Then forget about it. Do this with two other unrelated thoughts throughout the day.

3. In the evening, sit quietly and look at one thought. Think that same thought again and pay attention to what you are feeling now.

4. Write down what sensations you feel, and what you think you believe about that particular subject. Pay attention to what sensations are triggered as you write down the belief then write down what these sensations are.

5. Do the same with the other two thoughts.

6. When you are finished, put your notes away and forget about it.

Beliefs

What is a belief? *A belief is an unexamined truth you learned.* When you were an infant, your beliefs were created by what you experienced through first-hand physical sensation. As a toddler, these beliefs expanded to include what you observed and then attempted to mimic. Once you learned how to communicate through language, you began to absorb a new kind of information, second-hand information based on other people's beliefs. These beliefs largely account for 80% of what your operating data banks contain right now. This second-hand information also forms your current self-image and perception. Whatever your age now, you continue to operate from these same beliefs or, through conscious intervention, expand them to change your self-image and perception. You learned 40% of everything you now know by the age of four. So 40% of everything you now know was based primarily on your parents' or primary caretaker/s beliefs. Since you knew nothing about your world when you were born, these beliefs along with your own limited physical sensations and experiences formed the foundation of your identity and perception of your reality. Take a moment to reflect on that.

Between the ages of four and eight, you learned another 40% of everything you now know. This period emphasized both education and socialization. School education was designed to expand your knowledge of the world and acquire the reasoning and application skills to develop your own cognitive mental abilities. Regardless of your cultural background, you absorbed the same kind of information your classmates and peers did. You, your society, and peers then measured your identity against the beliefs and behaviors determined acceptable within that culture. How well you met the criteria greatly influenced your own self-image.

As a baby and toddler, your automatic reactions were a result of your own feeling sensations, based on whatever stimulation you received within your home environment. Through observation you then began mimicking what you saw others do and observed how they reacted to everything you did. The reactions that received the most approval in the eyes of your immediate family established your beliefs about how to get your *'feel good'* sensations. The reactions that did not get approval resulted in your *'feel bad'* sensations and established beliefs about what to avoid or suppress. Your automatic reactions now still rise from this early childhood conditioning. Unless you participate in your own mental processes, you still live your life today through the emotional reaction patterns established as a four to eight-year old child. So you only acquired 20% of everything you know now since puberty. Not a lot, is it?

Your existing beliefs are the result of your own mental system recording and compartmentalizing related information into files in your brain's storage compartment. An always-active comparing process first establishes, then reinforces or modifies your beliefs about yourself and your reality. The data reinforced the most becomes predominant and results in the conclusion that if it appears to be so, it must be so. These conclusions establish the operating data banks that create your self-image which determines how you see yourself and who you think you are. Your Ego, acting as a gatekeeper, uses filters at your interface in order to protect this self-image. The interface, where all information goes in then back out again, creates your conscious perception, a perception formed by your own core beliefs. As illustrated below, there is a great deal more going on in your reality than you realize. Your conclusions about reality are only based on what you learned to perceive within your particular family, society and culture, not what is really going on around you.

Model #2.

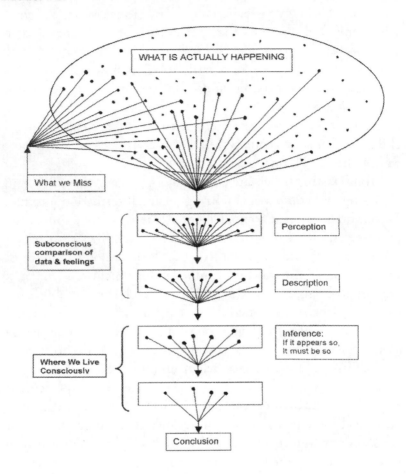

Although your interface is the point of change, *your subconscious actually creates your outer reality by what your inner self-image believes.* Your *imagination*, your spiritual 'imaging' tool, is the key to accessing the creative energy used to form a different self-image.

You were programmed by early childhood experiences, many of which were not uplifting and often included traumatic events or horrendous personal violations. In addition you were conditioned by all the other unexamined truths learned through cultural socialization and schooling. Regardless of what you believe up to this point, you *can* change your self-image by expanding these beliefs right now. You can reclaim your own authority over your life and become a self-thinking individual instead of living by other people's unexamined truths. There are several ways you can tilt the data bank scales in favor of what you want to image yourself to be.

From first-hand experience, I strongly suggest you seek counseling and whatever professional help is required if you have suffered early childhood violations that have not been healed. Seeking help to address childhood trauma and violation is the first step in reclaiming your own authority and authentic identity. These issues block your progress, particularly if you are in a state of denial for self-preservation. They are too deeply rooted in the very foundation of your core beliefs and self-identity. Early childhood abuse needs healing in a safe environment guided by a professional. There is no quick fix for this kind of trauma work. I know because I tried to do this work myself unsuccessfully. Although KEYS will be very helpful in your process, you will require other professional counseling if you have experienced abusive or deeply shameful violations.

Less than half of your current beliefs arise from your own first-hand sensory experiences. So 50% of your beliefs are comprised of unverified information based on what someone else told you. Since less than 50% of this information resulted from their personal experiences, only a small percentage of the data they acquired was actually examined and verified as being true. That would mean at least half if not three quarters of the beliefs perpetuated for generations are most likely hooey! However, once these beliefs are established they act as survival mechanisms and therefore you cannot just erase them.

A belief held by you as a three-year-old may have been essential to your survival then. For example: looking both ways and holding someone's hand before you crossed the street is a valuable belief for a small child. It is obviously still a good idea for an adult to look both ways, but no longer necessary to hold someone's hand when you cross the street. When you feel a moment's hesitation before you cross the street now, you are experiencing a residual of this conditioning or an actual fearful childhood experience. Some children have received such intense conditioning through fear; as an adult these fears have transformed into crippling phobias. *The power of any belief is governed by the emotional energy behind it.* Some of your beliefs are charged with such intense emotional energy not even a bulldozer could budge them.

You live life from the partial perception of beliefs created by unexamined truths. In other words, your belief system is a result of the existing knowledge within your immediate environment. This knowledge is generally unexamined or edited to meet someone else's criteria. Since your parents or caretaker/s formed your initial beliefs, more than half of your core beliefs result from what they learned. Since you accepted this information as being true, you would not have thought to examine it to see if it really was true. Although your mind and body work as independent mechanisms regulated by an automatic system that supports their functions without any direction from you, you can completely transform both when you begin to direct these processes.

The purpose of communicating with the outer world is to convey and/or exchange information in order to learn more about who you are while having this sensory physical experience. Ideally, you would view your beliefs with neutrality in order to draw new conclusions about yourself. You can see how problems arise when you try to impose your beliefs on others, or vice versa. At best, another person's beliefs can trigger an examination and expansion of your own, or at worst, prompt fierce resistance when they butt up against your filters. Beliefs are indicators of your current identity within any given situation. Since beliefs are learned, the identity they reflect is not necessarily a reflection of your genuine identity.

Our beliefs are the driving force in our lives. There was a time when humanity believed the world was flat, that if you sailed to the horizon, you would fall off the edge. Humanity accepted this belief as absolute fact until some curious soul did sail to the horizon and did not fall off, because there was no edge to the world. Thus, a new belief was born; that the world was a sphere. This new belief gained credibility with the safe return of many whose first-hand experience confirmed the horizon never ended no matter how far you sailed. However, when these adventurers took the news back home many people did not believe them despite the proof of their first-hand experience. This new information butted up against the filters that defined their known reality, based on the existing knowledge within that reality. If they accepted this new truth, they would possibly have to examine and change their mind about other things they believed were true, which would compromise their sense of security within their reality. Therein lies the key to humanity's overall resistance to change, particularly when one's personal identity and security is defined by the conscious beliefs of others.

Your mental systems automatically perpetuate these learned beliefs and trigger your automatic reaction tapes unless you participate in the process. As a child, you learned that in order to receive approval from others your behavior had to comply with commonly accepted beliefs. When your response fell outside of the acceptable, the 'feel bad' sensation of disapproval or exclusion prompted you to modify your behavior in order to get your 'feel good' sensations through the approval of your peers. You still do this as adults because your self-image is still dependent largely on your outer identity not your own inner sense of authentic self-worth.

You can even become so entrenched in your beliefs that regardless of proof to the contrary you will refuse to change your mind. When you become entrenched in this way, the consensus reached from filtering out all contrary points of view results in *judgments*. Judgments are strong points of view - *yours* - against which you compare all other information. The problem with judgments is that they result from your own mental abstracts called *ideals*.

Ideals

Your brain continually compares all the data in your mind's storage compartments. This includes your feeling-associations relating to the experiences recorded in these files. To your subconscious your need for survival and stimulation is always 100%. The desire to fulfill a real or perceived need or desire is always 100%. If your needs and desires are met there is no problem. However, if they are not, your 100% desire for fulfillment prompts you to envision the intended gratification as an ideal or unrealized *ideal abstract.* These ideal abstracts, based on the things you are NOT getting, become your *perceived desires.* Since your subconscious mind cannot distinguish between what is real and what you imagine, these perceived desires also require 100% fulfillment.

Most of your ideal abstracts result from your learned beliefs and not from you own genuine needs or desires. Since the majority of your beliefs originate from outside yourself, you are putting 100% of your feelings behind things you have learned to believe you should want. Although only perceived desires, your mind processes them the same way as it does your own genuine desires. The feelings attached to these perceived desires along with the feelings associated with your real needs and desires are recorded and stored in the same file. This distorted combination of your real and perceived ideals result in the abstract *'ideal'* criteria you currently use to judge yourself and others.

You have an ideal abstract for everything you think you are not getting in all aspects of your life. These ideals are your own interpretation of 100% gratification, a point of reference through which you consciously evaluate your own self-image and identity. Ideals and beliefs are passed on from one generation to the next. A historic ideal for women, like marrying well, filled a real need in past eras where it was essential to have a husband to support her and her children. To marry well ensured physical survival. Yet, in our era in North America where most women are able to sustain their own physical survival, many will still choose a partner who can offer materialistic security over a partner who is actually better suited to them. Your ideal abstracts become your points of reference that result in your *judgments*.

Others get defensive when you try to impose your judgments on them because you butt-up against their filters, which protect an identity based on their own beliefs, values, and judgments. You might as well take a sword and cut off their heads since you do the same thing to their identity when you disagree with them. To streamline the processing of these judgments even further, the consensus of all of your ideals is what you hold so dear - your *Values*. Values are not some God-given or universal truth. Values are a result of life programming. They represent *what you believe you lack in your life.* Your own mental processes draw conclusions based on judgments that result from the unrealized ideals arising from what you learned to believe.

Social Values

Society is a reflection of humanity's inner consciousness as it experiences itself within various interactive structures. Society creates a point of reference that reflects the thoughts and beliefs predominant within a particular human collective. The world contains many different types of societies, some which are similar and some very different. Some appear to work well to promote quality of life and others do not. Societies represent group experiments in how a collective of individuals operate under different kinds of belief systems. These collective beliefs are what form the group's overall social and cultural *values*.

You perceive society as an entity separate from yourself. Yet you help create and maintain it with the energy of your own thoughts and beliefs then modify your own self-image to fit the ideals society reflects back to you. You do not stop to consider who's values these are or if they are of benefit to yourself, your social grouping, or humanity as a whole. Many of you use social values like a rulebook formulated by an almighty power for what experiences you will allow yourself rather than as a point of reference reflecting an over-all social mind-set.

The Bible is a good example of such a rulebook. The fact that it has survived for thousands of years convinces many of you it must be true. If it was not, how could it have survived so long? Though written by men other than the Creator called God or his son Jesus, and continually edited and translated by man throughout history, many still perceive it as the definitive word of God. That is not to say it does not contain valuable truths originating from a higher power, only that much of it represents a cultural history of the changing beliefs and perceptions of society at the time. It reflects this culture's experimentation with a new belief structure injected by a prophet, to vitalize a mindset that had become stagnant in order to stimulate the expansion of human consciousness at that time. The early churches deleted much of the original Bible's message and teachings that would empower you in quite a different way for fear this information would strip them of their power.

The Roman Catholic Church also removed many remaining references to reincarnation in older versions of the Bible centuries ago. As well, original writings by this man Jesus, found in the area of the Dead Sea Scrolls, were secretly stored in the Vatican vaults that held a great deal of other sensitive material. What they contain would shake and dissolve the very foundation of western religions. What kind of information could this be? Perhaps, that everything you need is within you. Perhaps, that you are not separate from rather an integral aspect of the Original Creator. You have become the sheep dogs in your own sheep pens; monitoring each other's behavior, pointing out abnormalities, and even shunning or attacking those who question and live outside this social herd mentality. Yet, you each demand your right to individual choice of self-expression and resent others policing your choices and actions. Once you realize how ludicrous this is, you can begin to view society from a different perspective.

If you look at society and see things you feel are unprofitable and need to change, change your own thoughts. The energy impetus or e-motion behind your thoughts creates and supports the beliefs and values within any society. The injection of your energy can change the collective in what is referred to as the 100th monkey theory. Gandhi is a prime example of a man whose army was his own beliefs propelled by the e-motion of his peaceful intentions and personal integrity. His non-violent approach not only imprinted his society's consciousness with a new form of resistance to oppression, but also affected the consciousness of humanity all over the world to varying degrees. Although his actions did not eliminate oppression in his own country, he injected a new value, an alternative of challenging aggression in a non-aggressive way. Fighting wars in the name of peace has always proven contradictory and unprofitable. It is the ultimate oxymoron. How does violence achieve peace? The evidence of human history proves that all you gain by war is a temporary stimulation of some participant's economy at the price of a tremendous loss of life and devastating environmental and social destruction. Yet, wars continue, justified by a diversity of noble social and religious beliefs, ideals and values. The key to changing the things that do not uplift humanity is - to change yourself.

Personal Values

As a human being, your need to survive protects your physical form while your need for stimulation expands your soul's awareness of itself. Sensory feedback from your experiences reinforces the beliefs that form whatever identity will ensure your survival. Therefore, your operating data bank creates your *personal values*, in other words *'what is important to me'* in order for me to survive.

Your values are formed by the intellectual portion of your brain reaching a consensus conclusion. These conclusions are designed to ensure your needs are being met. *You value what you have very little of.* These values also determine how you think and act. Left alone, your values will never change, and neither will your experiences unless a shock or trauma shakes you out of your habitual patterns of behavior. Allowing new information into your data banks from an inclusive/expansive point of view will modify these values.

The bulk of your personal values are a direct result of cultural conditioning, known as traditional values. The dictionary defines tradition in part as, *'the handing down of information, beliefs, and customs by word of mouth by one generation to another without written instruction'* and as, *'an inherited pattern of thought and action'*. The problem with traditional values is not what they are in themselves, but that, as a by-product of the beliefs and needs of past generations, they limit your perception of the world you live in right now. Just as human consciousness needs to evolve, so do your personal values. Surviving in 400 AD, the 1100s or the 1500s required different values than those needed in the 1700s, your current historic timeframe, or the values that will be required in the year 2020. Yet, many of you operate from the same traditional values that applied to a world you know virtually nothing about, where the knowledge and conditions you take for granted now did not even exist.

In order to change your mind you need to broaden your values. This allows for new ways of thinking without eliminating or negating values that prove beneficial. Be willing to examine all your values. Then, be willing to expand those that diminish you or others. I find it soul-wrenching how many lives are still lost today through wars perpetuated by traditional resentments resulting from differences in ancient values established hundreds, even thousands of years ago.

Changing Beliefs

Your mind accepts whatever goes into your storage compartments, regardless of source. It can be a thought or feedback from your outer senses. It can come through your inner consciousness as a day or night dream or extra-sensory experience originating from outside this reality. The point of change is at your filters (interface), and the point of change is always NOW, since the energy for creation originates in universal timelessness. Since your thoughts and imagination also originate from this eternal source, they are not constrained by your conscious beliefs. If this was not true, you could not imagine anything that does not already exist. This is a fundamental key to making changes within this reality.

When you want to make a change to yourself, you first imagine a picture of this new version of yourself in your mind. Then you reinforce this new image by not only acting, but also *feeling* as if it already exists, even if it does not. For Example: perhaps you are shy with people because as a child you learned you have nothing valid or interesting to say. So how do you change this?

The next time you interact with another person, think of an experience wherein you did feel comfortable. Visualize yourself feeling that same feeling of comfort. Affirm that what you have to say is interesting because it IS interesting to you, or you would not want to talk about it. Acknowledge the fact that you are shy and give yourself permission to speak about what you find interesting. Your subconscious makes no distinction between what you call real or imagined because it accepts all data, regardless of source. It will allow you to bypass the filters that normally protect your shyness. It does so because you validated the fact that you are shy and reinforced the self-image your filters protect. You have just directed your filters to allow for a temporary one time exception to your existing shyness. The key is to focus only on the interesting information you want to share instead of how you think it sounds.

The next time you feel shy in an interactive situation again imagine a picture of yourself feeling comfortable and again focus only on what you want to say. Repeat what you have now already done before. Your usual sense of shyness will diminish because your feelings are always 100% and you are now energizing the feeling of being comfortable. Your current self-image will align itself to this new image not because it is right or better, but because that is where you direct your energy. It is that simple; what you focus on is what creates your feelings. You may have to do this many times to offset your habitual shyness, but your interactions will be far less uncomfortable.

Elfie H.M. Leddy

Your feelings are always 100%. If you experiment with your feelings, you will notice the e-motion of your feelings can move from shyness to comfort and back again very quickly, depending on your thoughts. *Your feelings are a result of your thoughts, not the other way around.* You may switch back and forth between the two, but you can only feel one feeling at a time because *'where the mind goes, the energy flows - all 100% of it'*. For example, try to laugh and be angry at the same time right now. You cannot feel these two emotions at the same time. You are feeling angry or you are laughing.

Beliefs exist to protect your identity and survival, even if you consider some of them outdated, silly, or restrictive. Whatever exists in your data banks now is the result of the automatic function of your mind's processing system therefore you cannot remove it from your memory banks. Many of you attempt to do that, in effect, you try to erase your existing identity. This makes your filters work even harder to protect the self-image you now want to change. Consequently, old beliefs continually re-surface to nip you in the butt in spite of practicing life changing techniques designed to eliminate them. What you can do is transform them by *expanding* them.

Another way to expand your beliefs and values is through the *suspension of judgment*. Give yourself permission to widen the framework within which you operate. Ask yourself this question: *"Do my beliefs help me sustain my needs and validate my individual experience or do they inhibit my creative expression?"* Your beliefs, values and ideals will automatically broaden when you allow for more and more exceptions to your existing perception. Your operating data banks will automatically begin to integrate data from your generic storage compartment given this kind of permission. It is all about AND, AND, and AND.

You can believe something to be true and that something else is true and that something else can be true at the same time. The truth is – it is all true – if you believe it. It is all about perception. By thinking about what you are feeling, and feeling your thoughts while having them, you reclaim authority over your own perception of reality. Your perception of reality will change as quickly as your beliefs do, if you allow your beliefs to expand. One truth that remains constant is that your perception of reality changes as your beliefs change.

Dogma is inflexibility in judgment. This means you accept only your own truth and creates a 'garbage in - garbage out' cycle of repetitive life circumstances. The proof of your convictions only makes you more dogmatic, which then perpetuates more of the same. If you allow exceptions, you will be amazed at how quickly your perception expands. Much like planting a flower garden, the more variety of seeds you sow, the more diversity of blooms will grow, in spite of the environmental conditions that may prevent some seeds from germinating. If you sow only sunflower seeds, that is all you get or if conditions are not ideal, you reap nothing.

Rather than attempting to delete an existing belief, validate it and expand it to include a one-time exception. That is why 'AND' and 'SO' are such powerful words. Begin to use them instead of BUT - a greatly misunderstood word. When the word BUT is used in conversation - disregard everything said before it. What a person really means to say is what comes after. For example, look at this statement: "I don't mind you just dropping in on me, but *next time, give me a call first.*" What came before BUT is either social window dressing or behavioral conditioning. When you hear yourself using the word, pay attention to what you say after it. Get your 'buts' out of the way could also better be phrased, *'get your own butt out of the way'* when you use it as an excuse for something you don't want to be accountable for.

If you acknowledge another belief can be true as well as your own, you give yourself permission to move outside your operating data banks and access other data in your generic storage files. This is where the X-File stuff that's not part of your operating data banks is filed. It holds entirely different kinds of beliefs based on your greater identity. These files contain blocks of exceptions to your conscious beliefs that would immediately expand your operating data banks and resulting perception of yourself.

The only conflict in contradicting information is your belief that there is a conflict in contradicting information. The universe operates on a principle wherein our concept of paradox, loosely defined in the dictionary as *'something involving an inherent contradiction'*, represents its own balance from a point of reference that is more expansive and comprehensive than the knowledge within your existing reality.

Many of your current difficulties result from thinking what you are in this life is all you are. You are so much more than your existing perception of yourself! When you adjust and expand your consciousness dial you can tune into the other band wave frequencies upon which you also operate. What prevents you from doing so is accepting only the official version of reality. You believe you can only tune into one consciousness station, the one you currently inhabit. It keeps you out of tune with your greater identity and prevents you from accessing your inner senses and own higher frequency knowledge. When you begin to align your mental, physical and spiritual aspects, you begin to resonate with your own higher frequencies. In tune with the cosmic pulse of your origins you can begin to access its vast universal storehouse of information. Through this alignment, the beliefs and identity created by your conscious programming and conditioning expands with relative ease.

There is nothing wrong with believing whatever you want to believe as long as you know they are beliefs *about* reality you temporarily accept in order have a specific kind of experience. Experiencing yourself through a variety of points of view is the overall intention of this sensory physical experience. Subconsciously you know you are more than you consciously *'believe'* yourself to be. You send yourself confirmation of this through your inner senses all the time. A belief which does not help you achieve your basic need for survival and stimulation will lose its power of influence, not because you deny it or try to bury it underneath all kinds of positive hype, but simply because you no longer energize it.

So where do you put your energy? Everything that comes from within you is 100% FOR YOU. The more energy you dedicate to the beliefs that allow for an expansion of awareness, the less energy goes to fueling beliefs that diminish you. In effect, you become a 'system buster' and break through your own conscious conditioning. To do so, you need to allow new information into your data banks. You also need to understand how mental programming works.

Chapter 3

MENTAL PROGRAMMING & CONDITIONING

"Information transforms beliefs."

I T is amazing how easily behavior is altered through mental programming and environmental conditioning. A variety of studies were conducted by the Jacob Blaustein Institute for Desert Research, Ben-Gurion University of the Neger supported by articles relating to the jump performance of seven desert fleas in Psychology Today. Researchers studying mind control and conditioning techniques devised a simple experiment using fleas based on these other studies. They constructed a 16-inch high glass box with a glass lid they could raise or lower at will. They then placed a bunch of little fleas in the box and put the lid on at its full height. Fleas habitually hop at least 12-13 inches into the air - which they did in gay abandon. Then they lowered the lid to 10 inches high. With this height reduction, at first the fleas banged their little flea heads on the glass lid when they jumped. Before long, they adjusted their spring to the confines of their new environment. The researchers continued to lower the lid by 2-inch increments and left it at each level until they observed the same adjustment to the fleas' hopping behavior. They then left the lid at a 4-inch height. Since hopping is part of their blueprint, future generations of fleas did not stop hopping entirely but adjusted their spring to fit the confines of this limited 4-inch height environment.

Then the researchers removed the lid completely. Although there was nothing to prevent the fleas from hopping right out of the box, the majority continued to hop only 3-4 inches high. The odd flea did hop higher, and one or two rebels even hopped right out of the glass box, but the majority maintained their hopping height of 4-inches. The researchers also noted that during the span of the experiment newly born batches of fleas did not hop nearly as high as the original batch of newborn fleas as if consciousness had imprinted this new limitation on their genes.

Although experiments with human subjects are conducted under different conditions, the results are the same. Repetitive reinforcement of gradual limiting conditions results in behavior modifications to ensure survival within any given environment. Your beliefs can be re-programmed just as easily since your beliefs create your existing environment. This process of mental self-programming is even more effective when triggered by real or perceived 'feel good' or 'feel bad' sensations. Feel good sensations satisfy your need for stimulation and 'feel bad' sensations, like fear, often appear to ensure your survival.

Humanity has much in common with the little fleas in a glass box with a 4-inch high ceiling. It has been suggested the Russians, still the world's forerunners in mind control research since the 1950s, have already engineered the cosmic longitudinal (EM) Scalar waves I referred to earlier for mass mind control experiments. This concept is not as far-fetched as you may think. A great deal of scientific experimentation goes on that the public knows nothing about. The human body acts as a biological dipole with brain wave patterns that operate on electromagnetic frequencies like all else within the universe. These frequencies can be altered without being detected since these longitudinal Scalar waves originate from outside our 3-D reality. Like radio frequencies, your senses respond to stimuli transmitted on these frequencies. Unless you become consciously aware of your own thoughts and beliefs, you won't know when your mind or thoughts is being manipulated.

Mainstream science has already proven that low frequency emissions limit the amount of neurological receptors triggered in your brain whereas high frequencies fire up more of these receptors. Using low frequencies, mental programming directly imprints your subconscious with subliminal messages designed to create a desired result. While working in advertising I too learned how to insert subliminal messages into print advertising. All advertising contains subliminal messages. Radio frequency waves are not as effective carriers of subliminal messages as television. Television alters more of your brain wave patterns because it stimulates three sensory levels - audio, visual, and emotional. These subliminal messages trigger your own feeling sensations, based on 'what you do not have enough of' in particular. Most of what you think you want is stimulated through television. Visual and verbal triggering along with second-hand affirmation from your immediate environment further reinforces your entitlement to have these material things. It is possible to reprogram a large portion of the population to change their beliefs about what they think they want or need. Two generations of parents in the 1960s and 1970s were unaware that while cute comic characters on Sesame Street or idealized family sitcoms were entertaining their children, their minds were altered by subliminal messages inserted into child-oriented advertising.

These programs and commercials designed to trigger specific desires resulted in a dramatic change in previous purchasing habits. If 'feel good' sensations did not hook you, stimulating your fears did by triggering your survival instincts. This economic agenda stimulated an artificial sense of materialistic entitlement resulting in mindless consumerism. Your perceived desires increase dramatically when you watch a lot of television. The more you watch, the more you realize you have 'little of' what you think you are entitled to have. While you are enjoying your favorite

Keys

programs, your minds are being altered. Someone else is writing the scripts that shape your beliefs, desires, and values.

Exercise # 2

You can prove this point to yourself by cutting out this kind of subliminal stimulation. For a one-week period, do not watch television, read newspapers or magazines, listen to the radio, or surf the Internet. Take walks in nature or pamper yourself in other ways like long soaks in the tub with herbal essences or meaningful conversations with those you have no time to spend with now. Within a few days you will notice a distinct difference in your thoughts. You will also have free time to examine your thoughts, beliefs, and emotions as well as feeling present in your daily experiences. You may think you will miss what is going on in your world if you cut yourself off from the news. Without this bombardment of primarily negative news underlined with subliminal messages, you will actually become more aware of what is really happening around you and within you. Raise the lid on the glass box that currently defines your limited identity and perception and begin to script your own dramas, comedies, and creative games by directing your own mental processes.

Bypassing Your Conscious Filters

Since beliefs protect your survival, at first it is necessary to trick your filters into accepting new data. You do this by *taking a conscious pause* to short-circuit your automatic reactions. Pause and mentally count to ten before automatically reacting to whatever is happening. Then CHOOSE a different response to how you would normally react. Your filters will not see a threat to your self-image providing you voice this exception in the NOW. This means using the present tense of I AM, not 'I will'. Then you simply insert one-time exceptions into your automatic reactions until eventually there are so many exceptions your beliefs have no choice but to expand. The more exceptions you initiate, the more expansive your operating data banks become. There is no point in resenting your filters for defending your existing beliefs and reactions, for they will as vigorously defend your newly expanded beliefs and responses.

You can also expand your beliefs with mental self-talk. Take the child who had the fearful German Shepherd dog experience. Confronted with another German Shepherd dog, you could mentally say something like, '*I am frightened of German Shepherd dogs* (reinforcing existing belief). *I now know it bit me only because poking that dog in the eye hurt him* (insertion of new data). *This dog on a leash is a different dog so I am safe with this dog*' (inserting an exception). You may need to self-talk this way each time you encounter a German Shepherd dog until you begin to feel more comfortable around them. If this kind of self-talk seems cumbersome, realize - you already use as much energy reliving the fears and horrors of what happened previously, or could happen again. All this goes on in a flash in your mind anyhow.

Your mind operates on the principle of the 100th monkey. Ninety-nine young monkeys will learn a new skill like drinking water from a bowl-shaped leaf by observing their elders and other members of their group. By mimicking what they see others do they too eventually learn the skill. When the 100th monkey learns the skill, it gets imprinted on the consciousness of all monkeys within that species. The energy of e-motion (energy-of-a-desire-in-action) propels thought into reality. Energy directed towards something repeatedly builds up enough of an electromagnetic charge to imprint the consciousness of the species as an intuitive knowing. When the same species of monkey on another land mass is thirsty, it will instinctively look for a bowl-shaped leaf. After some experimentation, it will fill the correct type of leaf with water and drink from it without ever having seen this done before in its own social grouping.

Another species of monkeys have learned to use rocks to crack open the shell of a particular kind of nut they relish. The adult monkeys gather these nuts and take them to a large slab-like rock in the middle of their territory. They pound the shells with smaller rocks they find strewn around until the shell cracks enough to get at the nut. Youngsters watch their elders and through practice learn how to crack these hard nuts themselves. Since they do not understand how consciousness and energy interact, this behavior still mystifies many scientists. Many human skills originated in the same way.

The energy generated by the repetition of either a thought or action builds up its own kind of electromagnetic charge. When this charge reaches a certain critical mass, it explodes into energy particles that seek out a compatible polarity frequency. By the laws of attraction, these particles merge with like-energy. Since thought is energy this is also how a new idea or inspiration spreads through human consciousness. We all possess but too-rarely use this ancient form of mental telepathy. This kind of consciousness transmission explains how ancient civilizations in completely different geographic locations develop similar skills and ideas without any physical contact with each other. As an artist, I see an obvious similarity in symbols and shapes used in the art and architecture of cultures that were unaware of each other's existence.

The same patterning exists in world religions. The creation story is essentially the same in every culture, just interpreted and expressed differently. Most religions contain one central God Creator or Spiritual Origin even though the religion may include a variety of deities. These religions also imply interaction with this source and salvation resulting in a glorious afterlife is possible, providing you meet specific criteria. Since they cannot influence our actions and choices directly, higher frequency entities like our own high-frequency identity can implant seeds for change into human consciousness through our subconscious.

Your Thoughts

Do you ever wonder where your thoughts come from or what happens to them once they leave your mind? Thought originates from your inner consciousness, outside of this 3-D reality; the part of you connected to timelessness. When you think a thought or get an idea you do not seize and use in this physical reality, it flows back into a cosmic energy consciousness collective, where every thought ever thought continues to exist. Some thoughts take form in other realities like your dream experiences, and others manifest on other dimensions in completely alien ways. The majority, if not seized and processed by an inquiring mind, flow back to this universal collective of human consciousness.

Your individual thoughts influence ALL human consciousness. All the thoughts ever thought reside in this universal thought-pool and are accessible to each of you. Your thoughts transform what this collective contains when you draw a thought into your reality, and process it through your consciousness. Then a new version of this original thought, transformed by your unique perception, flows back into this vast thought collective.

The energy of a thought and the energy-impetus of your desire to manifest it into this reality create its own positive and negative charge within the energy polarities of the human mind. This energy draws to you what is in alignment with your existing thoughts. You may get a new idea, information relating to something you are thinking about or revelations relating to issues you are currently resolving from many different sources. While doing my own deep trauma work years ago, I received much data in this manner to help trigger awareness of unhealthy core beliefs. It seemed like everything around me dealt with different aspects of the effects of trauma and shame I needed to heal. *The energy behind your thoughts sets the universe in motion.* Once you energize a thought, it continues to attract like information to itself like a magnet until you fulfill your intention or turn your focus towards something else. The more receptive you are on a sensory level, the more related information your thoughts will attract.

Your thoughts are your own, but once you dedicate energy to them they become accessible to all human consciousness. The more energy dedicated to your thoughts, the greater their influence. Since like attracts like, you can pick up similar thoughts, interpret them in your own way, and form similar or different conclusions. You are naturally attracted to those who think the same way you do or are dealing with issues similar to yours. The frequency of your beliefs naturally aligns your consciousness to those with similar beliefs. Utilizing this thought-pool enables individuals to influence and change mass consciousness by revitalizing ancient knowledge and transforming it into new thought-concepts.

Thought originates from outside of our concept of time. This means you can also access more advanced thoughts and concepts than the existing knowledge in your present environment. When humanity needs a boost this method often injects new ways of thinking into existing consciousness. I feel many inventors and innovators of new ideas have done just that. Like a time-consciousness traveler, their inquiring minds attracted form-constructs from the future. They interpreted these concepts and recreated the items they saw using the materials available in their timeframe. Over time, these inventions were refined as new materials become available and eventually resulted in the objects that actually existed in the future they had visited. To my mind, Leonardo de Vinci is a prime example of a time-traveler who sketched mechanical objects not invented yet for hundreds of years into the future. Inventions also rarely happen as isolated incidents. Your copyright or patent registration offices will attest to receiving a batch of applications from across the globe for the same or very similar inventions at the same time. I also consider Nostradamus such a consciousness traveler who recorded his impressions of probable futures in his prophecies. Past, present and future exist simultaneously as do many probable outcomes of all three. If human consciousness is not connected outside of time, foretelling future events would be impossible. This consciousness link would also account for humanity's Renaissance eras where a desire for creative expression through music, art and the sciences flourished all over the planet at the same time.

Any concept or belief can take root in human consciousness, be it for its expansion or enslavement. Mental programming implanted the seeds for much of the discrimination, hatred and other division between human cultures throughout history. By triggering survival mechanisms and an innate need for self-validation, people will embrace attitudes they would normally consider abhorrent. Although they would normally feel no animosity towards particular groups of individuals, brainwashing can induce them to hate or fear these individuals to achieve certain agendas.

One of the ways Hitler cleverly orchestrated resentment against the Jews was by using their own financial abilities against them. He perpetuated a belief that the Jews secretly controlled the economy and thus were taking jobs away from good hardworking German and Austrian people. Since I was born in Austria just after World War II ended, my parents experienced this programming first-hand. As a soldier in the German Army, my father had all his needs met providing he complied with the absolute and ruthless dictates of the military regime. On one occasion an Officer held a gun to his head, ready to shoot him on the spot when he hesitated to complying with an order. My mother reaped the benefits of her teacher's training through the Nazi job creation program only by agreeing to adhere to strict party requirements. Citizens were brainwashed to spy on each other and report any infractions to the Gestapo, which many, including some of my own relatives, did. Since personal survival was paramount, 'feel- bad' programming reinforced by fear was offset by 'feel-good' economic opportunities that enhanced personal survival and security. The Arian Race concept further fueled the nation's sense of a superior personal identity, also a 'feel-good' sensation. Aggressive propaganda diffused public scrutiny when political and ethnic undesirables as well as mental patients just vanished. By simultaneously energizing the 'feel bad' survival mechanism of fear, and the 'feel good' sensation of national superiority, millions of Jews were subsequently gassed in death camps with little public outrage or resistance. The stench of burning bodies that regularly hung over the countryside became an uncomfortable but accepted aspect of rural life.

The thoughts and emotions you energize influence mass consciousness. This is how excitement, hysteria, fear, and guilt can incite a group of people to act irrationally. In the same way, the higher frequency of love can also ripple through human consciousness to nourish it. When you do not direct your own mental processes, others can, will, and do, using the energy of repetitive reinforcement.

You reinforce or alter your programmed beliefs on a daily basis. However, it takes time to acquire 50 good dog-experiences to offset 50 bad dog-experiences to change your belief about dogs. Your own mental processes are automatically offsetting bad experiences with good experiences and vice versa in each of your subject files. Like a laser beam, when you focus thought-energy towards a particular intention, one you reinforce with self-talk, the e-motion behind your intention infiltrates your subconscious more quickly. Validating that you are worthy imprints this belief in all the data banks where a sense of unworthiness exists. Self-talk and self-validation through affirmations works. If you voice your affirmations in the NOW, they bypass your filters and directly influence your subconscious self-images.

You cannot possibly know or remember everything filed in your mind's storage compartments since one feeling or emotion represents many unrelated experiences. Several well-directed affirmations can alter the self-images within these cross-referenced data banks. One day you may suddenly realize you feel good about yourself and that a great many good things have been happening in different areas of your life.

For Example: to counteract your fears if you have many fears, you could affirm that *'each and every day, in every way, my fears are diminishing'* or *'This day, I have always been able to act despite my fears – effortlessly'*. Such statements voiced in the NOW, would affect any file in your data bank that has the emotion of fear attached to it. In time, if you have a fear of dogs you may find you have walked right past a German Shepherd dog without feeling afraid. Another affirmation like: *'Every day, in every way, my beliefs about myself are expanding'* affirms your willingness to allow new information into your operating data banks.

All human consciousness on this planet is connected. As much as your life is a singular experience of manifesting and experiencing your own thought projections, everything you think and do affects all human consciousness. The energy behind your own identity-affirming thoughts could be the 100th monkey that imprints others with a new awareness. An idea you formulate, one even you think is preposterous, perhaps about who is really running the world and controlling your mind, can be the 100th monkey that changes how humanity thinks and acts. What if your idea is the first monkey with the potential to seed a new concept or helps energize another person's good idea? You are unaware of just how much influence your thoughts have or that they are powerful enough to change the world. Perhaps you are already feeling more significant and empowered. Good!

Since your thoughts bridge both your conscious and subconscious identity, you can also change a belief by identifying its source. Pay attention to what you are thinking and how these thoughts make you feel. Your thoughts and feelings act as messengers from your greater subconscious identity. Although Ego controls what data is allowed into your operating data banks, Ego cannot control what you think. In spite of what kind of identity these filters protect, you still think what you think. You may not act on thoughts that are contrary to your existing self-image and values, but you will still think them.

Since your thoughts are always active, they can reveal core beliefs that impede success and wellbeing in various areas of your life. Once you identify the source, you can use this information to self-talk yourself into an exception or expansion of that belief. By the time you are thirty or forty, you've had a great many life-experiences and may have trouble remembering what you did three weeks, three months, or a year ago, let alone in early childhood. With the layering and cross-referencing of sensations and events, finding one feeling in what is now a vast network of cross-referenced subject and sensation files may be akin to finding a needle in a haystack. Since this process is also very time consuming - take a short cut. Acknowledge a belief that activates an uncomfortable feeling or automatic reaction and pause for ten seconds. Then simply add a one-time exception to your habitual reaction and choose a different response.

If a buried memory suddenly pops into your mind or someone tells you about something that happened in your childhood it is important to examine and process this new information. Every time you take a walk down memory lane, you have a new opportunity to redefine your identity. If, for example: you were just told that you had poked that German Shepherd dog in the eye just before he bit you, you can use this information to create an exception to diffuse your fear.

The simplest way to change your beliefs is to bypass your automatic reactions *by choosing all your responses.* Within each new experience pause and pay attention to what you are feeling. It matters not what you felt or did in the past, even if the results were beneficial or your memories are good. Pay attention to what thoughts come into your mind RIGHT NOW. Examine what you are feeling while you are thinking these thoughts, pause, and decide how you wish to respond. Certainly, scan past experiences, but make a choice based on the current circumstance, not past experiences. Choose an exception to an existing belief with self-talk that expands the belief and reinforce this new attitude with a self-validation affirmation. This is how you integrate your conscious and subconscious aspects and regain control of your own mental processes. *You live in the present by being present in all your moments.*

Conclusion of Exercise # 1 (Chapter 2 – p.25)

Go back to the exercise in Chapter 2 where you wrote down three random thoughts and how they made you feel. Review what you had written. I suspect you will view these thoughts with new awareness. Ask yourself the following questions:

1. Are these my thoughts or thoughts based on learned beliefs?
2. What kind of self-image did my feelings represent – and why?

3. Can you now identify what experiences or beliefs created these thoughts?

If you think doing this is too complicated or time consuming ask yourself this, *"Whose responsibility are your feelings and experiences if not yours?"* Being involved in every aspect of your physical, mental, and spiritual experience represents living through the 100% physiological sensations your body provides, something you already do. Your random thoughts already trigger automatic emotional reactions that affect your mind, body and feeling emotions. Give yourself permission to choose and activate feelings that validate and nourish your overall well-being. You may be surprised to discover what an interesting person you really are once you begin to explore your own identity.

Guilt

Guilt, fear, and shame are your most powerful negative emotions. All three operate on a low frequency that keeps you disconnected from your higher frequency self and its additional sensory resources. Guilt DIMINISHES you, fear IMMOBILIZES you, and shame DEVALUES you.

Guilt is a result of your mind's automatic comparison process to ideals created by your beliefs and fueled by your need for self-validation. Your guilt is yours - not anybody else's. By activating this automatic comparison process you can be manipulated by your own guilt.

Guilt feels uncomfortable because it diminishes your spiritual need for self-expression. You feel guilty whenever what you want or do not want to do is contrary to what you think you should do. Feeling guilty is a sure-fire indicator you have a belief you need to examine and expand. Key words indicating guilt are words like *should, have to, must, ought to, shouldn't, never, can't*, and *always*. These words indicate a belief has activated a filter that protects a self-image created by programming. You diminish yourself when you allow others to define your 'feel good' sensations. You have the right to exercise your own choice in any and every situation even if it is contrary to what others do or approve of. Only babies and toddlers do not have freedom of choice. Having said that, they too make choices based on their sensory responses and limited reasoning capabilities.

When you feel guilty, you need to ask yourself, *"Who gains, who loses, and who benefits?"*

Guilt always represents a loss to you when you surrender your own needs or desires in order to meet someone else's expectations or ideals. Your family, friends, social and political organizations, cultures and religions all utilize guilt to ensure you meet their needs and ideals. Many religions keep you bound to their dogma through guilt by reinforcing your unworthiness, even when you follow all their rules.

However, the guilt word ALWAYS is a flip word that can act as a powerful affirmation for change. It reinforces any new belief you want to energize, as you will see later.

You trigger your own guilt when someone places expectations on you that conflict with your own intentions. In order to belong, or be liked, loved, considered a 'nice' person, or whatever will give you 'feel good' feelings, you act contrary to your own needs. For example, you are feeling tired and planned a quiet relaxing evening at home. A friend phones and asks you to go out with them. What is your first reaction? How do *they* react when you just say 'no'? If they express disappointment or try to change your mind, do you feel guilty and capitulate? Do you justify your decision with excuses? Since your intention was to rest, why would you change your mind to fill a friend's need for interactive stimulation? When you do not respond based on your real feelings your automatic reaction tapes kick in. Your ideals of what is a 'good friend' coupled with your need for validation results in the conclusion that their need is more important than your own. Some of you would have to have had your leg amputated that morning in order to feel justified in saying NO. This is why guilt is so effective in the manipulation and control of others.

12-step programs utilize a 90-day format because the mental cycle of changing a belief takes about 81 days of daily reinforcement.

If participants can stick to the program for three months, they have conquered the most critical period in the process of breaking their addictions, whatever it is. However, according to spiritual resources that have tracked the workings of the subconscious mind, it takes about <u>THREE AND A HALF YEARS</u> for your mind to resolve guilt consciously. The process can be speeded up considerably by bypassing your filters and imputing new data directly into your subconscious.

When you act contrary to your own needs and feelings, you often set off a cycle of *punishment* and *absolution*, particularly if you have had strong religious programming that affirms you were born in Sin and thus are flawed. The problem with guilt, be it short-term or long-term, is that in order to maintain your self-image you think you must be punished for deviating from what your self-image dictates you 'should' do. In order to reinforce your innate worthiness - for you ARE a worthy person - you seek absolution for this self-punishment. Short-term guilt results in little fights and altercations or small accidents. Long-term guilt manifests as physical disease or disability - often so severe it can become life threatening.

Little fights and/or accidents are an expression of this cycle of guilt and absolution. For example: let us say you snap at your partner because you are annoyed that you committed to something you did not want to do. You feel guilty because you know it was not your partner's fault so you accidentally drop a glass in the kitchen *(self-punishment)*. You feel bad about breaking one of your best glasses and cut your finger while you pick up the broken pieces *(absolution)*. You swear, which is not 'nice', so you punish yourself again and then seek absolution for this self-punishment with another accident like staining your good blouse with blood from your cut finger. These kinds of physical events are not random. They are a physical manifestation of what is happening inside you.

Learn to recognize these subtle or sometimes not so subtle guilt/absolution cycles, and stop them. *You do not need to punish yourself for anything you do.* Learn from the experience and decide not to repeat it if you do not like the feelings or effects of your actions. Apologize to anyone you feel you may have offended if that is important to you, and let it go. Most guilt is a result of your own automatic reactions. You can diffuse much of this reactive guilt when you pause, then choose ALL your responses.

Fear

Just as guilt diminishes you, fear *immobilizes* you. The sensation of fear alerts you to possible danger or harm through a physiological heightening of sensory awareness transmitted through your whole body by your nervous system. This keen awareness of your environment enables you to anticipate and prevent harm to yourself. However, your mind's automatic process of comparison coupled with the randomness of your thoughts causes this survival mechanism to fire-up every time the sensation of fear is triggered - be it real or imagined. These are the woulda, coulda, and shoulda's in your life - the stuff you think will get you if you do not somehow protect yourself against it.

You cannot protect yourself against the unknown. Most perceived dangers result from your own mental fabrications or fears created by second-hand information. The majority of these fears will never materialize. Since your thoughts are fueled by the intensity of feeling behind them, your subconscious can't tell the difference between an immediate physical threat and one you imagine. What you imagine as possible IS real to the mind and therefore signals the presence of real danger. Yesterday's fears are not today's reality unless you make it so by energizing them.

Information transforms beliefs. You are born with only two natural fears: the fear of falling and the fear of loud noises. Both result from the shock of birth as you leave the protected safety of the womb. Your other fears were learned or result from first-hand childhood experiences where you did not understand what was going on. The conclusions you reached resulted from your own physical sensations and observing how others reacted to any given situation.

The word F.E.A.R. itself means <u>FALSE EVIDENCE APPEARING REAL.</u> In other words, based on your cognitive abilities and the information you have at the time, the evidence for a need to feel afraid appeared real to you. Relatively powerless as a child you observed and mimicked the responses of those around you. These sensations formed your fear-based beliefs and automatic reactions. Today, most of you still live your lives through this same childhood programming. Increasing your knowledge about what it is you fear helps de-energize these fears.

For Example: To a small child who awakens from a nightmare at night and sees the glow of their clown-face nightlight, the apparition can appear diabolical and frightening. The child does not know that nighttime shadows distort the grinning face of the daytime clown to give it a menacing cast. Comfortable with the daytime face, the child may never have seen the clown's face at night, particularly if waking from a nightmare. This event can establish a belief that clowns are not to be trusted despite their smile. If someone who smiled a lot also did something to frighten or harm the child, the conclusion could be that all smiling faces are not to be trusted. As an adult, you could distrust everyone who smiles a lot without knowing why. Several isolated events, linked by a strong common sensation and a lack of information, create beliefs that still define many of your emotional reactions today.

If you have had many fearful and/or traumatic experiences as a child you develop a form of sensory vigilance that makes you chronically alert to the possibility that the most mundane events or circumstance can threaten your survival. Be willing to examine your childhood experiences. You learned 40% - 80% of what you now believe during that significant block of time.

Nevertheless, half of the fearful things you think could happen to you never will because they do not directly affect you. Of the 50% left, half of these are out of your control. These are things like natural disasters and weather. The other 25% are fears based on what has happened to somebody else (second-hand information). Half or 12.5% of the other 25% are your own perceived fears and not real. The 12.5% left are valid fears, only half of which can actually harm you. Half of these can be diffused with new information. The remaining 6-7% is manageable. Therefore, only about 6 - 7% of the 100% of your existing fear is real and a possible danger to your physical survival.

Exercise # 3.

This exercise will help you become aware of your learned fear-based reactions. The more candid you are, the more you will learn about yourself. Write down all your fears; things like the dark, home alone, spiders, railroad tracks, big dogs, thunder and whatever else makes you feel afraid. Write them all down without judgment. When you are finished take another piece of lined paper and divide it into four columns. Write the following headings at the top of the first two columns: PHYSICAL and IDENTITY.

Examine each fear on your list and decide if it would cause harm to your physical body or self-image identity. Write all your fears under the applicable column.

When you have finished listing all your fears in these first two columns, write the headings LEARNED and FABRICATED in the remaining two columns. Start at the top of your fear list and say each one aloud. For Example: "I am afraid of heights". If this fear results from a first-hand experience, leave it where it is. If you experience strong physical sensation as you voice a fear aloud but have no memory of a past event, also leave it where it is. If nothing comes to mind, decide if it is a fear based on observing others react in fear, or one you may have fabricated yourself. Cross it off in the physical or identity column and move it to either the 'Learned' or the 'Fabricated' column. If you do not know its source, circle it for now and go on to the next fear. Once you have done this with every fear on your list, go back to your circled items. If you are still uncertain – just guess and put it in either one of the last two columns. Your chart should look something like the example below:

Model # 3.   MY FEARS

PHYSICAL	IDENTITY	LEARNED	FABRICATED
Examples:			
heights	looking stupid	Doctors	being alone at home
big dogs	speaking in public	the dark	thunder
spiders	being ridiculed	railroad tracks	railroad tracks

Items listed under the heading of <u>Physical</u> and <u>Identity</u> are your own fears. Put a capital 'T' beside the fears you know are a direct result of a childhood experience you remember. Cut the first two columns off your sheet and keep them in a file called your WORK-IN-PROGRESS file. These are your own real fears, fears you can begin to examine and modify by diffusing them with new information. Now look at the list of fears in your Learned and Fabricated columns. You are also dedicating 100% of your energy to this fabricated nonsense. Keep the list as a point of reference in the future should these fears arise and diffuse them as they do.

In a relatively hostile environment, early man needed these heightened sensations to protect his physical survival. Your indiscriminate triggering of what was an essential survival warning mechanism creates harmful energy blocks throughout your body's chakra systems. Unable to sustain this sensory vigilance indefinitely, your nervous systems seize up, blocking the energy flow between your conscious and subconscious self. Immobilized, you disconnect from the very senses that provide information to dissolve these blocks. I equate the expression *'paralyzed with fear'* more with a sensory and mental paralysis than the physical inability to move, although you can experience all three. With your emotions heightened by fear and your mental systems disconnected from your inner senses, it is easy to manipulate you. To regain a sense of security and safety, you will accept almost anything that will ease this tension without question.

What do you fear? You fear what you do not known and what you have learned to fear. You cannot know what it will feel like or what will happen when you do something for the first time *until you do it* in spite of how many times you play it out in your mind. The sensation of fear acts as a *feeling indicator* that you have moved outside your comfort zone or that your physical survival or identity, based on your beliefs, may be at risk. That is all. If you trigger fear by imagining or adding perceived risk to new experiences, you miss the signals designed to warn you when you really may be at risk. Each time you think of a fearful experience you re-live it 100% in the NOW: mentally, physically and emotionally. Pay attention to the physiological changes in your body when you think about something you fear or when you observe others expressing their fears. Your heart may pound, you may feel knots in your stomach, your skin may prickle, your ears may ring, or you may feel rooted to the spot unable to do anything. To your subconscious IT IS ALL REAL.

To diffuse fear, focus on your breathing and the memory of a circumstance where you felt safe and secure. With your energy directed to feeling safe, you disconnect from the low frequency of fear. You cannot eliminate the sensation of fear. In fact, you would not want to. It is still an important survival mechanism. What you need to diminish is the crippling effect of perceived fears. Courage is not a lack of fear, but the ability to reason and act in spite of it. Immobilized on a mental, physical, and emotional level it is difficult to reason through the validity of what you fear.

Toxic Shame

The feeling of shame is as immobilizing and diminishing as guilt and fear with the addition of feeling absolutely devalued as an individual. The dictionary defines shame in part as, *'self-reproach, mortification, feeling dishonored and discredited'* - all an amplified form of *self-degradation*. Shame is a learned emotion through life programming or perpetuated by early childhood abuses and violations. You were not born to feel ashamed of anything you do. In fact, you were born with a natural trust in your own worthiness, no matter what you do. Remorsefulness is a genuine response indicating you are sorry and apologetic, even seeking penance for actions that may have inadvertently harmed someone. Shame is a distortion of genuine remorse. You learned to feel shame as a regulating mechanism to elicit remorse for inappropriate behavior, generally by your parents or caretakers.

As a self-regulating mechanism of remorse, a momentary feeling of shame results from your own awareness that your choice of word or deed has unintentionally harmed another. You intuitively know that was not your intention and thus have a desire to make amends. The feeling of discomfort associated with this awareness helps you learn that your defensive or offensive actions and reactions have consequences. You do not need to feel shame for any of these kinds of mistakes. Learn from it, make what amends you deem appropriate, and let it go.

Toxic shame represents the most damaging form of self-degradation. This chronic shame generally results from early childhood abuses that may include both sexual and personal violations on a mental, physical, and emotional level. It encompasses guilt, fear, humiliation, embarrassment, awkwardness, and self-blame from a child's limited perception. A child is unable to understand what is happening or why someone would want to hurt them. If the abuser is a parent, family member, or caretaker, the feeling of shame is intensified. The child is unable to understand why someone they trust and love would want to hurt them. Something must be wrong *with them* for all these awful things to have happened *to* them. Particularly if the abuse is of a sexual nature, the child concludes that, *'It's my fault this happened so I must be flawed in some elemental way'*. Since the majority of these abuses are bound by secrecy, the traumatized child feels powerless. Unable to defend themselves against their abuser, they internalize their sense of helplessness by acting-in or acting-out in varying ways.

Believing they are to blame, their self-image freezes emotionally at the developmental age when the abuse occurred.

As a protective mechanism, they become hyper-vigilant so others cannot discover how flawed they really are. This occurs even if they have blacked the memory of the actual abuse. Their shame, fear, and guilt continue to trigger this defensive hyper-vigilance until they address the trauma and begin the healing process. I know because I lived with that internal hell for decades.

As an adult, many act-in their shame by self-sabotaging success or satisfaction in most aspects of their lives. Things appear to go well, then fall apart in a variety of ways that confirm they are not deserving of success or happiness. They may also act-out defensively by abusing others in a variety of obvious or not so obvious manipulative ways. Many become manipulative control-freaks in order to create some kind of stability in their own life. They remain a damaged, shameful child trapped in an adult body. They cope with life's challenges by using the same behavioral mechanisms they used to survive as a child. Their adult emotional reactions, although cloaked in a socially acceptable veneer, remain based on this same hyper-vigilance. This intrinsic sense of toxic shame results in a permanent sense of *awkwardness* as they interface in the adult world.

What is awkwardness? The 'awk' in awkwardness represents AWARENESS WITHOUT KNOWLEDGE. In other words, you are powerless in your ability to respond because you genuinely do not know what to do. This triggers uncomfortable sensations that make you feel vulnerable, like being *'bare-assed'*, or completely naked in front of the world. The words 'awkward' and 'embarrassed' are most descriptive of the feelings they experience inside themselves. Based on an elemental distrust of self, others, and life itself, toxic shame can result in an inability to interact at all. The good news is, providing you are willing to do the work, you can heal this toxic shame. Feeling awkward or embarrassed in a situation where you have no prior point of reference can result from a lack of healthy socialization as well. As an adult you ward off this feeling of embarrassment at 'not knowing how to act' by activating similar childhood defensive mechanisms. You believe you are supposed to know what to do as an adult, which confirms that you are flawed.

The simplest way to diminish guilt, fear, and shame is to acknowledge it, but not energize it emotionally. Divert your energy by focusing on something else - your abilities or something that interests you when you experience these feelings. Think of something that makes you feel good within the situation itself if you cannot divert your mind to more uplifting thoughts. It may be the fact that you did not scream like a Banshee and only squeaked a little protest, or that you stuttered but did not faint. A key to diverting your focus is to concentrate on your breathing. Focus all your attention on breathing and become fully engaged in each slow deep breath you take. This raises your frequency and interrupts your automatic reaction tapes. That ten-second pause of breathing deeply can make the difference between utter panic and getting through a difficult situation. Simply by diffusing and not fueling them, much of your guilt, fear, awkwardness, and embarrassment will diminish.

Affirmations for Change

The creative energy for change originates in the NOW timelessness outside of this reality. Affirmations are powerful tools in changing your self-image providing you reinforce each statement as if it already exists even if it does not. Say your affirmations aloud a few times and listen to the words you use. You can gather affirmations from any source but the words must sound believable based on what you intend to achieve. Rephrase them if they do not sound right, for what comes *from* you - works *for* you. Just be sure you do not *'I will'* your intentions away. Nothing will happen if you place your desire in this unspecific void. Every statement you make verbally needs to be said in the *present tense*, as if it already exists.

Using the phrase 'I AM' is initially how you affect the greatest portion of yourself. The more of your senses you use the more effective the results. If you write an affirmation and read it aloud with desire and conviction, you are using your visual, auditory and tactile conscious senses as well as 100% of your feeling desire to reinforce it. It is also important to EXPECT you will get what you say.

I am particularly fond of a woman who began a 90-day program of 33 positive affirmations that covered everything she wanted to change about herself and her life. She voiced her 33 affirmations aloud daily. Enthusiastic at first, she put a great deal of energy behind her words as she visualized herself in each new state of being. After the first week, her enthusiasm began to wan and she did not visualize as fully anymore. The next week she even skipped over a few. By the third week, she said her affirmations quickly and without feeling in an automatic monotone. Even the words lost their power, for many of these words were not hers and began to sound alien. After 60 days, she experienced some change, but not as many as she had hoped. Losing faith in the process, she decided affirmations were not effective and chucked her 90-day program.

Instead of trying to cover the specifics of every aspect of her physical, mental, emotional, relationship and material desires, she could have selected a few affirmations that would kick-start her intention and willingness to change beliefs that were sabotaging her intentions. I consider her a loving example because, yes, you got it . . . that woman was yours truly, many years ago. I sure learned what did not work from that experiment as well as from others. Fortunately, I shared my disappointment with a mentor who suggested I simplify my approach by asking, *"If I had the power to change only one thing in my life right now, what would it be?"* I concentrated on three things until change was evident in those areas of my life. Then I chose several more and so on. I soon became crafty and began to create open-ended affirmations that acknowledged my willingness to change. By making my statements vaguely specific and specifically vague, I found I could influence the greatest portion of myself in many different areas of my life.

I was amazed at my progress once I affirmed I deserved to get what I asked for and asked my higher self for help. After all, that part of me knew everything about me on a conscious and subconscious level. Many things I wanted began to manifest as a by-product of basic self-validation. A growing awareness of less desirable aspects of my identity I wished to change enabled me to address and change them as well. There was no end to the lovely surprises spirit awakened in me when I became interested in my own identity and individualistic desires. I began to realize that the very differences that I felt had always set me apart from others were aspects of an ever-changing consciousness I now cherish as an expression of my own uniqueness.

There is no end to the knowledge and information accessible to us when our mind is open. Just this past year I discovered an even more powerful key to enhancing the effectiveness of my affirmations. I watched an interview on Larry King Live with several spiritual teachers that included J.Z Knight, facilitator of the Ramtha teachings. They all responded to questions about spirituality, energy, and if the manipulation of energy was possible. When asked about the effectiveness of Affirmations, J.Z. Knight cited an example of an affirmation that included several important words designed to enhance their effectiveness. They were, "<u>This Day I have always been</u> (the content of the affirmation), and ending each with the powerful and emphatic word, <u>effortlessly</u>".

I felt a shiver run through my whole body as I heard these words and knew they were significant. I asked spirit to reveal the purpose and meaning of this feeling of what I can only describe in hindsight as excited anticipation. Over the next few days I contemplated the word 'effortlessly' and realized that based on my core life programming, I had always believed that to get what I wanted took hard work, time, and effort. Only then would I be deserving of having my wishes fulfilled. Many of us with European parents have a core belief that getting what you want results only from hard work and suffering. Aware hard work and suffering was a core belief of mine, I rephrased all my affirmations and chose those I felt would have the most encompassing effects.

I sat outside on my deck next morning, as I did every morning before daylight, with my coffee and at least one cat on my lap, and began my new affirmations. I choose the morning to say my affirmations in order to define my mind-set for the day. Once a day is all you need, preferably in the morning, though it may be helpful for the first few weeks to say them while driving home from work or at bedtime as well. Driving is an autopilot function meaning you are in a slight Alpha state while driving your familiar route home, which helps imprint your subconscious with your new intentions. You do not need to be concerned for your safety for you will immediately snap out of the Alpha state should any danger or need for vigilance on the road present itself.

My life completely changed within two to three weeks. Talk about sizzle and pop! Circumstances I could not even have imagined and desires buried within my subconscious began to manifest in my life so fast I felt like I was riding a celestial roller coaster of blessings and abundance. I could also hardly wait to share my discovery with friends and promptly emailed them about this exciting discovery, suggesting they add these power words to their affirmations. Some did, with evident results. I am profoundly grateful to J.Z. Knight for providing these powerful words.

Thus began a new creative game for me, of phrasing affirmations in the most specifically vague but vaguely specific way to affect the greatest portion of myself in all areas of my life. I also began to group my affirmations into segments that addressed specific aspects of my life, with a particular emphasis on my willingness to change previous patterns of thinking, perception, and behavior. Some affirmations that have worked well for me are:

<u>*Affirming Spirituality*</u>
"I AM a spiritual being having a physical experience"
"I know I AM here for a very specific purpose and have much to contribute to life"
"I AM always in the right place, at the right time, for the right reasons, for my higher good"

*"I AM here to create a safe, harmonious, and bountiful life -
effortlessly"*
"I know I AM, and have always been, a unique & valuable being"

Willingness to Change
"This day, I have always been open to change – effortlessly"
*"This day, I have always been willing to change my mind as
required to enhance my physical experience - effortlessly"*
*"I AM transforming my energy and healing all and any
imbalances within myself - effortlessly"*
*"I AM continually discovering newness about me each and every
day"*
*"I AM releasing all of my patterns of confusion and despair -
effortlessly"*

Self-Confidence
"I AM an interesting person with interesting things to say"
*"This day, I have always felt confident and at ease within all &
every circumstance - effortlessly"*
*"This day, I have always been able to communicate well with
others, even if their beliefs are different from my own – effortlessly"*
*"This day, I have always felt confident and secure within my
greater identity - effortlessly"*
*This day, I have always trusted my desires & curiosity lead me to
new creative adventures of self-discovery – effortlessly"*
*"This day, my mind has always been able to retain and recall all
and any information, as required – effortlessly"*
*"This day, I have always been able to learn and apply new
information & technologies – effortlessly"*

My Personality
*"This day, I have always been filled with so much love that it spills
over on everyone I meet and interact with – effortlessly"*
*"This day, I have always loved everything about me, seen or unseen,
known or unknown - effortlessly"*

"This day, I have always loved who I am and who I am becoming - effortlessly"
"This day, I have always been loving, compassionate, and understanding — effortlessly"
"This day, my life has always been filled with love, joy, and laughter — effortlessly"
"This day, I have always increased and expanded my ability to express love and be loved - effortlessly"
"This day, I have always chosen to be healthy, productive & wise — effortlessly"

Enhancing Intuitive Abilities

"This day, I have always used all my extended senses to enhance my physical experience - effortlessly"
"This day, I have always been able to manifest all my dreams, desires & intentions — effortlessly"
"This day, I have always felt safe to open my creative spiritual channels - effortlessly"
"This day, I have always trusted my inner senses to guide me towards my life's mission - effortlessly"
"This day, I have always been able to direct my energy towards what I want to experience — effortlessly"
"This day, I have always been willing to ask for spiritual help from my higher being — effortlessly"
"This day, I have always trusted my life is guided by Divine Grace — effortlessly"

Wealth & Abundance

"This day I have always been immensely wealthy — effortlessly"
"This day my life has always been filled with financial prosperity & continuous abundance in all ways - effortlessly"
"This day, I have always been able and willing to share with others the abundance that continually flows into my life — effortlessly"
"This day, I have always been immensely successful in all my business, personal & creative ventures — effortlessly"
"This day, I have always been creative, efficient, and effective—effortlessly"

Increasing Awareness of Self
"This day, I have always been willing and able to increase my awareness of myself - effortlessly"
"This day, I have always been willing and able to expand and change my beliefs - effortlessly"
"This day, I have always embraced the changes necessary for my continued growth - effortlessly"
"This day, I have always trusted that my feelings are safe, beneficial & expand my awareness of myself – effortlessly"

Body Consciousness
"This day, I have always been a beautiful woman/man, inside and out – effortlessly"
"This day, I have always been immensely healthy – effortlessly"
"This day, I have always loved my body the way it is & the way it is becoming – effortlessly"
"This day, I have always trusted my body to tell me what it needs for its health & wellbeing - effortlessly"
"This day, I have always trusted my body to operate at optimum efficiency – effortlessly"
"This day, my body has always been able to eliminate all & any toxins and negativity - effortlessly"
"This day, my body has always been slim, trim, fit & flexible – effortlessly"

Gratitude
"This day, I have always been immensely grateful for all the blessings and abundance that continually flow into my life – effortlessly"
This day, I AM always feeling tremendous gratitude for all that I AM, and that I am becoming - effortlessly"

How many affirmations you choose to voice is entirely your choice. May I suggest you begin with one from each category to influence your beliefs on a spiritual, physical, mental and emotional level. Alternating between affirmations that reinforce what you want as already existing and those whereby you give yourself permission to change your existing patterns is the key that allows spirit to direct you towards your authentic intentions via your own intuitive senses. "THIS DAY" ensures you are grounding your statement in the point of power of NOW. The 'I AM' ensures your expectation will materialize in the present, and the ALL WAYS reinforces consistent results. Since your mental processes do not judge the data coming in, 50% of assuring change is to trick your brain into believing these intentions already exist. The other 50% is the energy-motion of *faith;* that your new desire is an actuality, even if your outer reality does not yet reflect your intentions. *Faith requires no reasons* and *you will see it when you believe it,* not the other way around.

Phrases like *'I want to have', 'I will be',* or *'I'm going to'* place your expectations outside of the ever present now, thereby rarely materialize. The only thing that has effect now is a statement or belief grounded in the now. The past and future are memories (review of the past), and your idea projections (desires and intentions for the future). If you act *'as if'* what you want already exists magnetic energy will draw to you circumstances and events to reflect the 'image' you naturally expect. It happens not because some Almighty Deity decides you deserve what you want, but because the energy of your own desire and expectation sets the universe in motion whereby energy draws it to you.

If you want more prosperity in your life, a phrase like, *"This day, I have always been financially prosperous"* or *"Every day, in every way, my life has always been filled with prosperity and abundance"* is much more effective than *"I want to be prosperous".* As you will see later, abundance has little to do with your financial assets or material possessions, although there is nothing wrong with having an abundance of both. If you have to 'fake it until you make it', and act prosperous even if you are not - do it. Your subconscious cannot tell the difference.

Another important key to manifesting what you want is the amount of *dedicated energy,* or intensity of feeling behind your desire and affirmation. The more intently you visualize it, relish the feeling of having it, write it out and say it, the more quickly you will experience it. Since your thoughts and feelings are also recorded in your mental data banks, if you say you're prosperous but think you don't really deserve to get what you want, or you wonder how will it come, you scatter and disperse your energy into all these *'what ifs'*. Decide what you want and state it clearly in a matter of fact manner both in your mind and aloud, with the objective expectation of getting it. Visualize and feel what it is to have it, but once you have done so and placed your order, forget about it. What often prevents you from getting what you want is hanging onto a desire by continually thinking about it. What happens when you throw a ball but hang onto the elastic attached to it? It keeps zipping back to you. Desires need to be *released in order to be realized*.

Energy will manifest exactly what you believe you deserve, in spite of what you may consciously ask for. Whatever your glass ceiling on how much prosperity, joy, love or success you can have, that is exactly how much you will get. So raise your ceiling on what you believe you deserve. The universe just provides neutral energy to manifest your thoughts - *whatever* they are. You are already getting exactly what you believe you deserve based on your existing inner self-image.

How you order food in a restaurant is a good indication of how you order your life experiences. Do you scan the menu in anticipation and make a decision based on what your taste buds are prompting you to try or what sounds delicious? Do you even order what you want? Do you wonder what your dinner companions think of your choice or agonize if can you afford it? Do you order only what your diet says you can eat, or what everyone else is ordering? When the food comes, do you eat with relish, just pick at what is on your plate without interest, or wish you had ordered something else? You may not do this consciously, but you do this in your mind. It is the same thing.

How do you deal with mistakes in your order when it arrives? Do you calmly ask to have it fixed or choose an alternate item that also looks appealing? Do you take it personally, make a scene or bitch about it to your dinner companions because the situation proves once again that you never get what you really want? The universe is much like a cosmic ten-star restaurant with an unlimited menu. You can virtually have anything you can 'image', but you get only what you order. If the selection or results are poor, it is because these limitations are a result of your subconscious beliefs. Since your subconscious connects you to the source of your spiritual intentions, your Soul influences wish fulfillment in a way that is *for your higher good*. There may be a discrepancy between what you ordered and what you get since you are only aware of your conscious desires. You forget all about your higher frequency self's broader vision of your spiritual intentions and desires. You also forget you asked for spiritual assistance in the past so do not recognize what you get *is* what you need to fulfill these intentions. Your higher self will always promote the expansion of your consciousness. You also have so many thoughts, fears, and desires racing through your head, you cannot remember what you ordered previously or that the time-delay feeling-energy attached to those thoughts caused them to materialize in the most opportune way. You look at them and wonder what kind of a twisted mind could conjure up such a mess. Your mind did. Celebrate, for these circumstances affirm what a wondrous creative individual you are! Now begin to direct that creative energy so you can attract what you really want. Despite getting things you do not like, everything you manifest presents an opportunity to expand your awareness of yourself and and hone your desire-fulfillment skills.

If the methodology of how it comes is as important as getting it, your own criteria for '*how*' will greatly influence the '*when*'. For example: if you needed $1,000, you may have decided it can only come to you 'in an envelope edged with gold foil, held in the beak of a white dove, delivered on a Sunday morning via Albuquerque'. Silly as that sounds, based on some of your subconscious beliefs you may wait a long time for such synchronicity. You think the system is not working when in fact it works perfectly. It is your beliefs about how it '*should*' work that prevents the natural process of desire fulfillment, for your highest good. When you get something you do not want, find something beneficial in what you did get and place another order.

Your feelings, the carrier waves of your thoughts, propel energy to manifest what you desire based on what you subconsciously believe you deserve. *"As a man thinketh - in his heart - so he become."* There are no exceptions. State what you want and forget about how it will come. State what you desire as if it already exists, then act and feel like it already does. Trust the process and focus on something else. You will not get what you want until you decide what you want after you got what you wanted. Your purpose for being here is *your Soul fulfillment in its learning experience - both physically and spiritually.* Life is not about methodology or material props, although the former is an expression of your individual creativity and the latter an enjoyable byproduct of the former. Providing you do not intentionally harm another individual, you can desire and experience anything you want.

Many of you wage a battle between your desires and values. For Example: Two boys may want expensive roller blades. One does chores and has a part-time job to earn money to buy his. The other asked his uncle, who buys them for him with his credit card the very same day. Which pair of roller blades will have more value? How they got their roller blades is irrelevant. Both boys got what they desired based on their beliefs. Appreciation is not dependant on methodology, unless you believe it 'should' be. Do your beliefs and values dictate that you have to earn everything you want with the sweat of your brow, over a long period of time, and with great effort? Why not place an order and get it without expending any physical energy at all? You can – once you trust the process. The universe has unlimited creative ways of providing your needs and desires, if you do not predetermine how they should manifest.

You are here to learn how to direct energy within this three-dimensional reality. Learning something new takes experimentation and practice, so be gentle with yourself as you begin to use your inner resources to direct energy.

Chapter 4

YOUR SENSORY RESOURCES

"Your inner consciousness provides the keys to expand and enhance your outer reality."

YOU are an energy light being comprised of electromagnetic energy operating on different frequencies. This energy frequency circulates both within and around your physical body. The pulsing electromagnetic field that exists around your body called the AURA, is defined in the dictionary as *'a distinctive atmosphere surrounding a given source'* and *'a luminous radiation'*. Your Aura is in a continual state of fluctuation and transformation as it broadcasts your spiritual, mental, physical and psychological state of being. As an energy being, your body functions as both a receptor and broadcaster of energy frequencies. Thus, all your conscious actions, interactions, and experiences first occur on an energy level. There are no exceptions.

Although you generally accept the camouflage of an individual's interface, on an energy level you are always aware of their real feeling, intentions, and thoughts. The sensations and impressions you get from what their Aura broadcasts helps you understand their true position regardless of the persona they choose to project. On a sensory level you are aware of everything that is really happening around you at all times. Therefore, there are no secrets in the world. Your conscious focus just blocks all this extra information out. Consciously you only perceive what you learned to perceive. Subconsciously, you are aware of EVERYTHING that is going on around you on an energy level.

Chakras

Like a holographic projection of light and electromagnetic energy, your body is the thought projection of the energy being you really are. In actuality, everything around you, including your own body, is just a holographic projection and reflection of consciousness. None of it is real or solid. It just appears so because mass consciousness, the framework of this 3-D reality, and the root assumptions of your own beliefs support this illusion.

Your physical body has seven primary energy points along the spinal column called the Chakras, a Sanskrit word meaning *'wheel, plexus, or center'*. Sanskrit is a historical Indo-Aryan language of Hinduism and Buddhism. These chakra centers represent the energy circuitry responsible for different aspects of your whole identity like your mind, heart, feelings, psychological attitude, and physical organs within that chakra system. Although your chakras operate on different frequencies, they transmit information between the different aspects of your being.

Each chakra has a color that reflects the vibration of light and matter it represents on its particular frequency. When your hands are placed on an electromagnetic sensor device designed to measure these energy vibrations you can see which energies you are predominantly using at that moment. Every chakra also has its own frequency sound, much like the vibration or tone of an individual musical note. Some people chant while they meditate to connect with, align, and balance these frequencies to resonate with the higher frequency aspects of themselves. Particular tones stimulate and enhance the free flow of energy between all your charkas such as the high frequency of LOVE that dissolves blockages in your energy circuitry.

The seven points or chakras that represent these energy centers are:

Base	(red)	C note	- *tailbone*, most physical & elemental, survival
Sacral	(orange)	D note	- *below belly button* - emotions, sensuality/sexuality
Solar Plexus	(yellow)	E note	- *below ribcage* - communication & intuition
Heart	(green)	F note	- mid-point balance of outer/inner you, healing center
Throat	(blue)	G note	- *inner you*, love/feeling, communications with outer world
Brow	(purple)	A note	- *mental/reasoning*, masculine energy, aspirations & outward thrust
Crown	(violet)	B note	- *spiritual/inspiration*, feminine energy, creative & inwardly receptive

The first three, the *base, sacral* and *solar plexus* are the lower frequencies that maintain your biological existence and connect you to the supportive elements of Earth consciousness. The *base* chakra represents instinctive elemental behaviors associated with biological functions to ensure physical survival. The *sacral* chakra ensures survival through propagation and represents the emotional sensations associated with sexuality and sensuality. The *solar plexus* chakra represents your response feelings while you communicate with both your inner and outer world. It acts like a spiritual feeling center that interprets the physiological sensations triggered by all your physical experiences. It is from this chakra that your intuitive feelings, or gut feelings arise.

The last three, the *throat, brow* and *crown* charkas connect you to the Universal Cosmic Pulse. As the impetus for this physical experience, they represent your higher frequency identity. This Cosmic pulse is a kind of electromagnetic charge beamed at our planet from somewhere within the Milky Way. Picked up by the body's electric circuits, this pulse passes through the brain's micro-antennas to the heart and from the heart center flows to all other charkas in your body. The electromagnetic field of the Aura connects you to the Cosmic Pulse at your *crown* chakra, through which energy pours into your being. This energy flow maintains your biological form and synergy with your natural environment and inner consciousness. The human heartbeats aligned to this Cosmic Pulse before the Gregorian calendar intentionally disrupted this resonance. Disconnected from their higher frequencies and inner senses, humans could more easily be stimulated and controlled through low frequency emotions.

The *heart* chakra is the mid-point intersection of your higher and lower frequency aspects. It acts as a balancing point between your spiritual and physical self as they interrelate with each other. It is through your heart chakra that you express both the higher frequency of love and the lower frequency of fear. The low frequency of fear, expressed through a variety of emotions like guilt, anger, shame, aggression, judgment of self and others, blocks the flow of energy between your lower and higher chakras. These blocks immobilize the micro-antennas in your brain called amino acids, which act as connectors and carriers of information throughout your body's energy circuitry. They also interact with the data stored in your DNA. The more micro-antenna receptors are stimulated in your brain, the more sensory and intuitive information you can access to maintain a free flow of energy. Free flowing energy translates into a balanced spiritual and physical expression.

When you or others trigger fear and other low frequency emotions, your chakras are blocked and only part of your total micro-antenna receptors kick-in. Like eight spark plugs in a V8 engine, if one or two spark plugs do not work, you may not notice a power loss. When three or four of them do not fire up it affects the vehicle's overall performance. Accumulations of dense low frequency emotions block your charkas just as sludge blocks the fuel filter in a car. These blocks prevent energy flow between charkas and restrict access to your higher frequencies. Disconnected from the very senses that would signal manipulation and mental programming is taking place, you are unaware you are functioning and reacting on the most basic levels. Scientific research has proven the emotion of fear resonates on a low frequency as a long slow-moving wavelength that only triggers a limited number of the brain's antenna receptors. They also proved the higher frequency of love is a much shorter and fast spinning wavelength that stimulates more of the brain's amino acids. Loving yourself and others raises your frequency and activates more antenna receptors. These amino acids also stimulate your inner sensory resources. The more sensory resources you use, the more aware you are of what is really going on around you.

The heart chakra transmits any emotional imbalances between its upper and lower aspects. Imbalances caused by a discrepancy between your inner feelings and learned emotional reactions are passed upward to the mental aspect of yourself for evaluation. If not addressed on that level they move back down through the heart chakra into your other physical systems. The resulting blocks remain in any of the various organs connected to that particular chakra and manifest as physical symptoms or disease in order to get your attention. When chakras are blocked, your real feelings are unable to move through your heart chakra and reach the mental reasoning aspect of yourself for interpretation. The resulting physical changes are legitimate indicators of imbalance in other psychological aspects of your being.

Your chakras broadcast what is really going on inside you through the electromagnetic field around your body - your Aura. Your Aura generally extends about three feet around your body and looks much like a slightly pulsating rainbow of color. Representing the overall state of your being, these colors expand, contract, and change hue as you energize different aspects of yourself. When you consciously extend your Aura you can expand this sensory field to receive whatever energies enter it. For Example: You receive impressions from, or can even tune into the thoughts and feelings of anyone who moves through this extended field. Ever wonder where some of your *'mixed feelings'* come from when you are in a group of people, on a bus, or in a crowed Shopping Mall?

You can also pull you aura in close to your body and create a temporary energy shield around yourself others are unable to penetrate unless they know how. This blocks your own receptiveness when you do not want to receive random or negative external energies or when you want to prevent others from reading your energy signature. Often, those who trigger discomforting emotions in you use this method purposely to cloak their own aura. Shielded in this way, their aura acts like a mirror that reflects your own energy emissions right back at you. Not knowing you are viewing your own energy, you end up reacting to yourself. If you do not like what you are sensing, it is a wonderful opportunity to discover why. All kinds of interesting things can happen as you practice extending and contracting your aura in public places or during personal interactions.

Although you may not see this rainbow of colors around others, you all feel them on a sensory energy level. For Example: During a conversation with a friend, you unknowingly say something that triggers an uncomfortable or painful memory in them. As feelings are always 100%, your friend is now re-experiencing the past events triggered by these feelings in their mind. If you unconsciously extended your aura towards them during this interaction, you would intuitively pick up these feelings on an energy level. Consciously you sense something has changed without knowing what caused the change and may even begin to feel uncomfortable yourself. You become more receptive on a sensory level whenever you extended your Aura. Had you done so consciously you would know it was *their* feelings you are experiencing not your own.

Lower frequency emotions not only create blocks in your energy circuitry but also visually muddy the color of the affected chakra in your Aura. The denser and muddier a chakra's color is, the more blocks that system contains. Those who see and read auras can easily identify where your imbalances lie and what organs these blocks are affecting by the Chakra's color. Regular short periods of meditation and focused deep breathing keeps you attuned with your higher frequencies so you can use your own inner senses to identify, address, and dissolve these blocks before they manifest as physical symptoms. Whenever you express a genuine feeling of love, your heart chakra begins to spin at a higher and faster rate. This draws energy from the Cosmos into your body's energy network. The high speed at which this energy spins helps to dislodge blockages through a higher frequency awareness of the cause.

The higher your frequency, the more micro-receptors get fired-up in your brain and the more attuned you are on all sensory levels. Since feeling is 100%, you can only feel one feeling at a time. You are not energizing low frequency emotions while expressing the higher frequency of love. It can be done as simply as validating that you are a loving, worthy, and precious individual, which you are. You just forget this while experiencing low-frequency emotions. The triggering of all these antenna receptors affects how much of your brainpower you actually use. Most of you use only 6%-7% of your brain's full capacity – on a good day. You can significantly increase your overall intelligence and cognitive abilities by firing up more amino acid receptors. As these receptors also stimulate your inner senses, you will be amazed at the thoughts, ideas, and understandings that begin to flow through your mind. You all have the capacity to exceed the abilities of those considered geniuses when you reconnect with the free-flow energy of the Cosmic Pulse.

You are a far more multi-faceted energy being than you realize. You experience yourself through four basic energy elements - the physical, mental, emotional, and spiritual. Each of these provides you with a specific kind of energy power resource. Your spiritual aspect is the cosmic frequency through which your thoughts and impetus for the self-exploration emerge. Your emotional feeling center acts as the generator from which the curiosity and desire to realize these thoughts arise. Your mental aspect processes and utilizes the conceptual knowledge and experience you have acquired to choose your responsive actions and the body provides the physical actions that determine the resulting events in your life. When all these elements work in unison - when the mental and physical aspects of yourself are fueled by your inner feelings and desires - cosmic energy from outside this reality transforms your thoughts into what you experience within this reality. This is how you were fundamentally intended to explore your consciousness and identity within this 3-D reality.

Your Inner Senses

Your senses act as the spiritual interpreters of everything your consciousness experiences. As a light-energy being, this reality is only one of many frequencies on which you operate. Those other-frequency experiences along with your current physical experience are part of a much larger script for self-actualization than you realize. You could consider this life as just one spoke of many spokes on your Soul's wheel of experience. What prevents your awareness of these other spokes is frequency and conscious focus. Each of these spokes operates on a different frequency from each other yet are aligned through their connection to a common source: the consciousness of your greater spiritual or Soul identity. You can reconnect with these other aspects of yourself through a relatively small shift in consciousness when you enter the *Alpha state*. Bridging your conscious and subconscious, the Alpha state allows these two aspects to intersect in the timelessness outside this reality. Meditation and controlled breathing alters your brain's wavelengths by directing your attention away from this conscious focus. Although each of you operates within your own wheel of consciousness, as a light energy being you share a consciousness bond with all other light-beings. Were this not true, you would not be able to interact with the energy of anyone else within this reality.

Science says the geniuses of our world use 10-12% of their brain and that the rest of us use about 6-7% of our brain's capacity. What do you think the other 90-93% is for? Geneticists refer to junk DNA; the unexplained half of the double DNA helix they think serves no purpose. That is what they want you to believe because they have no knowledge of its real purpose. Based on Darwin's Theory of Evolution many scientists consider it the residual proof of this evolutionary process. This DNA is neither junk nor a residue of Darwin's linear and limited theory of evolution. It is in fact a powerful but dormant genetic resource awaiting re-activation. Each of you can activate aspects of this vast evolutionary database that contains the memory of your greater consciousness and celestial origins with your inner senses.

Your inner senses provide you with extra sensory tools such as Clairvoyance, Psychometrics, Telepathy, and Telekinesis, among others. Overall, scientists view these senses with skepticism and discount them as sensory abilities we all possess. The concept of 'normal' has come to represent the majority who do not use these extended senses. This was not always the case. Our genetic heritage is more expansive than we realize. These senses are legitimate and a more refined extension of our existing five senses. The difference is that they can bridge frequencies. The dictionary defines Clairvoyance as *'the ability to perceive matter beyond the range of ordinary perception'*. Psychometrics is defined as *'the divination of facts concerning an object or its owner through contact with or proximity to the object'*.

Telepathy, defined as, *'the apparent communication from one mind to another otherwise than through the channels of sense'* is discounted the most primarily because consciousness is not credited with the ability to direct energy. Telekinesis, *'the apparent*

Elfie H.M. Leddy

production of motion in objects (as by a spiritualistic medium) without contact or other physical means' is the ability to manipulate matter and alters the relationships between ourselves and the elements in our physical environment. I find it interesting that the two *'perceptive'* senses of Clairvoyance and Psychometrics are defined as abilities, while the two *'action'* oriented senses of Telepathy and Telekinesis, abilities that were they used, would drastically alter how we interact with our physical reality, are defined as *apparent* abilities.

Quantum Physics has long experimented with sub-atomic energy particles in order to understand their chaotic and random activity. Experiments have led several researchers to discover that a tiny sub-atomic particle can suddenly be in more than one place at the same time. Baffling as that was, a few even considered the possibility that this chaotic activity was somehow influenced by the fact that their activity was being observed by the researchers. Repeatedly noting the affects of this hypothesis, they do not know how to prove it to the scientific community. The idea that everything, including sub-atomic particles have consciousness and that consciousness influences other consciousness seems preposterous to the scientific community.

These extended senses and many others like moving objects with sound and tone frequencies, were utilized in daily life by ancient cultures such as Atlantis and Lemuria. *Tele-transportation* (moving your body from one location to another in an instant) or projecting a part of your consciousness to another location so you are actually in two places at the same time was a common place practice in the even older civilization of Mu, from which Atlantis and Lemuria sprung after a planetary axis shift. The use of these and other extended senses was a natural part of daily life in the more ancient cultures on this planet. Geographically located where Australia is now, remnants of the massive landmass of Mu still exist. It is no accident that the Australian Aborigines, their genetic memories largely unsullied by outside programming until this past century, have always considered the massive red rock in the center of Australia as the sacred womb of life. Despite the axis shift after the destruction of both Atlantis and Lemuria, California on the west coast of North America is also a surviving remnant of the ancient Lemurian landmass. The fact that any plant from any part of the world will thrive in the soils of this long narrow strip of land is no accident of nature.

Our creation story as a species is much grander and more interesting than scripted by religion, history, and science. Fragmented memories of this ancient heritage are still reflected in our art, myths, legends, and more importantly – in our own consciousness. Archeologists have already found convincing evidence for the historic existence and location of legendary Troy and mythical Atlantis. Arguments still rage over which of the three probable geographic locations for Atlantis is accurate. These include the mid-Atlantic ocean, the Mediterranean, and Pacific Ocean between North America and Australia.

Existing confusion results from not realizing that Atlantis was so large it spanned two of these areas, and that Lemuria's landmass, not even credited as being a legitimate mythical culture, spanned both the Indian and Pacific Ocean. Since each culture occupied one of only two massive primary landmasses of that time, archeologists are unaware that they have found remnants of both cultures in various unrelated locations. They are also unaware that central Australia is a remnant of the even older culture of Mu. Buried in our genes, in that dormant double helix, are the memories of our own existences in Atlantis, Lemuria, and Mu.

Within the dormant spiral of our DNA lie the keys to not only our Cosmic and authentic historic past as a species, but also the means to transform human consciousness into its previously 'Godly' consciousness. I use the term Godly because you only credit God with the ability to affect matter. Our extra senses are the inherent abilities of a greater identity intentionally suppressed. Using your inner resources, you begin to remember what a powerful manifesting light-energy being you were and still are.

One spiral of your DNA helix represents your outer consciousness and bloodline's biological genetic history. The other represents your inner consciousness and its more expansive genetic history. The Soul-memory of everything you experience as an energy-consciousness lies within this dormant half of your double helix. When you shift your consciousness to a higher frequency, you begin to realize just how multi-dimensional you are by how much more information these senses provide and understand what this game of self-exploration on Planet Earth is all about. When you ride the higher frequency of love as we once did, you trigger more of your brain's amino receptors, which result in a more expansive and creative physical existence. You experience your real physical TASK: Thought and Sensation = Knowledge.

Your inner senses provide the means to expand and enhance your outer reality. You can use these senses to link with someone's real feelings or tune into past-life interactions to understand the dynamics of your existing identity and relationships. These senses help you regain your synergy with the natural environment that also provides clues to your more expansive identity. This kind of sensory awareness may feel alien, uncomfortable, even frightening at first. You are not used to acting on feelings or impressions that have no 'reasons' to support their validity because of your current beliefs *about* reality. Yet, without reasons these senses ensure you are always in the right place, at the right time, to realize your spiritual intentions. The answers you seek are not out there, rather, they are 'INSIDE YOU' and accessed through your inner senses.

Emotions & Feelings

Most of you confuse emotions with feelings and consider them the same when they are not. Your feelings are the spiritual interpretations of your thoughts based on the physical sensations you experience while having those thoughts. *Feelings are sensations that spring from your inner consciousness.* With them, you feel your own thoughts on a subconscious sensory level before you respond on a conscious level. Since your thoughts and the life circumstances they manifest continually change, your feelings continually change. When your feelings change, your thoughts change. You have no idea how you will feel five minutes from now were your doorbell to ring. Even when you know who is at the door you are unaware of what kind of thoughts and feelings that person will trigger in you because you do not know what they will do or say.

Emotions are a reactionary byproduct of your learned beliefs. As the automatic reactions triggered by your mental systems, your emotions are predictable. Your emotional reaction to a new event or circumstance results from its similarity to past circumstances stored in your mental data banks. When you feel an emotion, you react *without* consciously processing the information as an independent experience. Your mind's automatic processes do it for you and trigger a reaction based on similar past reactions to similar past events. Yet, you rely on these automatic reactions to define your identity and response to a completely new experience.

If you need to justify your position or blame someone or something for what happens to you, you are responding to an emotion not a feeling. When you react to events only through pre-determined conclusions, you no longer express your true feelings. You believe these emotions are your feelings. As a result, you are easily triggered into reacting a certain way by those who wish to control the outcome of their interaction with you consciously or subconsciously. All they have to do is trigger certain beliefs, and the emotional reaction will follow.

Emotions perpetuate misinformation in the same way as the beliefs that created them. If your beliefs are inflexible, your emotional reaction will be as well. You may have noticed when you discuss a re-occurring sensitive issue with a family member, friend, or co-worker that you both react the same way when a specific recurring subject comes up in conversation. Your predictable reactions result in a superficial game of emotional Ping Pong rather than an opportunity to explore the underlying reason for your sensitivity on that subject. Many of you say, *"Don't go there."* meaning, *"you already know my position on that subject."* or you might say, *"I don't want to talk about it"*, meaning, *"I don't want to deal with the real issue."* Beneath these emotional reactions lie genuine feelings that relate to 'feel bad' experiences you have not identified or resolved. Such defensive reactions need investigation.

Despite your emotional reactions, you feel your genuine sensory response inside - the true indicator of your position in any given situation. You may be depressed or sad but act as if you are not because you think you should. You may be tired yet let yourself be convinced to do something you do not want to. Others can sense the discord between your real feelings versus what you project consciously. This is an important key to understanding how others know you are not telling the truth and therefore do not accept your excuses. When your response arises from your real feelings, they may not like it, but they will accept it. Many of your interactive difficulties are a result of this kind of sensory conflict. It can be confusing to be receptive to each other's real feelings subconsciously and emotional reactions consciously. The energy consequences for yourself when you act contrary to your real feelings create energy blocks that can soon manifest as physical symptoms. When you acknowledge and express your genuine feelings, you release the energy dedicated to them. If another person does not like it, it does not matter. You are responsible for your overall wellbeing.

There is nothing wrong with expressing how you feel even if you believe they are 'bad' feelings. All your feelings are valid because all your feelings are 100% from you and 100% for you. Your feelings are the means through which you understand yourself. Without feeling sensations, your experiences would consist of robotic action without meaning. Your particular programming and self-judgment defines what feelings you think you can or should not express. Allowing yourself to express love is of paramount importance to your well-being. Your feeling of love towards someone does not need reciprocation but it does need expression to set the universe in motion. The frequency called love is much more than a sensory byproduct of relationship and sexual intimacy. It is a powerful energy vehicle for creative self-expression, and self-transformation. It is the universal frequency of creation itself.

The feeling of love opens *your heart chakra* so high frequency energy can move through all aspects of your being. You *allow* someone or something to trigger the sensation called love to activate more of your own amino acid receptors. The 'feel good' sensations you experience when you fall in love, when your own perception sees the world as wonderful (full-of-wonder), is the higher frequency state of being you want to feel within all your physical experiences. You are able to express more facets of yourself to expand and nourish your self-identity. You have learned to direct this energy just towards your love interests on the lower frequencies of neediness and possessiveness as expressed through sexuality. Anything or anyone in your environment can trigger this high frequency of love in you. You allow love to be triggered not only through human contact, but also by music, art, nature, animals, and any sensory experience that stimulates 'feel good' sensations within your being.

The more you can find in others, in your environment and circumstances to trigger this feeling of love within yourself, the more love you will feel towards yourself. The more love you feel towards yourself, the more love you express towards others. The more love you express, the more love you attract. The more love you attract the more love you feel. The more love you feel, the more you set the universe in motion to fulfill your own desires and intentions. Sharing and exchanging love is the means through which we help each reach a higher state of being that results in a meaningful life for us all. So, by all means, feel as much love towards as many people as you can, whether they reciprocate or not.

If you feel defensive within your interactions, you need to ask yourself why. Defensiveness is a disguise for vulnerability and insecurity. Ask yourself what expectations are not been met? What inner fear, guilt, or shame are you protecting? Anger is also a disguise. Anger is fear turned inside out - a need to protect against real or perceived harm. Knowing this, you can stop taking another person's anger personally. Their anger belongs to them. You can choose a compassionate response rather than a self-defensive reaction to their anger. You can say something like, *'I can understand how you would feel that way'* or *'I'm sorry you feel that way'* to validate the inner cause for their anger. Then send them love to help diffuse their anger. All you have control over is yourself. What you have no control over is others - what they think, feel, and do. You may not change their position even if you do send them love, but it is impossible to send someone love without feeling it yourself. This changes your own perception within the situation, which changes your response and then the interaction.

Your emotions reinforce your conscious sense of security. As long as you react as others do, your identity within your social environment remains intact. Emotions allow you to abdicate responsibility for your real feelings and their effects were you to express them. What if you expressed your real feelings and others ridicule you? What if you hurt or anger someone you care for? What if saying what you really feel compromises your future at work or changes your personal relationships? By running your emotional tapes, you also do not have to examine or change your beliefs. Fueled by your own imagination, all these perceived *'what-ifs'* running through your mind keep you bound to these programmed reactions.

You maintain a natural state of well-being through *expression,* not *suppression.* To suppress your feelings will not change them or make them go away. The discrepancy between what you really feel and what you express emotionally causes most of the energy blocks within your system. A build-up of these blocks eventually leads to illness or disease. Despite medical advances, disease, mental illness, addictions, and environmental sensitivities are on the rise. If you ignore the messages your heart chakra sends your mind, they are sent back through the heart chakra to your physical body to get your attention in a way you cannot easily ignore - through DIS-EASE. Disease signals the presence of imbalance caused by beliefs that do not nourish your well-being.

Expand your sensory awareness by taking time to explore your natural curiosities and personal inclinations. Conditioned to race through life at warp speed you have learned to expect instant gratification in all areas of your life including your emotional feeling center. Life is not a horse race or a destination. It is a moment-by-moment interpretation of your thoughts and feelings within all your experiences. When you rush from one emotional reaction to another, you de-sensitize your real feeling responses. Nevertheless, the 100% energy behind your suppressed feelings still needs release. Spiritually creative, you fabricate artificial emotional traumas or dramas to trigger this essential release. If you still do not express your feelings, like a crack addict, you seek a higher high to release this imbalanced state. Eventually you have a grand mess of energy blocks that result in mental, physical, and emotional illness.

Real feelings can be more difficult to define than emotions. Like a kaleidoscope of fleeting colors many conflicting sensations can be triggered by a single event or circumstance. Some, though deeply felt are also ephemeral. For example: your body may tingle and tears may flow at the sound of a piece of music that touches you so deeply your feelings cannot be contained within one sensation or a fleeting scent can trigger a rush of unrelated memories with their own sensory feelings to cascade through your body. Since emotions follow your beliefs, they represent only a limited response to a more expansive sensory experience. Yet you experience these emotions with the same 100% intensity as your real feelings. Your mind, during its comparison and cross-referencing process, creates sub-files that record all your sensory responses, be they real feelings or emotions. To *'get in touch with your feelings'* means just that - to seek out your real feelings and allow yourself to explore and express them. That is why you chose this sensory physical experience. Action in itself is meaningless. *Your feeling responses define your identity.* Therefore conscious living is experienced inside out - through sensation, not outside in - through re-action.

Model # 3.

99% OF WHAT IS HAPPENING - IS HAPPENING IN
THE SUBCONSCIOUS...
BUT... IF YOU CLOSE YOUR EYES FOR A SECOND –
IT'S CRUCIAL!

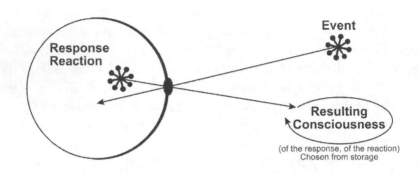

So, how do you short-circuit these emotional reaction tapes?
The most effective way to stop your automatic reactions is to do or
say nothing for at least ten seconds. It is harder than you think, for
you have learned to react to all exterior stimulation, particularly
in conversation. This ten-second pause gives you time to connect
with your real feelings and choose a response. Unpredictable
responses also interrupt automatic reactions and programmed
patterns of behavior. Do something out of character. When a
situation triggers anger in you, say nothing and smile. When you
feel you should defend your position, lightheartedly agree with
the other person's opinion, no matter how mistaken it is. That
they believe something about you does not make it true. A good
response if you need to respond is, *"I find it interesting you would
think that about me"*. You can also say, *"Really? That's interesting."*
There is no need to defend against someone else's opinion or even
respond to it. What another person thinks of you is none of your
business. *What you think of yourself is your business,* for it is your
own thoughts that create, maintain, and change your self-identity
and reality.

In spite of your answering machines, cell phones, voice mail, text messaging and other technologies, when your phones ring, many of you answer even if you are in the middle of a task or conversation with someone. You automatically interrupt what you are doing in case the call is important. What is more important that what you are currently doing? If you utilized more of your inner senses, you would intuitively know who is calling and if the call is important or not. You also feel compelled to say something when asked a question or someone makes a comment. You do not take time to think about what was said, what you want to say, or if you want to respond. If asked a question you do not care to answer, a good response is *"Why do you ask that question?"* This puts the ball right back in their court. What are they going to say, that they are nosy? Most questions asked in conversation rise from idle curiosity and social programming rather than genuine interest. Their minds are already on what your response triggered in them and what they plan to say or ask as soon as you are finished talking.

Next time an acquaintance or co-worker who always asks, "How are you?" or "What did you do last night", make up something outrageous like, *"I'm fantastic! My basement flooded, my underpants are riding up the crack of my ass, and I just found out I'm illegitimate."* Standard responses will range from an automatic, *"Oh"* or embarrassed mumblings and stunned silence. Many do not care or even listen to what you have to say and play this conversation game for self-validation. When these people ask how you are in the future, smile and say nothing. There is great wisdom in the old expression, *'Silence is Golden'.* Many of you find it difficult to be silent even when you have nothing to say. You do not have to respond when you are addressed or in someone else's presence unless you have something to say. A good rule of thumb is that your immediate reaction to any situation is likely a programmed reaction, particularly if you need to explain or defend yourself. Pay attention to what you are actually feeling when you have a compulsion to respond automatically without putting thought into what you intend to say.

The sensations that make the least sense to you consciously most often reflect your real feelings. If you hear yourself say or think, *'Every time I', or,' this is just like',* you can be sure you are running an emotional tape. *A different response will always produce a different result.* Without participating in the process your mind just replays its automatic reaction tapes. You can only over-ride this automatic function and change the nature of your interactions when you choose all your responses.

When your physical/mental/spiritual aspects are in alignment and work in unison, you act upon the thoughts and feelings that spring from your inner self. Your *'dream eyes'* open, and you begin to see how directing your mind changes how it works. Changing your mind changes your experiences. So, how do you choose to play your role? You can say your lines in a monotone and react to everything that happens like a robot, never knowing why your life is a cycle of repetitive circumstances. Alternately, you can follow your inner senses and feelings towards discovering and expressing your authentic identity within all circumstances. This is how you begin to explore and understand your own consciousness.

The dictionary in part defines understanding *'to achieve a grasp of the nature, significance, or explanation of something',* and *'to have a clear or complete idea of'.* You are unable to have a complete idea of the meaning of something or understand its significance if you have not processed it through your inner consciousness. *Understanding rises from the conscious application of your subconscious senses.* Intellectually or mentally, you may know a lot but understand little. Until you process your experiences through your inner senses, you possess information but not necessarily understanding. Understanding something means the information flows from your mind, through your heart chakra, to be subjectively experienced on a sensory level before you form an intellectual opinion. The word itself, *'under-stand'* means to know what is underneath or beneath any piece of information so your position or stand results from a combined mental and sensory evaluation.

Beliefs are not understandings. They are information requiring further examination. The word 'believe' itself contains the phrase be-lie-view. In other words, this information can be true or it could be a lie, based on someone else's view. If you hear yourself start a sentence or phrase with, 'I believe ' you are expressing unexamined information, not an understanding. A phrase like 'to my understanding', 'in my opinion', or 'I think/feel/ sense', bases your statements on your own inner perception, providing you actually use these inner senses to process the information.

Once a belief evolves into an understanding, it is no longer a concept separate from yourself. Integrated in both your outer and inner consciousness it reflects your authentic personalized perception of any subject at that time. As you continue to validate existing and new information, these understandings will also change and expand.

Intuition

The more you activate all your senses the more effectively you can operate from both your inner and outer consciousness. In spite of communicating from partial perception, your intuition, positioned in the solar plexus located below your ribcage, constantly provides you with sensory feedback that many refer to as your gut feeling. The literal interpretation of the word intuition is most appropriate, 'IN-TU-IT'. When you pay attention to these sensations, you can get into what is really going on beneath your conscious experiences on an interactive energy level. You already act on this data to whatever degree without being aware of doing so. Your interactions will significantly expand when you align yourself to the frequency of the Cosmic Pulse, the love energy that stimulates and aligns your heart and mind. Without this alignment, you miss a great deal of what is going on around you and the significance of all your interactions. Ignoring these intuitive messages perpetuates a partial and highly edited version of reality.

Your intuitive senses automatically pick-up and record all energy activities around you. When you walk into someone's home, you intuitively scan the energy signature of that environment. You have all had experiences where you instantly sense something is amiss. For Example: even though your hosts are pleasant and welcoming, you may feel a tension or discord in the air when you visit friends. Consciously you are unaware they have been arguing before you arrived, and have been doing so all week. In spite of their interface (the face they put on for you), the discordant energy present in their auras and imprinted on their environment makes you feel uncomfortable. These energies are the source of the expression *'bad vibes'* or *'good vibes'*. You are intuitively aware of these energy signatures wherever you are.

You *'intuit'* in the same way during conversations. Your body may send you a signal that there is a discrepancy between the person's outer demeanor and inner feelings and/or intentions. Realize that conscious communication happens in four primary ways: through ENERGY, BODY LANGUAGE, TONE, and WORDS. The first, which is always 100% and all-ways active, is energy. Everything happens first on an energy-exchange level after which 50% of conscious communication happens through body language, 40% by the tone of your voice, and only 10% by the words you use. This is one primary reason your physical body is so valuable; not because of how it looks, but because of the physiological sensations it provides. Even if you were mute, others could sense your true feelings via energy and body language.

Your conscious senses first interpret the meaning of the words, then facial expressions and finally body language to see if it fits the words. Your inner senses work the other way round. They first register the energy transmission, secondly any discrepancies based on body language and tone, and lastly the words you use. Many people adopt a physically self-protective and defensive stance to prevent harm to their identity, be it real or imagined. Despite speaking with confidence and projecting self-confidence, their body language transmits this inner defensiveness if that is what they are feeling. A prime example of this is someone standing with their arms firmly crossed over their chest, as if to ward off access to their Solar Plexis from where their inner insecurity and feelings arise. The energy you continually broadcast not only imprinted on your environment but also the personal objects you handle regularly. This includes positive high frequency and negative low frequency emotions. That is how Psychometrics is applied. The more you wear an item like a favorite watch or ring, the stronger the imprint of your energy on that object.

Many years ago I lost a valuable Austrian Gold coin pendant I had worn around my neck since I was about eighteen. In my late thirties, while working on my self-image, someone stole my car from outside my house. In the car were my pendant and other jewelry I was taking to a nearby jewelry store to have cleaned. I was not terribly upset about the car theft for my husband and I had fallen in love with a new one at a car show a few weeks earlier. In fact, the insurance settlement from the theft financed the purchase of this new vehicle. What I was really upset about was the loss of the coin pendant. It was my most valuable piece of jewelry, one I had worn daily for almost two decades. I felt an immense void within myself at losing this precious item. At the time, I was unaware the unresolved trauma experienced since early childhood was imprinted on this gold coin. The gold, which acts as a conductor, had actually amplified all the emotions attached to the shame-based unhealthy identity I was working so hard to change. Intuition had whispered that I should leave the car running while I dashed into the kitchen, just 10 feet from the vehicle, to pick up the gloves I had left on the inside bottom step. With no one in sight I did so. From a conscious point of view, I did the wrong thing but from a spiritual perspective, my wrong-action proved highly beneficial. The loss of the necklace helped release many of my accumulated and amplified emotional attachments I could not release consciously.

Your energy continuously imprints itself on your environment. A sense of peace, comfort, tension or discord will dominate your personal space at different times. Attuned to your inner senses, you would be aware of the energy frequencies you are projecting. Your work place is imprinted in the same way by the staff's collective energies and may have an invigorating, calming or stress filled atmosphere. Historic buildings and ancient sites still broadcast energy from the past, particularly if intense emotions or traumatic events occurred there. Residual energy is more potent if these sites lie along Ley lines, the earth's natural electromagnetic energy grid lines. Structures located on Ley line intersections, as in powerful sites like the Pyramids and Stonehenge, still broadcast ancient energy. You can feel this energy because your inner senses exist outside of time.

You can all read energy to varying degrees. If you are psychologically perceptive, you can easily evaluate body language, tone, and words to determine another person's true position during your interactions. Many fake Psychics us this method to hoodwink you into thinking they know and see what you cannot. Those who are genuine Psychics or Mediums use their own extended senses to help you be more aware of what is happening within you. Depending on their particular sensory strengths, they can tell you about your fears, unfulfilled needs and desires, past and probable future events, and other significant data your energy broadcasts. The more emotional intensity behind your thoughts and desires, the stronger its imprint will be on your Aura. An Empathic, who has the unique ability to tap into your feeling vibration and feel what you are feeling, can generally identify the source of your emotional blocks.

Since all consciousness has its own bias based on conscious programming and perception, a Psychic always interprets the information they pick up through their own perceptions to varying degrees. *Mediums*, during an altered state called *trance channeling*, bypass their own consciousness, move onto higher frequencies, and connect with your own higher frequency identity, or Soul essence, while in this altered state. Information channeled from this higher frequency source can often be cryptic and symbolic though relatively untainted by the medium's own conscious interpretation. However, these frequency sources have their own interpretive biases.

When you reconnect with the Cosmic Pulse, you can use your own inner senses to perceive what is really happening in your life on an energy level. What comes from you is for you. In an altered state like the Alpha state, you can interact with your own higher frequency identity, inner consciousness, and other Soul entities on their own higher frequencies. You do not need to have a Psychic reading unless you want validation or another perspective on an issue once you activate your own extended senses.

You become *responsible* and *accountable* in a completely different way. You strengthen and expand your *'ability to respond'* based on your own senses in order to fill your needs and desires. You become accountable for your own physical, mental, and spiritual well-being. You are *'able to account for'* both the cause and effect of your choices since YOU are directing the process instead of just reacting to what happens to and around you.

If you are willing to explore your consciousness, the evidence of your own subjective experiences will provide the proof of your own greater identity and validate these sensory resources.

Chapter 5

Your Inner Consciousness

"Desire creates the energy to satisfy itself."

WERE it not for your inner consciousness, you could change nothing in your outer reality. It is the generator that propels your thoughts into 3-D life experiences. Although Ego protects your conscious identity, it does not interact directly with your inner consciousness until certain conditions are met. Only then does it allow your operating data banks to accept input from your X-Files. These X-files support the memory that you are a spark of Prime Creator, the creative energy that thought you into existence. Therefore, you are still connected to both it and all its other aspects of consciousness even if you don't acknowledge or believe it to be so.

All of your Soul experiences are recorded in your generic data banks. You are in fact walking around with an infinite history and toolbox of knowledge and resources that would change your concept of who you are and your whole perception of physical reality. When you alter your focus and direct it inward, you can begin to access this information. The game plan is to trick your

Ego into bypassing your filters and accepting this new data into your operating data banks.

Because of your life programming, you move through several frequency levels of consciousness as your overall perception evolves. These stages of development fall within FOUR ENERGY FORCES or energy frequencies that characterize these four types of perception.

Model # 4

THE FOUR FORCES

FORCE # 1.   (80-90% of people think this way)

MOTIVATION:	**BIG** cause, **SMALL** effect. Everything is ALWAYS and FOREVER.... And SLOW
VIEW OF GOD:	God is an Englishman – fearful, reproving, and vengeful
CHARACTERISTICS -	Everything is either' Right' or 'Wrong'
-	Plays & recites repeat tapes in their head
-	Makes, follows, and lives by rules & a rigid hierarchy
-	Enforces the rules that control them
-	Has labels for everything & loves cliché's
COMMUNICATIONS: -	favorite saying, "I know" and "You can't"
-	Either/Or – top dog or bottom dog
-	Rituals and tapes – loves sage sayings

TRAITS: - predictable – when in doubt, guilt yourself
- Lives in fear & is afraid to rock the boat
- Generalizes everything to de-guilt self by blaming others

NEEDS: - Learn the rules to fit in and belong (likes to belong to clubs)
- Stratify (but layered thinking) & have everything in its place
- Leave themselves an alternative if backed against a wall
- Operate from a 'blind' view – manipulates others from that view
- (Examples: Governments, Army, Charities, Economics)

FORCE # 2. (Rule-breakers, just for the sake of breaking rules)

MOTIVATION: **BIG** cause, **IMPRESSIVE** effect.
Everything is NOW... And FAST

VIEW OF GOD: God is an Englishman, an Irishman, & possibly even a heathen

CHARACTERISTICS: - Two types – reactive & smooth
- Acts & reacts to laws & flows with an unfixed status
- "I have no tapes – I even have a tape that says I have no tapes"
- Has no sympathy for Force #1

	-	Constantly tries to establish alternatives
COMMUNICATIONS:	-	EITHER/OR – of which I SAY
	-	When something is explained, says, "Now I Understand" and thus I KNOW
TRAITS:	-	Strives to grow – breaks molds while fighting to expand
	-	Into mind stuff, meditation, Yoga, and Eastern Philosophies
	-	More sophisticated way of enforcing than Force #1
	-	Can appear reckless & hates 'haters'
	-	Revolts against Force #1 – tries to beat them at their own game
NEEDS:	-	Find it necessary to teach new rules & how to break molds
	-	Wanting to grow is a two-way thing

FORCE # 3.

(Practices Refinement & Exercises Playfulness)

MOTIVATIONS: **BIGGER** effect than cause

Everything is TIMING

VIEW OF GOD: God is everything and more

CHARACTERISTICS:	-	A SUBTLE FORCE
	-	Rises above Force 1& 2 – uses them for his/her own purposes
	-	"What programming & Tapes?" Importance of opposing states diminishes
	-	Invents own tapes – has CHOICE
	-	The 'slogan' writers

	-	Attitude of: and… and… and…
COMMUNICATIONS:	-	"Now that I UNDERSTAND that" - I can understand other things
	-	Aware of own greater identity
TRAITS:	-	Appears as a leader – a Guru to Force #2
	-	Starts to lose importance of other forces
	-	Casts their own individual mold
	-	Communications – it's all the same
NEEDS:	-	Teach the rules and more to others
	-	Help others break out of their limiting molds

FORCE # 4.   (The actualizers! – Everything is important, yet nothing really matters. It's all creative play)

MOTIVATION: **SMALL** cause, **LARGE** effect
                     Everything is CIRCUMSTANCE

VIEW OF GOD: EVERYTHING IS MORE and far beyond description

CHARACTERISTICS:	-	Subtle – shifts according to needs for self-actualizing
	-	Everything is circumstance & appropriateness
	-	Inconsistent & unpredictable – have movement of action
	-	"Maybe it will" or 'Maybe it won't"…it doesn't matter
	-	Invisible fineness – can be chameleons but are always appropriate

	-	Empathy and compassion for everyone
	-	Why are we discussing programs and tapes?
COMMUNICATIONS:	-	"I am pleased I did not fully understand" is the general attitude
	-	"Thus I can learn more…"
TRAITS:	-	"I never thought of that!"
	-	No hidden agenda
	-	Always appears relaxed & charming to the other forces
NEEDS:	-	De-guilt Force #1 so they can move forward

These four forces align with Maslow's Pyramid and represent the progressive levels of development of human consciousness in order to reach higher awareness. By utilizing the inner resources available to you, you can move through the first two forces relatively quickly.

Your Dream Reality

You also possess four levels of brainwave activity: *Beta, Alpha, Theta* and *Delta*. *Beta* is your normal physical waking or daytime conscious state. *Alpha* is the state beneath your waking state, just before you enter your dream state. You enter this Alpha state during relaxation, meditation and prayer. Acting as the doorway to your subconscious, when you are in Alpha you have one foot in conscious reality and one in your subconscious reality. It is also from here that you draw your memories and imagination. In *Theta* you are asleep and in your dream reality but still connected to this reality enough to feel and respond to physical sensations like pain. In the deepest state of sleep, *Delta,* you have entirely disconnected from this reality. Your spiritual consciousness has left your physical body, but remains connected to it via the *Silver Chord* in case of physical emergency.

The Silver Chord is much like an energy umbilical cord attached to your body at the belly button. Without it, you could not find your way back into your physical body when your consciousness leaves. Astral traveling is the result of self-directed other-consciousness experiences while your body is in a meditative or rejuvenating sleep state. Unlike deep sleep, in this state you can see the Silver Chord that connects your consciousness to your sleeping body. The most important of these levels of activity is the *Alpha state*, the state that bridges both your conscious and subconscious identity.

In your dreams, while your body lies in the rejuvenating stasis of sleep, your consciousness is completely free from the limitations of this reality. To your dream self this reality is like a fuzzy memory of dream-like experiences much like your memories of your dreams are now. In your dream state you can monitor your progress and set up new scripts for yourself in this reality, learn and teach within the framework of other frequencies or visit your other lives and parallel realities. Some dreams are just creative play to satisfy your soul's need for self-expression, particularly if self-expression is stifled in your conscious waking reality. Many aboriginal cultures use the Alpha state to glean inspiration, maintain cultural direction, and strengthen their connection to their spiritual ancestry. This kind of intention-directed dream work helps maintain a more interactive balance between their physical and spiritual aspects.

Your dreams are important. Disconnected from your natural environment and real feelings as most of you are, it's often the only way you can freely experience yourself and maintain an interactive relationship with your higher frequencies and greater consciousness identity. Among other things, dreams allow you to design and experience the probable outcomes of your physical circumstances and challenges in ways you cannot during your waking state. Although your dream activities are also recorded in your mind's storage files, you often wake with either no memory or only a distorted memory of these dream experiences.

Dreams often make little sense because they occur on frequencies that have a more expansive framework than this 3-D reality. If you think of some of the things you do remember from your dreams like flying, or changing your age, appearance or surroundings in the blink of an eye, you get a glimpse of how thought creates reality when not impeded by conscious limitations. What prevents you from expressing yourself in the same way in this reality is conscious programming. As you move down through different frequencies and settle your consciousness back into your physical body, your dream memories are often hazy. Your experiences may have been so grand within a completely different context you are unable to translate them with your existing perception. What survives as memories is often only a symbolic or indistinct residue of disconnected impressions for which you have no conscious point of reference.

You can have similar experiences during the Alpha state. I remember a particularly awesome experience while in a meditative Alpha state. First, I became the sound waves upon which the musical notes I was listening to rode. Then I felt myself dissolving and transforming into various geometrical symbols these sounds represented on a different frequency. It was exhilarating to experience myself in this way but discomforting to realize that I had actually felt my identity dissolve and change into something else. Obviously, my consciousness was still intact or I would not have remembered losing my identity. I can still recapture some of the feeling of that experience but can't describe it in words since it was completely subjective on a sensory level.

Your subconscious uses your inner senses to trigger thoughts that draw dream information into your conscious awareness. You may have a wondrous inspiration, reach a surprising new conclusion, or suddenly have completely different feelings about something you have always taken an adamant position on. New information can filter into your operating data banks to broaden your perception when you consciously validate these kinds of subjective experiences when they occur.

Although your consciousness is more active at night than in your waking state, few of you remember your dreams for two reasons. First, you sleep far too long in one stretch. Secondly, you have not programmed yourself to remember your dreams before you fall asleep. Your conscious and subconscious aspects ideally work together so that information can flow freely between the spiritual and physical aspects of yourself. When you sleep for eight to ten hours in one stretch this link is severed. You feel groggy, cranky and out-of-sorts when you do awaken, not because you are not a morning person but because your energy upon waking is completely focused on kick-starting your body after such a long separation.

The more connected your conscious and subconscious states are on a consistent basis, the smoother the waking transition, and the more inner senses you use in your daily lives. A 5-6 hour block of deep sleep a night, supplemented by a short rejuvenating power-snooze during the day when you need it helps maintain this link. You may only need 4 hours of deep sleep or you may need 7 after a stressful or exhausting activity. You could say the ideal is somewhat like operating in a light Alpha state all the time. I find it amusing that new sleep studies try to prove you need at least 10-12 hours of sleep each night. Right-e-ho – and it is Zombie Time! Go for it - if you want to be so disconnected from your inner consciousness you have no clue how you are being manipulated, and so dopey you do not care.

People who do not appear to be *'all there'* probably are not. They are partially in another reality or bridging realities while still partially functional here. In the Alpha state your *Base* chakra or visceral brain, responsible for your automatic biological functions, takes over. The same thing occurs while driving a car on a familiar route when you cannot remember parts of the journey. You often slip into Alpha during habitual and repetitive activities. Your conscious focus also relaxes somewhat when you are mentally tired or your body needs to rejuvenate. This triggers the Alpha state and puts your conscious focus on autopilot.

I have often experienced periods of Alpha where returning to this reality and my conscious focus almost felt like a surprise. For a few seconds I would be befuddled and even wonder where I was until I recognized familiar elements and remembered. On occasion I have even felt disappointed that it was this reality I was settling back into since the ones I had just left afforded me much more freedom of expression.

Exercise # 4.

You can instruct yourself to remember your dreams before you go to sleep. Wait until your mind has stopped rehashing the day's events and all the 'woulda', 'coulda', 'shoulda' you are projecting into your tomorrow. Once you're completely relaxed, in that slightly fuzzy state just before you feel yourself drifting off, simply tell yourself that, *'Now I will sleep and awaken refreshed, energized, and revitalized, remembering my dreams'.*

I suggest you keep a dream journal by your bedside where you can record your dream impressions upon awakening. Also, keep a day journal to record any significant feelings, impressions or events experienced throughout the day at the end of each day. Do this for one month and remember to date your entries. You will be surprised at the correlation between your dreams and conscious experiences when you compare them. By recording both, you also begin to recognize what kinds of feelings or events your dream symbols represent.

When you first awaken in the morning, lay perfectly still for a few moments and keep your eyes shut. Allow your dream impressions to flow through your mind freely without judging them. There is no need to get disheartened if all you first get are faint impressions that make no sense rather than memories of specific events. Before long you will remember more and more. Your nightly instructions and morning receptiveness will begin to draw them into your conscious awareness. If you still have no success, add the phrase to your daily affirmations, saying, *"This day, I have always remembered my dreams upon waking – effortlessly."*

Dreams are a doorway into your more-expansive spiritual activities and therefore are extremely valuable interpretive tools. You can learn to direct your dreams and through them begin to practice conscious thought-manifestation. Many of your dreams are precognitive trace memories of setting up future events for this reality anyhow. When the event does materialize, you have what we call a *de-ja-vous* experience - the recognition of what you set up for yourself in your dream. The more *de-ja-vous* experiences I have, the more I know I am on my intended path.

I feel only you can interpret your dreams accurately since your sensory associations and symbols are uniquely yours. For Example: fire can symbolize warmth, danger, comfort, fear, depending on your past associations with fire. Water can symbolize peace, feeling out of your depth or lost, fear, tranquility, freedom or expansiveness of spirit. Not all of these feeling-associations rise from this lifetime. You may have an unreasonable fear of water due to the residual memory of death by drowning in another existence. When you have a dream about water, it may indicate a need for vigilance in order to avoid a potentially harmful situation. Dream books can be useful once you begin to explore your dreams. Someone else may interpret your dreams with some accuracy, particularly if they are empathic, intuitive, or know you well as a friend or companion. However, only you can truly understand their meaning since only you can correlate your sensory impressions to your feelings based on your previous experiences.

Many dream events never materialize. Dreams allow you to play out various scenarios to review their possible outcomes before deciding which you will manifest into this reality. Many of your desires and random thoughts are played-out in dreams to see if you like the results or if they should be manifested into this reality. If you have only invested a little energy in these thought projections, you often release this dedicated energy in dreams.

If you have a question or a problem you are struggling with ask that the answer is revealed in your dreams just before you fall asleep. People who have trouble expressing their real feelings or are unable to defend themselves against physical or other violations tend to have highly emotional dreams and nightmares. I certainly did through my fear-based and traumatic early years. Nightmares are actually a dramatic form of creative sensory release in order to maintain a certain balance within an imbalanced physical life.

Young children, who are relatively powerless within their environment, use dreams to act out self-empowering scenarios. To them nightmares are both frightening and exhilarating. They exercise their sensory perceptions within dramas that involve both real and fabricated characters. As a rule, they grow out of their nightmares once they have more information about what frightens or diminishes them. As their cognitive abilities develop, so do their abilities to reason. My own nightmares stopped once I related them to fearful childhood events. When I do have unpleasant or disturbing dreams, I know I am dreaming and can pull myself out of such situations at will. That is a whole other game you can play in dreams – consciously manipulating your dreams while you are having the dream. In fact, *that is exactly what you are doing in your life right now from the perspective of your higher frequency identity.*

You may not have a violent or aggressive nature yet in dreams you may act violent and even kill someone you know in this reality. You play out many suppressed feelings in this way to release the energy dedicated to your resentments or vulnerabilities when others repeatedly trigger them. Not allowed to express my opinions and feelings as a youngster, I used to scream at and argue with everyone I knew in my dreams to release this kind of blocked energy. Since time is simultaneous and your soul experiences itself on many different frequencies, if you do not choose to manifest something into this reality, you will do so in dreams or in other realities. Nevertheless, *all your thoughts* will manifest somewhere once you have emotional energy attached to them. The understandings you reach through your dreams also get recorded and are integrated with your consciousness. The key that opens the doorway to this creative dream world is the Alpha state.

Energy

Energy is the fuel of creation. You can have a vehicle with all its parts working perfectly, but without gas it can't move. The fuel moving through the mechanical components sets the car in motion. Your mind and body are the mechanisms through which energy transforms pure thought into 3-D experiences.

When you want something, you create a desire to fulfill this need for either self-expression or sensory stimulation. If you can make yourself want something, what is termed MOTIVATION, you attach energy to that desire. This energy is now *dedicated energy*. Your body acts like a battery whereby the desire is one charge and the dedicated energy the balancing charge. You will have at your disposal exactly as much energy as is required to get what you want. How much energy that is depends on how much you want what you desire. Once you get it, this block of dedicated energy is released to flow back into the universe. There is always more energy available from this unlimited source so you never run out of energy. You just think you do.

The intensity of your desire is the e-motion or *energy-in-motion* that determines if you get what you want. It also determines how quickly this desire will manifest. This feeling-intensity directs the energy attached to your thoughts like a laser beam. Having a lot of energy equates to VITALITY. Your level of vitality is the mechanism through which energy pours into your being. The more in sync you are with the Cosmic Pulse and your higher frequencies, the more vitality you will have.

You often lack vitality when you have a lot of energy tied-up in 'nots' such as the random and perceived fears your thoughts create. You often attach so much emotion to these random thoughts and fearful images you actually propel them into existence. Long after you forgot you had these thoughts, unexpected and unpleasant situations pop up in your life. They are generally the things you mentally hoped *would never happen* but unconsciously energized. Since your subconscious can't tell the difference between a real fear and mental fabrication, to your mind it's all real once you dedicate energy to it.

Although your subconscious acts upon your mind's directives it is unable to recognize the word 'DON'T'. The directive DON'T is a 'do' and 'do not do' at the same time. When an action 'do' directive is followed by an in-action 'do not' directive the 'not' cancels out the two 'do's'. For example, when you say, "I don't ever want to be hurt like that again", what your subconscious hears is "I want to be hurt like that again" and guess what happens? Like a Cosmic magnet, when energy is attached to what you do not want, it draws it to you. The more intensely you do not want to be hurt again, the more you actually energize it. This same magnetic charge also draws what you *DO* want into your life. So pay attention to your words. They are powerful and they have consequences.

If you have a lot of don't that have a little energy attached to them, you also create a knot of energy that blocks the flow of energy between your chakras. To release these blocks find one beneficial aspect of each undesirable situation and focus on that. Then replace your don'ts with an affirming statement that reinforces what you do want for yourself. In the example of continually being hurt in relationships, you could recognize that your expectations are highly idealized. You feel hurt because you did not get what you believe you want and/or deserve. Examine your ideals. You can say something like, "This day, I have always been happy about what my relationships teach me about myself - effortlessly." This kind of affirmation gives you permission to have experiences that are satisfying because you are willing to learn, despite the fact this learning may involve some pain.

Your thought processes are all-ways active. A lot of your energy is also dedicated to imagining yourself in a variety of scenarios triggered by random thoughts. You can choose how much energy you dedicate to these thoughts and therefore what kind of circumstances will appear in your life. You are already an expert at this, for your existing circumstances are the result of energy dedicated to previous thoughts.

Your thoughts create your reality. When you direct a lot of e-motion towards what interests you or what you really desire, you give it form in this 3-D reality. The trick is to avoid attaching energy to mental fabrications and random thoughts unless you want to experience them. Love all your thoughts, for they are the impetus for your physical experiences. Allow the thoughts you do not want to manifest to flow through your mind without fueling them.

When you are stuck in a rut, those periods where nothing seems to be happening, you dedicate as much energy to staying where you are then you need to change these circumstances. Such plateaus often result from a fear of moving forward and taking responsibility for your choices. Stifling your need for sensory stimulation is positively exhausting! It is like trying to stop breathing. When your mind is not going anywhere but around the same loop, you are dedicating all your energy to maintaining inaction.

Realize that nothing in life is interesting until you become interested in it. Find something beneficial or interesting about the situation when you are stuck in this way. Consider it a rest period to marshal your resources before your next grand adventure. Then become interested in something new. Inspiration is SPIRIT-IN-ACTION. Explore new thoughts to break through these energy blocks. Even a small shift in focus will set the universe in motion.

If you feel like you have no energy and want more energy, simply do more things you want to do. *Desire creates the energy to satisfy itself.* Instead of waiting until a friend can go with you, take yourself to the movie you want to see. Buy that book you were meaning to get, a new CD from your favorite musical artist, or take yourself out to dinner to that new restaurant you want to try. *If not now, when?* Take charge of your own experiences by directing your thoughts and desires, for they have consequences, particularly if you suppress them. Everything in your life is there because you drew it to you with the e-motion of your thoughts. Therefore, thought can be as much a source of dissipation as inspiration, depending on what you energize. You dissipate energy when you continually envision what will happen in an interaction or situation that has not happened yet. This also applies to all those mental sitcoms involving imaginary conversations and interactions you continually play out in your mind. They generally consist of idealized circumstances and your clever responses to what you think another person will say which usually corresponds to what you want them to say. What actually may happen in your interaction in reality rarely plays out the way you envision. You can choose what you say or do but you are unable to control what another person will say or do. Absorbed by these kinds of mental designer scripts, you often try to manipulate a real interaction to duplicate this pre-fabricated scenario. The problem with this kind of mental activity is that you are not participating in the present and miss what *is* really going on during your interactions with others.

Caught in repetitive thought also prevents you from getting what you want. Because your beliefs influence your thoughts it is important to continually expand your beliefs. If you are unwilling to do so, you create a *garbage-in-garbage-out* cycle of automatic reactions that predictably give you the same results. Use the 10-second pause or Alpha state to access your inner senses and disrupt these automatic processes. The more you shift your focus away from your habitual mental aerobics, the more you can direct what thoughts you wish to energize.

Exercise # 5.

Deep even breathing stills your mind and enables you to access your inner senses so you can examine your thoughts on a sensory level. Close your eyes and focus on a spot of stillness in the middle of your forehead, be it a white spot of light, a peaceful pond, an enchanted forest setting, a flame, or whatever appeals to you. You can do this anywhere: on the bus, at your desk or while engaging in mechanical tasks. For those of you who say you have no time, you can do it while you are in the bathroom, for in spite of your busyness you will all sit there at least once or twice a day. The more you take these little journeys into the inner landscapes of your mind, the easier it will be to isolate and identify your own thoughts. Once you have created this empty or peaceful space, you can pluck a random thought from your mind, examine it without emotion, reach a conclusion, and release it.

It was during these exercises that I learned the wonder of the word 'INTERESTING'. I became most interested in and amazed by the convoluted diversity of thoughts that flowed through my mind. Possessing a creative, imaginative, and passionate nature I had actualized far too many of these bizarre fabrications in the past. The more imaginative you are and the more you suppress your real feelings, the more fabricated and idealized thoughts will swirl around your mind.

Stress, impatience, frustration, and constant fatigue all signal that your Chakras are blocked. You don't need to sit on the top of a mountain in a Yoga position to find inner peace and balance. Regular meditation can be as simple as taking a few minutes throughout the day to focus on breathing and being still. You can also re-align yourself by connecting with nature's grounding energies. Go outside and breathe in the air deeply. Touch a leaf, a flower, the trunk of a tree or the grass and earth. When you ask Mother Earth to ground you, she will infuse you with her energy, which activates your heart and solar plexus chakras. Your heart chakra can then send her balancing energy throughout your systems. These periods of stillness also create a pocket of space in your mind where you can dedicate energy to your overall well-being and the desires you wish to manifest.

Just like planning a vacation, you need to script your life intentions. I found the best results come from being *vaguely specific* and *specifically vague*. By taking a thought, perhaps of well-being and self-worth, you can energize into existence the kind of experiences you are not quite sure you deserve. Use affirmations to validate your willingness to embrace a more expansive view of yourself. You can also be very specific about what you want. Announce your intention in the present tense as if it already exists, imagine it visually and feel having it with all your heart. Trust it will come to you in its own way and forget about it. If it is for your higher good, it will come. If not, that is also for your higher good. When something does not manifest it often means you have energized ideals or that what you wanted was a perceived desire that is not to your benefit.

Real and Perceived Desires

You have complete control over what you want, but no control over how it will manifest. Once a desire is voiced and released into the universal energy pool it can come back to you in the most unusual and unexpected ways. Your spiritual intentions, beliefs, and thoughts all influence how you get what you want. *The less expectation you place on the how, the more quickly you will see it in the now.* Whether you are specific or vague when you place your orders, they will arrive in a manner that is to your highest good. Since your spiritual needs are different from your conscious desires, you may not get something the way you expect. Based on your beliefs, you will get it in a way that expands your understanding of yourself and greater consciousness.

The e-motion of your desire coupled with the energy of the initiating thought undergoes a transformation wherein all the required elements come together to create what it is you asked for. On a sub-atomic level, energy is in a constant state of chaotic magnetic activity to orchestrate the manifestation of your desires on a multitude of energy frequencies. These sub-atomic energy particles utilize your whole consciousness signature, not just your 3-D energy transmission. That is how your spiritual intentions enter the mix and more often than not, influence the outcome in unexpected ways. You interfere with this process when you pre-decide how you should get something when you place an order. You may wait a long time for the synchronicity of time, circumstance, and energy frequency resonance to fulfill a desire in the manner your beliefs dictate. In spite of this, you always get what you order based on what you believe you deserve subconsciously.

During my own Alpha Training, I loved the example of a young woman who tried to manifest a red convertible sports car. She cut out a picture of the car she wanted, taped it to her refrigerator, and envisioned it sitting in her driveway. About a year later, she still did not have her red sports car so thought visualization and wish fulfillment did not work. Then she got a promotion, sold her house, and relocated to another part of the city. Several months later, she happened to drive past her old house on the way to visit a friend and could not believe her eyes. In her old driveway sat a sparkling red convertible sports car, the very car she had envisioned for herself. Only it belonged to the new owners of her house. She got exactly what she asked for but forgot to visualize herself driving the little red sports car. Just imagine the cooperative universal synchronicity it took to make that happen!

The unpredictable wild card in the deck – your higher spiritual self or Soul - makes your earth games most interesting. It continues to respond to the appeals for assistance you have forgotten you made when you were distressed in the past, both consciously and in your dream state. Your Soul, through your subconscious, is your hidden partner in creating the manifestation that *allows for the greatest awareness of yourself.* Given permission by a silent appeal for help, it will translate your desire into events designed to expand your consciousness. Remember - spirit IS you - the greater identity not limited by your conscious perception and beliefs. You need to examine your beliefs, for they form your inner self-image and influence how your desires manifest. What you manifest could also result from one of your random thoughts with a lot of e-motion behind it come to nip you in the butt! No matter which it is, it always reveals more about you.

Your desires rise from both your conscious and subconscious identity. Therefore, you have two kinds of desire - your subconscious *real* desires, and your conscious *perceived* desires. Consciously, a great deal of your energy fuels perceived desires; getting all the material stuff that represents success in your society. These perceived desires are a result of life programming, media brainwashing, and your existing need for outer validation. Once you get something from this conscious 'want' list, you immediately dedicate energy to something else you want. These materialistic desires represent a sense of self-worth or temporary gratification you could more easily achieve without spending a dime. Underneath these perceived desires lie your real spiritual desire for creative expression and your spiritual intentions or TASK: Thought And Desire = Knowledge.

Materialistic possessions serve two purposes: functionality - to make your physical tasks easier, and pleasure - to give you 'feel good' sensations. Take a moment to look at your possessions, all that wonderful stuff that fills your home or personal space. If it is not functional and time saving, or gives you pleasing sensations when you look at it, it is an encumbrance and a no-thing. Some of you fill your homes with memorabilia from family and friends. If looking at it triggers a fond memory or a 'feel good' sensation, it serves a purpose. More often than not, you hardly notice these things. You feel obliged to display these props because you care about who gave them to you and feel guilty if these items are not on display. A gift does not oblige you to either display or keep it, no matter whom it is from. Learn to say thank you with a smile, then tuck it away in a box with all the other stuff you get but are not particularly fond of, want, or use. When the box is full, take it to a second-hand store or donate it to those in need. Once a year you can also plan a no-charge mini 'TREASURED GARBAGE' exchange amongst your friends.

The spiritual fulfillment of your real desires has less to do with the objects you may manifest and more to do with the feelings these objects trigger in you. Some material things may be deeply significant because your energy resonates with them due to the memory of having owned something similar in another existence. Spiritual desires most often manifest as AWARENESS and UNDERSTANDINGS that enhance your sense of well-being and increase your appreciation of all your subjective and sensory experiences.

The reason you want financial prosperity appears obvious. It enables you to buy all the swell stuff you think you want, need, and should have to make you happy. There is nothing wrong with having lovely possessions. However, maintaining all this stuff can be as enslaving and as the tied-up energy of not having your desires fulfilled. What wealth and financial prosperity really buys you is time and freedom - the freedom to do what you want to do as well as the time to explore personal interests and curiosities. You can have anything you want in the way of materialistic possessions as long as you own them, not the other way around. You can measure your attachment to your stuff by how you would feel if you have to release it, if you lost it or it was damaged. The more devastated you feel, the more your possessions own you and support your conscious self-image.

Disconnected from your inner consciousness, your conscious beliefs and life programming trigger your conscious desires. In spite of this, your higher spiritual self uses every opportunity to bring you back to an awareness of your real desires – the desires that enhance a self-identity of well-being. It does so via those fleeting little impulses that tickle the edges of your consciousness. By delivering your perceived desires in unexpected ways, your resulting frustration often helps you re-define what it is you really want and need. It is all about developing a balance that satisfies both your physical and spiritual needs. To do so you also need to understand the important role your physical body plays in this grand game called life on Planet Earth.

Chapter 6

Your Physical Body

"Your body just reflects what your mind thinks."

HEALTH is your natural state while in your physical body unless you chose to be born with a physical handicap or deformity for a particular purpose. All disease has *psychosomatic* origins that indicate an imbalance within this natural state. The word psychosomatic discomforts people by its implication of a mentally fabricated versus a genuine biological cause. They are the same.

The word psychosomatic originates from the Greek word *Psycho Soma Tic* - meaning *'mind, body; condition of'*. As an indicator of your overall state, your body reflects the condition of all aspects of your being. However, *the feeling starts in the mind*. The body just reflects what your mind thinks. You create your own psychosomatic illness and you create and maintain your own psychosomatic health. An illness or disease is your body's way of letting you know you have imbalances or blocks that need addressing.

Suppressing the most important element of your identity - your spiritual essence - is the primary cause of nearly all illness. Your spiritual essence is the source of your very being. When integrated into your conscious experience it maintains a balanced existence reflected by a healthy body. Every aspect of yourself serves an important purpose in how you experience this 3-D reality. As a conscious and biological vehicle, your body's senses enhance your sensory expression and allow you to maneuver within this reality. Your mind is an efficient mechanism designed to catalog your experiences for effective viewing, evaluation, and application as directed. Your feeling sensations are sensory indicators of your beliefs about yourself. Last by not least, your subconscious is a vast storehouse of resources rising from the expansive Spiritual Being you really are. The more faith you have in these perfectly working systems, the greater your capacity for self-knowledge, awareness, and physical wellbeing. Therefore, your higher frequency self, or Spirit, will use a variety of methods to draw you back to your natural state of wellbeing.

Your body possesses an energy circuitry that controls all your physical functions within this polarized reality. Although the Chakras represent key energy points that relay information to different aspects of yourself, your brain is the mechanism through which you direct everything but your most basic biological functions. Considered the visceral reptilian brain, this aspect of your brain takes care of the biological functions that ensure your physical survival. The parietal lobe in your brain, defined as *'the middle division of each cerebral hemisphere that contains an area concerned with bodily sensations'* is from where your thought intentions first emerge. From there, they translate thought into physical action through the body's energy circuitry. When you want to initiate a physical action, you create a split second image of your intentions in this part of your brain. This image causes electrical neurons to send charges of electricity to your brain cells. These charges relay your commands in the form of energy frequencies to the appropriate parts of the body.

Researchers have mapped this process in order to help stimulate movement in the limbs of partially paralyzed individuals. By implanting a chip in the brain activated by an exterior device, a reactive flow of energy between the brain and the affected limbs can be re-established. Despite their success in helping the partially paralyzed, these medical researchers are still unable to decode the energy patterns of the neuron activity created by the thought images of a healthy person. Busy trying to simulate the mechanics of how this electrical circuitry works, they have not even begun to map how *thought directs consciousness.* An individual's thoughts create a healthy body or one that is not.

Difficulties resulting from a separation between the mental, spiritual, and emotional aspect of your identity arise through your lack of trust in the expansive support system in which you operate. You no longer trust the integrity of the earth and your intimate connection to it. Consequently, you misuse its resources and consider it a threat to your material constructs. You no longer trust your intuition and feelings as the spiritual resources they are. You bury them deep within your psyche and rely on your automatic reactionary programs. As well, you no longer trust the integrity of your own body consciousness to help maintain your physical well-being, and thus it has become diseased. To compound the problem even further, your beliefs and social programming support this overall distrust of your body.

When you are out of balance all kinds of interesting things begin to happen. Initially Spirit may give you a little nudge in your dreams or through an intuitive sensation or insight. If you ignore these prompts, you begin to experience challenges in various aspects of your life. If you still refuse to pay attention to the messages your heart chakra sends to your mind, your body itself makes you aware of an energy block in a way you cannot easily ignore - by manifesting the symptoms of an illness or disease. Most of your mild physical discomforts are indications of small energy blocks caused by low frequency emotions and limiting beliefs. When you accumulate numerous blocks of this kind, they reach a certain critical mass that needs to be shaken loose. And Spirit helps do just that.

Imagine for a moment that you are Spirit looking at the physical form you currently inhabit. As Spirit, you see your physical self in a state of imbalance due to a variety of energy blocks. Since the free-will principle of the universe prohibits intervention unless asked, you arrange a dream interaction wherein your physical counterpart asks you for help. You can then use your higher frequency to direct energy to bring this imbalance to the conscious attention of your physical counterpart. Since Spirit is aware of all your subconscious beliefs, it knows what kinds of triggers will be most effective to get your attention. On the physical level you consider these triggers annoying or frustrating problems. I call these spiritual promptings loving reminders or *'messages from the universe'* based on having received *many* on my personal journey. First, you get a nudge, then a prod, and then a 2 x 4, and sometimes a 4 x 8 will hit you over the head. And, if you happen to be as strong-willed and stubborn as I often was, a honker of a tree may fall on you to get you to change the beliefs that compromise your own well-being. It often takes a grand mess to trigger awareness if you are particularly resistive, like I have often been in the past.

Your Physical Identity

Your body mirrors your identity. Many of you are dissatisfied with your body, and therefore, with your identity. North American society has become increasingly obsessed with physical appearance - how you 'should' look vs. how you do look. Women in particular are influenced by these fabricated ideals. You nearly all think you are unattractive and overweight, and rarely consider yourself too thin. You think your eyes are too small and your nose too long, short, hooked, thin or wide. Your hair is too thick, stringy, curly or straight and your breasts are generally too small and nearly always too saggy. You think your waists are too thick and your belly too flabby, and you see your hips as too wide and your buttocks too flat or large. If I have missed anything, it's because the list is as long as imagination and dissatisfaction is limitless.

You picked this body as your physical vessel for self-expression, period. You can starve it, overfeed it, plump it up, suction it, nip and tuck it, deny it, camouflage it, hate it, ignore it or tolerate it - but it is still your physical vessel within this reality. Although you can make modifications, it is your body for the duration of your physical life so you might as well accept it and love it!

Most of you do not question the origins of an ideal weight and shape, an ideal that has continually changed throughout history. You buy into the current image and expend a great deal of time, energy and money trying to emulate it. Over the past two decades, body image has become the defining yardstick for self-identity. The ideal is that the more undernourished and lean you look, the more beautiful, fit, and healthy you are. Obsessed in reaching this ideal you have compromised your physical, mental, emotional, and spiritual wellbeing. You are body, mind, and Spirit - as one. Each is an aspect and reflection of the other. Your beliefs about how you look in the name of beauty, fitness and health has nothing to do with providing your body with what it actually needs. This obsession also diverts your attention from your real TASK: Thought And Sensation = Knowledge.

If a slender body is not your natural state, that's the truth of it. You can't do much about your height, can you? There's no fitness regime or nutritional program that will make you five foot eight if you're only five foot three. In spite of how you feel about your height, you know your genes determine it. Genes also determine your features and overall shape, a gene pool YOU chose when you decided to have this physical adventure.

You are being fed several illusions about your appearance, the foremost being that you are healthier and more attractive if you are thin. A medical study of obesity conducted over an eight-year period in the United States confirmed that many individuals considered overweight (20 to 40 lbs. over the existing normal height/weight ratio guidelines), were in fact healthy and fit. After thorough laboratory testing of internal functions and the external physical capabilities of the over 1,000 participants, the results proved the researcher's assumptions incorrect. Based on their own criteria the evidence of this study as well as others disproves the untruth health practitioners continue to promote.

Most of you also believe you need to adhere to a specific exercise and dietary regime to stay healthy. You do not. Your mistake is in believing you are not already healthy. You never question the belief that you should fit within the parameters of a specific model for fitness and health. Thus, you diet and strain your body to attain a shape that may be genetically unnatural to you. Your body is unique, just as your consciousness is. Some of you are naturally slender and some of you are not. If your job requires exceptional physical mobility or you enjoy sports the very act of doing these things keeps your body toned no matter what your height, shape, or weight. However, if your tasks and interests don't require this kind of mobility, what are you straining, starving, or building your body up for?

It has not been long since your ancestors forged their living directly from the land. The same Mother Earth who sustained them still provides the food that sustains you now. Your biological body is designed to interact with your environment, a synergy now compromised by several factors that have directly affected your physical well-being.

Your body acts as both a receiver and transmitter of energy with every breath you take. You inhale the energy of the world around you and a portion of your own energy consciousness (comprised of your thoughts and beliefs) is released back into your physical environment when you exhale. This is how you interact with the physical world and how disease infects you. I am not only talking about the air-borne organisms you believe cause illness. You have as much control over these microorganisms as you do your physical imbalances. When you maintain your own well-being and choose not to become a host to these microorganisms, they cannot survive in your body. On an energy level it is as if your body is toxic to them.

This symbiotic relationship with your natural environment also affects how your body assimilates the nutrients in the food you eat. You absorb and process the energy essence of the food you eat in the same way you absorb and process all other energy in this reality. Food polluted by chemical additives, preservatives, and those altered through genetic manipulation inhibits the efficiency of your body's own biological regulators. Processed and convenience foods contribute to obesity and disease because over time these foods have changed your body and brain cells. Your body now has more difficulty eliminating toxins than it did a few decades or ago.

You may not wish to grow your own food or raise your own livestock but you can change your attitude towards food. Your beliefs *about* what you eat are as important as what you eat. When your thoughts support a respectful and loving attitude towards food, your body more easily assimilates the nutrients and more effectively eliminates the toxins it contains. Since your body follows your mind, many food sensitivities or allergies are a direct result of your fear-based beliefs. These you can change. It is a testament to the power of brainwashing that North Americans, who have access to the largest variety of fresh food on the planet, consume more processed and fast food than the rest of the world.

Historically, your diet consisted of what was indigenous to your geographic location. People worked with the cycles of their natural environmental and appreciated what Mother Earth provided because it sustained their survival. Despite our manipulation of the physical environment that has altered this synergy, Mother Earth continues to sustain us. There is in actuality no food shortage on the planet - yet. Greed, waste, and disrespect for the natural environment will lead to this eventuality unless we change our minds. When we do, we can again nourish the biological synergy essential to the well-being of both our bodies and environment.

Do not for a moment think this era's health consciousness has anything to do with genuinely promoting healthy bodies. Were that the case, government and health professionals would ensure animals were not fed chemical bulking agents, were not raised in appallingly conditions or slaughtered with disrespectful brutality. Grocery stores would not be stocked with foods preserved with addictive and mind altering agents were there genuine care about your physical well-being. You would also not be encouraged to medicate yourself the moment you experience any kind of physical discomfort – a trigger to inform you of an existing imbalance.

Were your health important, the health practitioner's prime agenda would encourage trust in your own body. Advertising that triggers you to purchase toxic foods or products to enhance your appearance to meet fabricated ideals far outnumber the few that promote genuine health. Advertising encourages you to keep you spending your money while you seek validation outside yourself. You are confused about your physical identity and wellbeing because what is being promoted is starvation consciousness. Your spiritual self IS starved. You seek physical validation, for health is created in the mind. When you love who you are, by utilizing your heart, mind, and senses to nurture your own wellbeing, you create a healthy body regardless of its shape.

The irony of this starvation consciousness is that it exists in an era where there is actually an abundance of food on the planet. Political and economic agendas interfere with the fair distribution of food to those in need. Even the world's charitable organizations use the bulk of your donations to finance their costly administrative hierarchy or to pay off corrupt officials in needy countries. Large quantities of food designated for third world countries lies rotting in warehouses while political red tape prevents its distribution to the needy. While you compassionately donate food to your food banks, your local restaurants and grocery stores throw out enough food each day to feed every hungry person in your city. Globally there is great profit in promoting poverty of body, mind, and spirit. When you open your eyes and look at what is really going on, you would quickly realize it doesn't make sense. It is not meant to make sense; it is meant to keep you off-balance, for many corporations glean huge economic profits from your overall imbalances.

How you look in no way affects how you express yourself as a human being unless your self-image derives from your physical appearance. Your beliefs about your appearance, health, and fitness are just that, unexamined beliefs you accept as truth. You are healthy and happy when you love and accept yourself the way you are and listen to what your body tells you it needs. If you consider your body and food as suspect or if your program for improvement includes one of the Deadly three D's - discomfort, denial, and diet - forget it! Nothing you do on the outside will change who you are on the inside. The changes you make will only last as long as you maintain any unnatural shape-changing regimes. When you love your body, your outward appearance will reflect this inner wellbeing. If your outer body does not change much, no matter because you love your body however it is.

Spirit loves your body because it's the sensory feedback the body provides that makes it so precious. Additionally, fear of disease and death has you thinking otherwise. Media advertising generated by beauty, medical and fitness oriented organizations fuel these fears for profit. Information on what helps maintain a healthy body is useful but not essential once you begin to resonate with and listen to your own body. In most cases, the conflicting information these organizations provide only confuses you and prevents trust in yourself to nurture your own mental, emotional and spiritual wellbeing.

Bombarded by highly physical and sexual triggers, your appearance has become the yardstick for your developing identity at a younger and younger age. Your emerging sexual awareness stimulated during adolescence obviously ensures propagation of the species down the road. However, it does so much more. Sensual and sexual stimulation generates a powerful kind of creative energy intended to expand your consciousness. The feeling of pleasure you experience during your sexual attractions stimulates all your senses, including your inner senses. When you feel love, your sensory receptiveness expands. When you are in love, the whole world is wonderful! You feel *'wonder-full'* – filled with spiritual energy. The object of your love triggers your pheromones, which stimulate your amino acids to trigger more of your own micro-antenna receptors. The more micro-antenna receptors that are triggered, the more sensory and intuitive information is available to you. This expands your awareness of yourself and the environment so you can integrate the extra sensory resources stored in your generic X-Files into your operating data banks.

You use both your mind and senses to maintain your physical wellbeing. It is your responsibility because you have the mental 'ability-to-respond' to the sensory messages your body conveys. The Russians have long been forerunners in exploring the potentials of the mind and extrasensory abilities, although more with the intention of developing and refining mind control techniques. To determine how much control a person has over their health, they initiated one of many interesting clinical studies in the early 1970s with a randomly chosen group of pre-school children.

In a boarding school setting, they could eat whatever they wanted from a broad spectrum of foods that included both junk food and nutritional food within this controlled environment. There were no restrictions on what, how much, or how often they could eat throughout the day or night. Staff recorded their individual eating choices and patterns during the three-month study. After evaluation, researchers noted their choices were highly individualistic. Few ate what we consider a balanced diet yet all met their body's nutritional requirements. In spite of odd food choices, many children showed a marked improvement in their health by the end of the study. If young children can intuitively maintain their health without food guidelines, why can't you?

Your beliefs, racial heritage, metabolism, and what stage of life you are at influence your individual nutritional needs. The kinds of foods available in different climatic zones across the globe perfectly matched humanity's need to either maintain body warmth in cold environments or disperse body heat in hot countries. Whether you are a child, adult, pregnant woman, senior or if you have a physically taxing or a cerebral and sedentary lifestyle also influences your nutritional needs. A twenty year old who works at a computer all day would compromise their physical well-being if they consumed a construction worker's daily carbohydrate intake. By strengthening your body-mind-spirit connection, you can realign any physical imbalances you have created, regardless of source. When you ignore the messages your heart chakra sends to your mind, your body will quickly let you know something is out of alignment.

You create a physical imbalance and you fix it with your mind. Commonly known as sugar pills, placeboes work because your body follows your mind. With your mind, you also give doctors and holistic practitioners the authority to participate in your healing process. Your belief that a certain remedy or procedure will cure you is what makes it work. That is why Traveling Medicine Shows did so well in their era. The alcohol and herbal content in these medicinal compounds relaxed people's conscious filters. Therefore, their conscious minds didn't interfere with their body's healing processes. You could dance naked around a tree stump with a string of garlic or Chipotle peppers around your neck to cure an ailment if you believed it would. Belief not methodology induces healing and you choose your methodology, based on your beliefs. The reverse is also true. The best holistic, herbal, or pharmaceutical remedy will not cure you if you do not believe it can.

Healing and wellness starts in the mind as does discomfort and disease due to imbalances. Despite your interference and unloving attitude towards it, your body continues to maintain your biological functions. It hasn't arranged a mutiny because of your beliefs - or has it? Change your attitude towards your body's physical maintenance, towards food, and your physical appearance. When you listen to your body, your cravings will indicate what it needs and your sensitivities what to avoid. This has nothing to do with what anybody else's body needs. Reclaim your authority over your body and pay attention to the messages your physical sensations are sending you, for that is their job – to increase your awareness of yourself on all levels.

Become more flexible in your attitude towards food. You can be a vegetarian and still eat fish or the occasional meat dish. Follow your ethnic preferences. Choose the foods that appeal to you regardless of the current fad food others are eating. Be willing to try new foods and listen to your body. It will let you know if it likes these new additions. Although it is beneficial to eat as much fresh organic food as you can, the key to maintaining and enhancing your physical wellbeing lies in your mind, regardless of what you eat.

Your desires also influence your body. If you want chocolate and deny this desire, you still have dedicated energy attached to the desire. When you finally do succumb, you will most likely eat the whole chocolate bar instead of the few pieces that would satisfy your initial craving. You then tie up more energy with guilt or self-loathing for having done so and set one of those automatic punishment and absolution programs in motion. If you had a few pieces of chocolate, half a piece of cake or pie, or a little gravy on the mashed potatoes you love, you would release the dedicated energy attached to these desires. Your body metabolizes these foods without harm to your health because you derived the sensory gratification you were initially seeking.

Denial leads to over-indulgence and self-depreciation. *Your food cravings are not about food.* They represent a built-up denial of sensory gratification in other aspects of your life. Allowing yourself these small sensory pleasures will not harm you. Denying them will. Honor and enjoy your food, believe it is good for you, trust your body to metabolize it, and stop fussing about it!

Just as you do not participate in the sensory enjoyment of food you've become spectators of simulated life rather than active physical participators in your own. Your physical environment has become a backdrop for your fitness initiatives and other self-absorbed activities. The fulfillment of your spiritual need for sensory stimulation is rarely self-generated anymore. You satisfy it through your computers and television. Although the Internet is a rich information resource, you need to examine your thoughts and feelings while you are absorbing all this data. It is thought AND sensation that equals knowledge. Watching a lot of television also disconnects you from sensory participation in your own experiences and allows these sensory triggers to stimulate your perceived needs and fears. The more artificial stimulation you get, the less you pay attention to your own thoughts and feelings.

The less you are thinking, the less attention you pay to what you are feeling *about* what you are thinking. When you do not direct your own processes, others can, will, and do.

Choosing a Body

Disregard everything you know or believe about your body for a moment. You are a spiritual light-energy being having a physical experience. You are not your body, yet your body is an extension of who you are. What your body looks like matters little. Yet, it all-ways reflects, *though not defines,* your identity. As an aspect of your higher frequency consciousness, your physical senses enable your spiritual self to express and view itself through this 3-D holograph. Physical incarnation is highly coveted because of this unique kind of sensory expression of thought. Your feelings are different from anyone else's because you have your own Soul identity, history, and accumulation of experiences. The blood flowing through your veins carries the imprint of its ancestral existence, which is why bloodlines are important to those who control you on this physical plane. This human experience is both coveted and a pre-requisite within the universe if a Soul is to move onto other frequencies. If you think as Spirit you just float around the cosmos willy-nilly or sing praises to a higher deity in heaven after this life, you are mistaken. You continue to learn and expand your consciousness through self-expression. That is the nature of the Consciousness you are. Therefore, this human experience is an elective, one you have joyfully chosen.

If no one ever told you what you should look like, you would think there was nothing wrong with the way you do look. Take time to watch small children. They think their bodies are wonderful no matter what they look like. Hang on to that thought, for you can change your reality with it. To Spirit, your body is a wonder-full reflection of its own consciousness. So it matters not which one you pick. It is the very differences and intrinsic characteristics that make each body so unique. I feel intrinsic is such a beautiful word. The dictionary defines intrinsic as, *'belonging to the essential nature or constitution of a thing, i.e.: the worth of a gem'.* Each one of you is such a gem. The word intrinsic is also defined as, *'being or related to a semi conductor in which the concentration of charge carriers is characteristic of the material itself instead of the content of any impurities it contains'.* What impurities you may think you possess are a result of your beliefs, all of which you can change.

Your subconscious is the energy-conductor that translates the spiritual ancestry of your greater consciousness into this physical reality through your body. If you are a woman, how does this relate to the fact that you are thirty pounds overweight, have stringy hair, small sagging breasts, and thunder thighs? If you are a man, how does this relate to the fact that you have a paunch, hair on your back but none on your head, and a honker of a nose? It matters not. Your personal judgments are a result of your programmed and self-constructed ideals. These ideals have no relevance to your actual worth as an intrinsically unique reflection of your spiritual identity unless they actually support this view of yourself.

Why do you have your body, rather than another body? Spirit has its own criteria, and it is not at all what you might think. Before you enter this reality, you embark on the grand adventure of planning your physical incarnation. You first decide on the lessons you wish to learn, for you come with specific intentions in mind. I will expand on this aspect of your physical experience in the next chapter. You then choose whatever historic era and ethnic expression via race, culture and geographic location appeals to you. Having done so, you communicate your intentions to other Souls planning their own physical existences, or those intending to have children. Whatever loose script you have designed for yourself, when these elements are in place, you enter this reality through the birth canal like everyone else and begin your physical experience.

You choose parents whose bloodline contains characteristics that will enable you to learn your intended lessons. Each family's bloodline not only carries the DNA blueprint of your physical appearance, but more importantly, the cellular memory of its consciousness ancestry. Bloodlines carry the accumulated knowledge of all the experiences, lessons, skills, and personality traits acquired by that bloodline through physical expression. You are, in effect, the evolutionary repository of the whole of your genetic ancestry when you are born into a pairing of two bloodlines. You in turn imprint your bloodlines with what you add to its Soul memory throughout your life. The chains of harmful cycles like addictions, family dysfunctions, and other abuses can be broken, healed, and transformed into understandings that raise the frequency of your whole bloodline ancestry.

The paradox of how you look physically is that *it does not matter a wit!* Your physical appearance is just part of the whole package. Disappointed? Your higher frequency aspect is not. Regardless of how imperfect you consider your body, it is loved and treasured by your Soul. This life is not about how your body looks, rather, how you experience your consciousness *through* it. If you have had more than one past life regression you know you've inhabited many different types of bodies of both genders, some of which you liked and some of which you didn't. Once you understand this, you can release your judgments on outer appearance, love yourself the way you are, and begin to enjoy the grand game of life on Planet Earth.

Body Consciousness & Health

Your body has its own self-regulating consciousness without which your cells and organs could not perform their functions. You do not have to get up each morning and direct these functions. Although body consciousness handles these processes automatically, it also reflects what your mind thinks. Each morning when you look at yourself in the mirror, you subconsciously re-create and reinforce the image you expect to see, based on your self-image. Since your body follows your mind, when you change your perception of yourself the outer reflection in the mirror also changes. Your reflection will not actually change your features, the color of your hair or your weight, but you'll appear more slender and attractive to yourself and others. The reverse is also true.

Your physical body is capable of lasting much longer than you suppose, hundreds of years in fact. Your beliefs about aging direct it to deteriorate at a pre-determined rate. In isolated locations of the globe, there are many vital 100+ year-olds who are still very functional on both a mental and physical level. You will follow the aging pattern of your parents and grandparents unless you envision a different picture of yourself at their age. If you think you will be pudgy and unattractive at forty, useless and lonely at 60 or hobbling like a hunchbacked at seventy because your parents and grandparents are, you will too.

You will also follow ancestral patterns in how you experience your life. I feel we choose particular bloodlines because these patterns serve our intentions. Sometimes our intention is specifically to heal a corrupted bloodline while expanding our own consciousness. The evidence of my own family history confirms my ancestors were highly task-driven but late bloomers when it came to personal achievements. Most of my ancestors never got kick-started until they were in their late forties. Until then they just survived their many life abuses with outer courage and inner self-pity. I am slightly embarrassed to say I followed suit until my forties.

There is also a pattern of longevity in mental alertness until their mid-90s providing they live past 60 in both my bloodlines. My mother only started to learn languages by correspondence when she turned fifty. Ninety years old now, she has five languages to her credit. Despite her beliefs about life's many burdens and the physical pains associated with old age, the belief that her mental abilities would stay sharp made it so.

I fondly call my bloodlines 'experience-gatherers'. Lacking the knowhow, they were unable to examine and utilize their experiences to change their circumstances and just perpetuated more of the same. Nevertheless, within my genetic heritage flowed an indomitable fortitude and will, strengths I use to change my own life programming. The difference lies in focus. Their focus perpetuated their dysfunctions whereas mine energizes discovering, releasing, and healing them. Consequently, I heal my whole bloodline as I continue to heal genetic imbalances within myself.

Your body is a wonderful repository of multi actualizing functions. The automatic process of breathing not only keeps you alive but also acts like an energy-transmitting generator. Whatever this energy, be it negative and toxic or loving and healing, it is continually released, absorbed, processed, and exchanged. Notice your feelings when you are in an angry crowd, an emotionally charged situation, or around someone else's imbalance. Controlled breathing and meditation helps move these external energy influences through your body without creating energy blocks.

Why do some people never fall victim to colds or seasonal illness and how is it that some of these people are overweight, do not eat a healthy diet, or do not exercise regularly like you do? Why do you get sick and they do not? These things do not create illness whereas your fear-based beliefs do. Exhaled through your breathe just like airborne viruses and other infectious organisms, your energy draws what you fear to you like a magnet. Some of you are so entrenched in these fear-based beliefs, like a prophet you can predict what illness you will get, how it will make you feel, and how long it will last. You are always right, for the body follows the mind. One dictionary definition of virus, *'something that poisons the mind or soul'*, validates this process.

A viral or bacterial microorganism needs a willing host in order to survive. When your natural immune system is weakened by the constant use of suppressing medications and you are afraid you'll catch something, you become that willing host. One person may get the same illness but have only a day or two of mild discomfort while you may be very ill. It all depends on how much energy is dedicated to what you don't want, and how many energy blocks you already have in your system. Creating disease does not make your body your enemy, rather a loving partner that always informs you of any existing imbalance.

Heart-related diseases are on the rise because the heart represents love. Stress and dissatisfaction created by society's expectations are low frequency energies that limit your ability to express love. When more of your energy is directed towards making money, advancing your careers, and all the busy stuff you do rather than loving yourself and others, the heart chakra itself becomes blocked. Designed to beat in time to the cosmic frequency of love that carries the joy of spiritual self-expression to all aspects of yourself, the arteries of the heart contract to let you know you have reached critical mass.

Cancer is also on the rise in both men and women. Cancer represents low frequency emotions like deep hurts, secrets or grief eating away at you, longstanding resentments or hatreds, and an overall 'what's the use' attitude towards life. These feelings indicate you are unable to forgive and love yourself and unable to forgive others. It generally indicates an inability to release the past. A woman's breasts represent mothering, nurturing and nourishment. Breast cancer represents over-mothering, over protectiveness, overbearing attitudes, and always putting others first. Always putting others first is a decoy for a refusal to nourish the self. Since the uterus represents the home of creativity, female-organ cancers represent a rejection and denial of the elemental feminine principle and expression.

Prostate cancer is also on the rise in men. It represents unexpressed guilt, mental fears they believe weakens their masculinity, a fear of aging, and an overall sense of giving up. Cancer in both genders represents an elemental lack of self-love and worthiness. I recommend an excellent little book by Louise L. Hay called *"Heal Your Body"* if you want to become more familiar with the mental causes of physical symptoms and the thinking helpful in changing these conditions. The more I have used this little book over the past few decades the more I appreciate the synergy between the body and mind. Your body perfectly mirrors what kind of energy blocks you have.

Just as your chakras represent your body's energy control centers, your thoughts also have neurological centers that connect to different parts of your body. The dictionary defines your nerve impulses as *'the progressive alteration in the protoplasm of a nerve fiber that follows stimulation and serves to transmit a record of sensation from a receptor or an instruction to act to an effector'.* Simply put, your thoughts direct your nerve impulses to trigger a response in specific parts of your body. Imbalances in any aspect of your thinking transmit discomfort to your body in the same way that loving thoughts transmit health and wellbeing throughout your body.

As an electromagnetic energy being, your body responds to all energy fluctuations within this reality. The insertion of a higher frequency has already altered the frequency upon which humanity had previously operated. Some of your existing physical discomforts are a result of your body's self-regulating process as it establishes balance within these frequency changes. Many of you are experiencing periods of accelerated dream work and other consciousness expanding sensations to prepare you for upcoming frequency changes. These fluctuations may cause you to feel sluggish, heavy or unusually sleepy. Conversley, you may feel light-headed and disconnected, as if you are viewing your actions from a distance. Even if your energy is balanced, you will still be affected by these frequency shifts to varying degrees. The difference is, you are aware of the cause and can better manage the effects.

Some of you have developed sensitivities you have never experienced before. You may be more sensitive to noise and large gatherings, certain foods, and people who emulate energy no longer compatible with your own. The more you raise your own frequency, the more sensitive you become to all energy transmissions. You need to eliminate what has become toxic for you and begin energizing what nourishes you. You may also experience periods of physical cleansing while undergoing energy frequency changes. Left alone they will stabilize with minimal discomfort unless you compound the process with mental resistance and/or suppressing medications. Avail yourself of herbal detoxifiers to cleanse your system of built-up toxins if need be. Despite these temporary discomforts, allow your body to realign itself and avoid cloaking unpleasant side effects like body odor or skin eruptions when they do occur.

Hygiene and beautification products that mask natural secretions have suppressed many of your body's own natural cleansing and detoxifying processes. Bad breath or a bad taste in your mouth is often the first indicator of a toxic buildup or impending illness. Deodorants prevent your body from releasing these accumulated toxins through your glands. Chemical accumulations from years of use has altered you body's natural chemistry to such a degree that were you to stop using these agents you would smell unbearably vile even to yourself until your body eliminated these toxins. Many of you feel offended by your own natural body odors. Where you attuned to your body, you are intimately familiar with all your body scents, thus aware of any subtle changes.

Myths about Health & Health Foods

Many of you pound the sidewalks with expensive air-cushioned runners or contort your bodies in the newest rendition of the Inquisition's contraptions at the gym to keep fit. Consider just walking about a 1/2 hour a day. If you feel you have to sweat to stimulate circulation, climb stairs, briskly walk up a hill, or participate in a physically stimulating sport you enjoy. Whatever you do to vitalize your body do it because you enjoy that activity. A taut belly and firm thighs will not make you a more nurturing parent, supportive and stimulating friend, uplifting mate or creative and productive human being if you hate the regime that that keeps you looking lean. Thoroughly enjoying a silly game of ball in the park has greater overall benefits than these regimented 'have-to' workouts.

When you breathe deeply, you oxygenate the whole body. This automatically raises your energy frequency. Reconnect with earth energy by walking barefoot on the grass or soil, leaning against a tree or immersing your feet in the ocean, a river or a lake. Then breathe deeply to relax and be receptive to all your senses. Each deep breath absorbs earth's healing and balancing energies and strengthens your attunement to your own higher frequencies. Give yourself time to simply BE. Allow yourself to experience whatever sensations arise while you are in the natural environment.

Unless you participate in a sport or other activity requiring specific conditioning, all you need is some physical activity on a daily basis to keep your body toned. Frequent cat-stretches and walking will suffice. You could as easily lie on the couch each evening and visualize yourself exercising with your mind. The results will be the same. I once received a nightshirt with a slogan on the front that said, *"Honey, when I get the urge to exercise, I just lie down until it goes away."* I lay me down and visualized myself physically doing a regime of Yoga exercises. During this visualization, I focused my energy on my breathing and the feeling of my body actually doing the exercises. It works because your subconscious does not know the difference. Accept your body, love it, trust it, and stop making such a fuss over it.

Intense physical activity alters your body chemistry much as fear does. When you reach those adrenaline peaks while you strain at the gym or pound the pavements during your daily run, your receptors trigger your nerve impulses to put your body on a high state of sensory alertness. If you take pleasure in the activity, this also triggers the release of 'feel good' pheromones. When it doesn't trigger your pleasure endorphins this tension creates a state of hyper-vigilance that needs to be de-energized. Add the expectation that you must always be doing, doing, doing, you are moving so fast you forget where it is you are going, or why.

For many of you, your days consist of mental activity without being present in each moment, followed by intense physical activity without being present in each moment, and emoting without acknowledging your real feelings in the moment. Busy as you are, basically, you are generally not present in any of your moments.

The expression *'lighten up'* relays a powerful message. It not only implies adding humor to your life but also adding the light-energy of your higher frequencies to your conscious perception of yourself. If your weight makes you physically uncomfortable, love yourself anyhow and just eat a little less or change what you are eating. If you lack stamina or vitality, love yourself anyhow and just walk more and /or breathe more deeply. You body knows exactly what it needs and will prod you towards those needs as long as you use it as your yardstick for well-being, not some exterior criteria. Chart your cravings for several weeks to see what your body is lacking. It matters not if you go on binges where you have a craving for only one kind of food for a time to nourish an existing deficiency. A balanced diet does not mean you have to eat something from every food group each day. Balance is providing what your body needs in order to maintain its natural state of health.

Next to telecommunications, health foods and holistic supplements have become one of the largest growing industries of the last two decades, an industry that generates billions of dollars each year. Why do you think the FDA, who have previously regulated only chemical pharmaceuticals, are now attempting to do so with holistic and herbal products? It is not because they support this mushrooming market to ensure your wellbeing. They can't prevent a renewed interest in natural and herbal remedies so now want to control and cash in on it. If you intend to use real herbal supplements, I suggest you see a genuine Chinese herbalist, ideally one who also does acupuncture and Iridology. They know how to read your eyes, ears, tongue, and energy meridians on your wrists to determine which organs are blocked and what you actually need to fortify them.

When you think you are buying organic food, consider how it's grown. I find it hard to believe that the soil in the fields where supermarket organic food is grown is immune to the pesticides used on neighboring fields. If you think Eco and Free Range eggs are lain by chickens that actually range free and happily peck untainted grain from the earth, think again. What these chickens eat may be a fraction less toxic, but they are eating it in indoor/outdoor enclosures almost as cramped as the cages stacked one atop the other where mainstream grocery eggs are laid. The eggs they lay absorb the stressful energy of existing in these confined quarters.

Unless you know the farmer who is growing your produce and grains or raising your livestock, you haven't a clue as to how it is really produced. You also do not know if the produce labeled organic didn't come from of the third bumper crop of a thousand acre plot right beside the pesticide-sprayed acres that grow regular produce. It is amazing how a little organic sticker and slick advertising can hypnotize you into paying more for something only a fraction less polluted. With an increase in consumer awareness and subsequent demand for organic foodstuffs, the need for multiple harvests to meet this growing demand has also risen. Labels do not tell the whole story. It is your belief that makes this food better for you.

Unless you buy your eggs from a farmer you know feeds them natural rather than chemically engineered grains, you can bet these eggs are only marginally healthier. Many of you think a bright orange joke means a natural healthy egg. I know of a specific additive to their diet that makes the yokes bright orange because we raised chickens when I was young. Over the past 20 years, seeds and grains are all genetically engineered and pre-treated with chemicals. Talk to the farmers. Independent farmers who previously harvested and sowed their own seeds must now purchase this genetically manipulated seed. If they refuse, they lose their subsidy entitlements, meaning they cannot market their crops. All phases of the production of the food you eat is controlled and regulated in this way.

Having said that, everything you eat is good for you if you believe it is. Just be aware you are being brainwashed. Trust your senses and read the labels. The fewer the ingredients listed, the better this food is for you. Seek out the most natural foods you can afford and reduce if not eliminate processed and convenience foods. A good rule of thumb is to buy the majority of your food from along the perimeters of the grocery store. That is where your fish, meat, vegetables, fruits, dairy products, breads, and grain, nut and legume bins are located. The processed foods that contain the most preservatives are located in the center isles along with all the toxic household products you use on a daily basis.

Increase physical activity somewhat and reduce the quantity of food you consume slightly if your body mass prevents you from feeling vital. You will intuitively begin to seek out better foods, and eliminate unhealthy habits that are the residuals of brainwashing over the past few decades. Stop eating on the run, out of boredom, or with disinterest. Mealtime is a richly interactive experience on many levels. When you begin to listen to your inner senses, you will also begin to experience the sensory enjoyment of the preparation, texture, and flavor of fresh food again.

Making Changes to Your Body

It is no accident that body consciousness is a key to determining your well-being, for your attitude towards your body is a reflection of your overall self-image. Until you accept and love your body the way it is right now, you will not achieve and maintain any of your desired modifications on a lasting basis. How you look may be the result of years of poor thinking. Nevertheless, it is how you look right now. If you want to change your physical appearance, I suggest you do this exercise.

Exercise # 6.

Take a sheet of paper and divide it into four columns. Number the columns 1 to 4 and write down your answers to these questions:

1. *What do I want to change about my physical appearance?* List everything about your body you don't like and want to change in column #1. Be specific and don't leave out anything.
2. Read your list aloud then ask yourself *'If there was only one thing I could change on this list, what would it be?'* Circle

that item with a red pen. At the bottom of the page, write what feeling you think you would get *(benefit)* if this one thing about you changed.

3. Start at the top of your list again and ask yourself '*Would changing this enhance how others see me, would it make me feel better emotionally or would it increase my inner well-being?*'

    Then put an <u>O</u> for how others view you, an <u>E</u> for your own emotional gratification or <u>I</u> for a sense of inner well-being in column #2 beside each item on your list.

4. Start at the top of column #1 again and ask yourself these two questions for each item:

    a) *Does this inhibit my normal physical mobility?* If so, transfer that item to column #3.

    b) *Does this prevent me from feeling joy and satisfaction in what I experience each day?* If so, transfer that item to column #4.

    c) Write the heading <u>Physical</u> at the top of Column #3, and <u>Emotional</u> at the top of Column #4.

The items that have an 'O' beside them are desires based on ideals and social programming. The items with an 'E' beside them are perceived needs resulting from unmet real needs you've transferred to your physical appearance. This dedicated energy will be released once you discover what real needs each of these items really represent. The items listed in columns #3 and #4 can be addressed as legitimate intentions for change.

Read what you have written about your circled items aloud. Can you get this feeling another way, and if so, how? Write down the other ways you can get this 'feel good' sensation and do it!

If you do not accept and love yourself now, what makes you think you will once you change your appearance? Many who have lost a lot of weight continue to see themselves as heavier then they now are when they look in a mirror or at another slender woman. Your outer reflection will not change if you do not also change your inner identity. Women who lose weight to attract a mate quickly gain it back after they are married and over time often gain even more weight. The cause is starvation consciousness. Once the euphoria of the weight loss has worn off and others stop commenting on how amazing you look, then what? The test of any physical change is what happens when you stop the regime that created the transformation. When a substantial weight loss is contrary to your existing self-image, your body will instinctively begin to hoard fat to prevent future violation of this self-image. Your body's cellular memory automatically reverts to its prior form unless your inner beliefs about your physical identity and food have also changed.

You need a physical body to maneuver in this gravity-based reality. Yet this body does not define your consciousness. You will not take your body with you when you leave, yet your consciousness continues to exist. Consider how those who have left this physical plane still influence you. Their spiritual influence can be so great you often pattern your beliefs after them even though they no longer exist. Spiritual beings that have never been physical cherish the possibility of experiencing themselves through a body no matter what it looks like. They would jump at the chance to have the body that dissatisfies you.

You have lived other physical lives and will live many more. Therefore, you have and will inhabit many bodies, both male and female. You have been tall and short, skinny and plump and all the variations between within as many different racial bloodlines. No matter what kind of body you chose, every one is a beautiful gem to Spirit. The concept of beauty in this reality is a perception that continually changes. Open an art book or National Geographic magazine and see the variations of beauty idolized by the world's different cultures and races throughout history. If you do not happen to meet the current ideal, change the ideal to how you look. Then you will be just perfect!

How you view your body affects your self-image and vice versa. If you were born with brown hair and are not happy with the color you can shave it off, camouflage it, or dye it. However, at the root of the matter is still your brown hair, and an unhappy brown-haired person is no different from an unhappy blonde-haired person or red-haired person. You can have fun with your appearance and change it as long as you do it to please yourself. Better to dye your hair green for fun than to loathe your natural hair color. If you make changes to seek outer approval by looking like everyone else or to get attention by looking different, your 'feel good' sensations will be short-lived.

Energy Management

Each body has its own energy patterns. Called *biorhythms*, these energy flux patterns are your individual biological frequency pattern signature. They represent your unique energy ebbs and flows. In order to discover yours, track your high and low energy periods throughout the day for several weeks to see what times of the day you energy peaks and sags. There will be periods when you are more mentally alert or have more physical stamina than at other times during the day. Most work-related accidents, mistakes, or poor mental choices occur during low energy periods when mental or physical fatigue dulls both your physical acuity and cognitive awareness.

Once you become familiar with your personal patterns, align your tasks to these patterns as much as possible. Utilize high-energy periods for your mental and physical tasks, and low energy periods for routine functions to maintain a higher level of productivity, awareness, and creativity. Begin to use low energy periods to realign and rejuvenate your body. When your energy is low, breath slowly and deeply until you are completely relaxed. Close your eyes and instruct your body to rejuvenate itself. You can do this anywhere - on a bus or at your desk while staring at your computer screen. You already take these time-outs, but use them to worry about stuff that has not happened yet or to condemn yourself for something done or not done. If you can, go outside and breathe in the air slowly and deeply. Fatigue often results from a lack of oxygen circulating through your system.

Take mini energy-breaks throughout the day when you feel imbalanced or overwhelmed in any way. When you slip in and out of these meditative rejuvenation periods during the day, you will notice a marked improvement in your overall vitality and level of efficiency. Restructure your activities when your energy levels change. You will enhance your productivity and begin to enjoy what you do more.

Within our current time-oriented frequency, your mind utilizes what equates to a 45-minute cycle to process information. Self-awareness instructors optimize their effectiveness when they format their presentations to conform to this cycle. It consists of 15 minutes of new data input, 15 minutes of comparison to what is already in your data banks, and 15 minutes of review, from which you reach your conclusions. This three-segment pattern follows the pattern of your mental systems although the actual time this process takes will vary and can be much shorter. When instructors review important points during the last 15 minutes of this cycle they do so to reinforce the conclusions they want you to reach. Until the late seventies mainstream education structured classroom subject periods to align with this cycle.

Television commercials interrupt this mental cycle intentionally to scramble your mind. Formatted to last 29 seconds, the first 5-15 seconds of a commercial mixes new data input with triggers that activate specific desires and fears. The last 5-14 seconds mix comparison of your have and have-nots that reinforces of the ideals they want you to satisfy. The next commercial starts this process all over again before you can review and reach your conclusions on the previous data. On an energy level, this interrupts your mind's natural processing system by introducing data to trigger new perceived desires and fears. When you watch 7-8 of these commercials in a row, your brain stays in new data input and comparison mode without reaching any conclusions. Emotions are triggered but never satisfied, after which you immediately return to your secondary reactionary processes when the program you were watching resumes.

A compressed form of this cycle occurs during your personal conversations regardless of the length of the interaction. Consider those times when you *'tap out'* during a conversation. Programmed to react, you move from absorbing input to comparison then to review and conclusion while the person is still talking. Consequently, you often react by saying something you did not intend to say. It is only after you complete the comparison process that you reach your conclusions about what has been said and know how you really wanted to respond. Pausing for ten seconds ensures you have time to process the data and form the response you want. The higher your energy frequency, the more quickly your mind moves through this cycle. Some people are able to compress this process into a few split seconds, while others operating on a lower frequency need more 'time' to complete this process.

You also lose about 2-4 hours a day in playing out mental fabrications where your energy is focused on reviewing all your perceived desires and fears. When your energy is engaged only with the present moment, you become more creative and productive. Take time to clear your mind, take a stroll, enjoy your sensory pleasures, assess your tasks and progress, or relax. Although time is an artificial construct of this 3-D reality, everyone operates within a 24-hour day. People who do more have no more time than you have. They just structure their time differently. They have more vitality because they do more things that interest them. In a balanced state of free-flowing energy they utilize more creative ways to approach tasks and resolve challenges. You can expand or compress time when you reorganize your priorities, re-arrange your sleep patterns, and work in alignment with your own biorhythms. The resulting vitality makes you more focused on whatever you are doing. Then everything you do is both interesting and meaningful.

If you are self-employed or raise children at home, you have greater flexibility than if you work in an office. However, you can still do this at work during your coffee and lunch breaks. Whenever possible, go outside and breathe fresh air or bring an oxygenizing plant into your workspace. Any concentration of a specific kind of energy creates its own magnetic force field. As an electromagnetic energy being, these force fields affect your own energy signature. Office buildings with their florescent lights, computers, and re-cycled air create magnetic fields that literally suck energy from you. If you work in this environment go outside as often as you can to rejuvenate yourself. You will cleanse the stale air recycled through office air-conditioning systems out of your lungs and counteract the effects of the electrical hardware in your office.

Everything in life will begin to look better - even you! How you feel about how you look physically is of paramount importance. If you are unhappy with how you look, you are unhappy with who you are. If you are unhappy with who you are now, you will continue to be unhappy no matter what exterior transformations you make. Appreciate and love what you are – a beautiful gem, inside and out. Love your body and approach any changes you want to make with a light heart and loving intentions. Your intrinsic uniqueness is cause for celebration not denigrated. Love yourself and others will respond to the love you broadcast. Once you realize you are just fine the way you are, you will stop obsessing about your body. Adorn it, camouflage it, modify it, or leave it as is because it matters not what you look like. What matters is how you use your body's wondrous senses to achieve your TASK: Thought And Sensation = Knowledge.

Chapter 7

KEYS TO YOUR SPIRITUAL AGENDA

"Knowledge Expands Your Soul"

THE *more you know, the more you grow.* You chose this physical experience to learn through thought-manifestation. Consider it an informal and elective school where you script your own lesson plan in order to explore and expand your Soul consciousness within the sensory-rich framework of this reality.

Certain lessons are *core lessons*, elemental rites of passage of every Soul's evolution on this 3-D frequency. Despite your proficiency on other frequencies, learning how consciousness works in this reality can be tricky business. Once your consciousness settles into a body, its physical sensations and the beliefs you acquire through life programming sidetrack you. Because you are sidetracked, you keep coming back to finish your lessons. Some are group lessons, where you participate in cultural or racial experiments while learning your own lessons and some are new lessons created by the choices you make within your existing experience.

All of these adventures contribute to the expansion of your Soul's consciousness, whether you learn these lessons or not. Every person, event, and circumstance in your life is there to teach you something about yourself in order to remember who you are and why you are here. Once you do, you can begin to use your thought-energy to influence and change your experiences within this reality. You are a precious aspect of Prime Creator's consciousness, a consciousness with a desire to learn more about itself through its own explorations and what all its multi-aspects experience on different frequencies.

Core Lessons

A core lesson fundamental to all souls within this 3-D is to remember that *you are a spiritual being having a physical experience,* not the other way around. What makes this physical experience so challenging is that from the moment you are born you have to learn everything in order to become functional in your human form. It is *what* you learn that either nurtures or blocks the awareness of your spiritual intentions. Instead of using all these extended sensory resources, your experiences become limited to what your beliefs will allow. In spite of this, once you access your inner senses you can begin to expand these beliefs.

You will live as many physical lives in as many variations as needed to remember who you are and to complete your intended lessons in order to raise your consciousness to a higher frequency. Then you can leave the cycle of physical lives, merge with your Soul consciousness and the God-Consciousness and move on to other frequencies. Once you do, you may decide to come back to this reality specifically to help others in their journey. These enlightened trailblazers help uplift humanity by inserting their higher frequency knowledge into the existing stream of human consciousness.

Another core lesson is to realize *you create your own reality* on this frequency, just as you do on all other frequencies. Although events and circumstances seem to happen to you, you drew these experiences to you with your own thoughts. Your thoughts create the holographic manifestation to which you respond on a sensory level. You then interpret your own response to hopefully understand the effects of the original thought. What disrupts this natural process of self-awareness are your programmed beliefs and learned emotional reactions. As an energy-being you continually transmit your energy outward like a cosmic magnet to attract people and circumstances through which you can learn these lessons. The kinds of experiences you attract is determined by your inner self-image. Although your root assumptions maintain a common view of your environment, you 'see' this common view through an individualized perception formed by your own beliefs.

Universal Free Will, by its very definition, allows each of you to experience your own truths through your interpretation of these beliefs. One definition of the word free is, *"not determined by anything beyond its own nature or being: choosing or being capable of choosing for itself"*. Freedom is also defined as, *"the absence of necessity, coercion, or constraint in choice or action"*, and, *"the ability to choose between alternatives so that the choice and action are to an extent creatively determined by the conscious subject."* That conscious subject is you. Truth IS subjective and reality is all about perception. For, whatever you believe to be true *is true for you*.

For example, I always believed my prime spiritual intention was to understand human nature even if I did not understand what that meant when I was younger. Although my early life programming and resulting beliefs did not support this spiritual agenda I have always attracted people, philosophies, and circumstances that inspired me to continue exploring human consciousness. One of my most significant sources of inspiration since the early 1980s has been *"The Evergreens"*, channeled through deep-trance medium Michael Blake Read. Their book, *"The Evergreens' Gentle Book of Practical Living Pointers"*, was instrumental in helping me examine and expand my beliefs about reality. Dog-eared, taped together, and without a cover, I still reach for their book when I lose sight of my task. On the purpose of life, The Evergreens say:

"The purpose of life is to learn, and share learning with others."
"The purpose of life is to work so that there is manipulation of the world, not the world that it would manipulate you."
"The purpose of life is to experience the experiencing of experience."
"To the total life, there are five points to be taken here. The first one is the expression of love. The second is the expression of a helping hand. The third is the expression of physical sharing. The fourth is the growth of physical and spiritual links. The fifth is to aid the growth of those that have found themselves stultified."
. . . *The Evergreens*

Intellect is a result of mental conclusions based on evidence of the existing knowledge within your environment. Spiritual understanding results from the expanded sensory interpretations that include the broader knowledge existing *outside* this reality. Your lessons were designed by you to gain this broader knowledge. Not based on the social programming through which you pattern your lives, it is difficult to learn your lessons if you are unaware this is what you are here to do. Towards this end, Spirit will use a variety of methods to help your conscious perception expand – when asked.

The changes many of you are willing to make fall within the parameters of what your self-image allows. Sensory data that would help expand your perception and identity is obstructed by the very beliefs that maintain your limited identity. Although Ego protects this identity, Spirit uses the X-files in your data banks to trigger inspiration and intuition. When you begin to use these resources, your senses trigger insights that help you see the lessons beneath your conscious experiences. Hindsight is always 20/20 because you already know what is going to happen and why. You know because you scripted it.

You can attract an experience that enables you to learn many different things like patience, love, and forgiveness all at the same time. For Example: You may be in a committed relationship and discover your partner was unfaithful. Are you interested in what you can learn about yourself through this experience or is your reaction based on social programming that has you thinking, *"How can that bastard or bitch do that to me"?* Can you forgive them and continue to love them? Are you so wounded you leave the relationship or are you willing to explore your partner's motivations as well as what this can teach you about yourself? Are you willing to rebuild trust between yourselves? Such events enable you to examine beliefs about *your own self-image.*

How you set up your lessons is as creatively unique as you are. Although the opportunity for many understandings exists within any one lesson, you can choose to learn everything, only a part of what you intended, or nothing at all. Although the latter is generally the byproduct of your own limited beliefs, that's OK too. You will just set up another circumstance to learn the same lesson. Everything is learning in order to expand awareness of yourself and within all your thought manifestations is the opportunity for more learning. Therefore, choosing not to learn is also learning.

What often perpetuate the continuation of problems and undesirable circumstances, *lessons that persist because you resist,* is the conscious judgments and automatic reactions you use to process your experiences. Spiritually you know why you create a problem or challenge for yourself. Consider the problem the conscious half of a lesson and the solution the subconscious portion - temporarily hidden from conscious awareness. If the problem gets resolved, you learned the lesson. If the problem remains, you are not finished yet. If a similar problem resurfaces, you did not get it the first time or you have decided to expand your explorations of that particular theme. You may even develop a fascination for a subject and manifest variations of this theme to become experts by understanding it from many different perspectives.

You sabotage yourself when you use the same problem-solving tools for everything. That is fine if your method works and the problem is resolved. If it is not, you are trying to fix a symptom of an underlying issue you have not yet addressed. You will not know this unless you use all your senses. You were intended to approach every event in your life with curiosity and without judgment, evaluate the sensations to reach your understandings, pat yourself on the back for getting it, and joyfully move on to the next adventure. Despite the fact your beliefs compromise this natural process, Spirit ensures you never miss an opportunity to learn your lessons. The same issues will repeatedly crop up in different guises. The ease with which you learn your lessons is dependant on your willingness to examine and change your beliefs.

Life is an informal school where you can bounce between lessons or work on one or many themes and projects at the same time. You may arrange lessons one after the other in a linear fashion or deal with several unrelated lessons all at once. You can even decide to avoid learning your lessons, for a while. The very fact that you are still in this physical reality means you are still learning. When you get down on yourself for all the 'issues' in your life, remember, you created these challenges for your own understanding.

Many of you take life far too seriously. The paradox of life is that *everything you do is of paramount importance yet it does not matter what you do.* It does not matter what you decide to do because it's all learning. When you approach this physical experience with a light heart and playful attitude and view the changing circumstances of your life without judgment they become creative projects. I often find myself thinking, *"What a mess! What's here for me to learn about myself and others that isn't immediately apparent?"*

Maintaining your problematic circumstance takes as much energy as changing them. Your resistance is 100% for you and your willingness to change is 100% for you. You choose to dedicate your energy to the problem or the solution. Although your lessons are 100% for you, they are never one-sided. Everyone in a shared experience has an opportunity to reach many different understandings. Just as you script your own dramas and play the lead role in these creative productions, you have a willing cast of thousands who facilitate your lessons. Within their dramas, they play the lead role wherein you are a member of their willing cast. Take a moment to think about the loving synchronicity that transforms energy into physical experiences where you all act as mirrors to help each other learn. Your spiritual ancestry rises from a vast creative consciousness source that ensures every thought-manifestation creates endless opportunities for everyone.

So, where does all this learning lead? It leads to experience and the understanding that you are a spark of God, the Prime Creative consciousness within all things. As a light-energy being you are here to learn how to manipulate energy in the framework of this reality. Think of yourself as a God Energy Scout who is sent out to research what energy can create in many different kinds of frequency environments. The understandings you reach through your individual experiences is imprinted on your consciousness and also filters through all human consciousness. These understandings also move through your higher frequency identities and eventually cycle back to the originating God-Source. This expands the thought-consciousness of the God-Source itself. Everything that then springs from this God-Source expresses itself in a more creative and expansive way because of the inclusion of *your* individual experiences. You have just forgotten what an integral and powerful aspect of universal consciousness you really are.

Reincarnation

Although humanity's spiritual identity has been lost within the purposeful editing of history and religious scriptures, traces and clues remain to this day. From Pagan Celtic lore comes a phrase: *'In Ochi No Sharin'*, meaning 'the wheel of life'. If you viewed the concept of reincarnation as a wheel, the axle would represent your higher frequency Soul identity I refer to as your Oversoul. Your Oversoul decided it could experience more aspects of its own consciousness through more than one physical life in one historic timeframe. To this end, it split its consciousness and sent fragments of itself into different historic timeframes in this reality. The spokes of the wheel, these separate identities, represent different physical aspects of the one Oversoul. Although they are part of, and connected to their common Soul-source, each of these spokes exists as an independent consciousness that begins its own evolutionary path.

For Example: Right now, you may be one spoke of the wheel in your life in the year 2009 as the person you are right now. Meanwhile, another aspect of your Oversoul may be living a life as a wine merchant in Venice in 1473, another as a poverty-stricken mother of 11 children in the 1920s in India, as a devote priestess in early Atlantis, as a barbaric warrior in central Europe in 923AD, and as a galactic explorer in the year 3073, and so on. Each of these alternate personalities is as unaware of you in their reality as you are of them until certain conditions are met. Yet, you are all connected by and are different facets of one consciousness; the Oversoul at the axle center of your wheel of physical lives. Your experiences are all separate and unique, yet shared with all aspects of your own greater Soul consciousness.

To your Oversoul these different physical aspects of its consciousness exist simultaneously, as if layered one upon the other on different frequencies within the same reality. I prefer to call them alternate existences rather than past-lives. If they did not exist at the same time outside of this 3-D reality, you could not access them, nor could one existence influence another. In the same way, your Oversoul is only one aspect of its own higher frequency consciousness identity, and so on. Your Oversoul may have kick-started your physical existence as you know it, but once this portion of its own consciousness splits away, you exist as an entirely separate consciousness. Yet, since your Oversoul connects you to your other aspects, any one of you can balance the karma created by another in these various existences. These alternate lives are all aspects of your Soul's greater identity. Much like an extended Soul family, the family's knowledge continually expands through the experiences gathered by all its individual family members.

When your own cycle of physical existences is complete and you move onto higher frequencies you may also decide to split your own consciousness into aspects you also project into this and other realities. Only this time you are the Oversoul at the axle of your own wheel of human consciousness experiences. That is why world population on this planet has increased so dramatically. As consciousness evolves on a global level, more Souls are sending fragments of themselves into this reality to experience the exciting shift in consciousness now taking place. The concept of human consciousness as one global family originates from this evolutionary process. I consider this a more credible version of evolution than Darwin's Theory of Evolution.

Integrating all these other aspects of your Soul consciousness is necessary before you can raise your own frequency. Entities from all corners of the galaxy are gathering to observe and participate. They are curiously interested since they too are part of your celestial ancestry. Caught in your own limiting beliefs it may be difficult to comprehend that you can be a separate consciousness yet part of a greater consciousness at the same time. The thought of merging with a higher aspect of yourself may feel like losing your own identity. It actually expands it so you can experience yourself through any form you desire. That is how powerful a Light Being you really are.

Frequency and belief are all that separates you from these other existences. You already interact with your Oversoul and counterparts in your dreams through your inner senses and during the Alpha state but don't realize it. You can call your Oversoul your Spirit Guide or Guardian Angel. Whatever you choose to call your spiritual counterparts, all you have to do is ask for assistance. If you think you have many different Spirit Guides, you most likely already interact with these other aspects of yourself. Often your Oversoul will project itself into the various guises you subconsciously create for yourself. You will see whomever you envision as a spiritual authority, be it the Virgin Mary, a Native Shaman or Wise old Wizard. These visual illusions arise from the same source, your own higher frequency identities. You have many, many higher frequency entities, all willing to help you.

Understanding reincarnation is simply to realize you are much more than you believe yourself to be. Taught to limit your perception of yourself, you can more easily be controlled and manipulated within this reality. Living just one life does not even make rational sense in light of the existing imbalances in human circumstances. You may well ask *'why was I born into this race?'* or *'Why is that person born into better circumstances than I was?'* There is no imbalance if you view this existence as one of many from a larger perspective. Then the diversity of life circumstances makes sense.

You go to school for many years because you cannot learn everything you need to know in just one year. The same thing applies to this physical experience. Few can learn how to manifest thought and manipulate energy in just one lifetime although Jesus and other trailblazers did. In this reality, most Souls have to learn how to function then unlearn the limitations of the beliefs acquired. The subjects and themes you choose to explore are as unique to you as mine are to me. This applies whether you are new Souls still getting the hang of this physical existence or an older Soul who has gained expertise in thought-manifestation and is ready to move on. Since you are all at different developmental stages, it is unreasonable to determine your progress by comparing yourself to others. Your Soul experience is unique and has nothing to do with what others are here to learn, even when you are working with each other on various projects.

Like a grand kind of thought-feeling play, you will not know what the effects of one of your thought projections will be until you manifest it and evaluate its sensory effects. Although your prime responsibility is to experience yourself as fully as you can in this lifetime, what you do or do not choose to learn in other existences is also part of your consciousness experience. Therefore, some of your lessons may be the flip-side of lessons another you is learning in another existence. The understandings reached are imprinted on your consciousness, your Oversoul's consciousness, and the other spokes on your wheel of physical lives. You will each interpret these inspirational understandings through the beliefs and existing knowledge in your historic timeframe on your particular frequency. In this way you all have the opportunity to expand your awareness through the understandings other aspects of your identity reach.

You determine and change your Karma with every choice you make. Karma is defined in the dictionary as, *"The* (energy) *force generated by a person's actions held in Hinduism and Buddhism to perpetuate transmigration and in its ethical consequences to determine his destiny in his next existence."* Transmigrate is defined as, *"1. of the soul – to pass at death from one body or being to another."* Karma is not a punishment for a poor choice in another life, rather a continuation of learning within different circumstances. Karma enables you to understand cause and effect from many perspectives. Since all these lives exist simultaneously, you can balance Karma within any of your other existences. However, once you set a spiritual lesson in motion you will complete the lesson no matter how many lives it takes, not because you have to, but because you want to.

Another core lesson is to understand *the ramifications of taking a life*, a lesson every consciousness is required to learn. Humanity has largely expressed a historic disregard for the value of life. Taking a life is the intentional annihilation of another consciousness. Taking lives for self-preservation or for some cultural, religious or national value has kept human consciousness on its low frequency and prevented it from operating through the higher frequency of love. In one life you may be righteously hacking off heads during the Crusades in the name of your faith, in another you may be a murder victim, and in this life a parent struggling to understand the senseless death of their child by a drunk driver. Each of you will reach your own understandings from your own perspective and add this knowledge to your individual and collective Soul consciousness.

Once you ride the frequency wave of love you realize life is priceless – ALL LIFE. Taking a life for any reason whatsoever diminishes all consciousness. That is why fighting for peace is the ultimate oxymoron. Experiencing death from a variety of perspectives is how consciousness comes to understand its connectivity to all other consciousness. I like to envision a day where somebody calls a war and nobody shows up on either side.

Your inner senses are awakening to prepare you for a higher frequency existence. You will need all your conscious and extended senses to not only survive this frequency transition, but to maintain your identity within an expanding reality. Some of your sensory experiences have already bridged the veils between realities and your other existences. You may even be aware of events on these frequencies but cannot interpret and integrate them into your present consciousness. If you cannot comprehend that you are many different individuals at the same time, how can you deal with their intrusion into your reality? How will you maintain your identity when you start to experience your own past, present and future at the same time? How will you maintain your conscious focus? You learn how through practice, through your own subjective sensory experiments.

If you think yourself insignificant and your life pointless, why escape into a rental movie when you can experience your own greater identity and its many aspects first-hand? You will automatically expand your identity once you explore your other existences. Experiencing yourself as entirely different individuals, particularly of the opposite gender, will not only expand your concept of yourself but also your attitude toward those who are significant in your life now. Your relationship with these Souls in other existences influences and helps you understand the dynamics of your relationship with them now.

The residual memory of highly charged emotional experiences in other existences is often the source of many of your instinctive fears and phobias. Under Hypnosis, many people have discovered these did not result from early childhood events, rather traumatic experiences in another existence. During the 1970s and 80s when hypnotherapy first became popular, traditional therapists were initially caught off guard when their subjects regressed to another life. Directed to go back to the event that triggered their problem, their subconscious took them right out of this life and into the existence where the trauma actually originated. These repeated occurrences led some therapists to explore the validity of reincarnation and thus was born the new practice of past-life regressions.

For Example: Stabbed to death in another existence may be the cause of your unexplained fear of knives now. Until the trauma is resolved, the energy of emotionally charged events or a sudden violent death stays in your consciousness. It may have happened to another 'you', but you can resolve many of your existing fears by exploring your other lives. An irrational dislike of a person can also be the trace memory of an unpleasant emotional experience in another existence. You all experience these trace memories and feelings to some degree when you meet someone new. It can be either a pleasant sensory feeling or one that triggers discomfort, revulsion, or even fear.

Many aspects of your whole identity are often working on similar lessons or a common theme. This synergy acts like a conductor that creates an energy resonance that allows access to each other's frequency. There may be little similarity in these lives, but on an energy level, you are linked through your aligned focus. When your focus changes so does your attunement with other existences. A guided or spontaneous regression will always connect you with an existence that resonates with your existing focus now in some way. Once this frequency connection is made with any one of these existences, it becomes easier to access other existences on your wheels of life.

During the mid-1980s a Past-life Regression Practitioner I had sponsored asked me to assist in the regression workshop I had signed up for myself. I took a grand leap of faith and impulsively said yes. I was both excited and scared silly because my twelve charges assumed I knew what I was doing even though I didn't have a clue. Once everyone was in a relaxed Alpha state and directed to a relevant life, I lost some of my initial fear but still was not sure just what I was supposed to do. Slightly panicked, I extended my Aura to see what would happen and discovered I could link with their experience whenever I moved into their aura's field. Completely engaged by this discovery, I could guide them through highly emotional periods when they needed help. I became so absorbed in their experiences I forgot all about my initial fear and lack of confidence.

Dale Snook, the workshop Instructor, knew I had the skills and created a circumstance where I had no choice but to draw on the intuitive abilities I had already developed in another existence. Of course, he omitted to share this tidbit with me until after the workshop, bless his crafty but loving heart. I think of that experience as a valuable lesson in *'necessity is the mother of extension'*. I used these skills because subconsciously, as an Empath I intuitively respond to emotional distress because I feel it myself. Once I connected with that aspect of myself, I just did what I had to do. Just think what inner resources and skills you may discover when you take your own leaps of faith!

The workshop participants each experienced at least one event significant to their current lives. They also recognized at least one individual they know now through the *'Windows of the Soul'*, their eyes. These are your Soul-buddies who play different supporting roles in your various existences. Only one fellow said he had not experienced anything. Since he was in my group, I knew differently but said nothing. Several months later, he showed up at one of my self-awareness classes and confessed he was so shocked at being in a woman's body in that existence he had blocked it out for weeks.

Many of your natural abilities and talents originated from other existences and your current bloodline ancestry, which includes many of these other existences. As a Soul grouping, you have an expansive identity and personality you can utilize at will. Your Soul is as partial to bloodlines as it is to gender, race, historic eras, and geographic locations. You may be good with your finances now because you refined this skill in other existences or if you are not good with finances, you can access an existence where you are and begin to draw on those skills.

Your current interests often reflect what you are actually doing in other existences. You could develop a sudden interest in Indonesian architecture because you are building a temple or other structure there in another life, in another timeframe. The interests you explore also influence these other existences in the same way. Your extensive gardening project in this life could trigger a desire to till a new plot of land in another existence. You each translate the information that bridges your existences through your individual perception and the existing knowledge and circumstances in your particular timeframe.

When I discovered an intuitive talent for figurative clay sculpting, I wanted to know the source of this talent. After doing several Alpha cycles, I discovered I was a tablet scribe, brick maker and pyramid artist in several old Egyptian eras, a stone carver in both the Aztec and Mayan cultures as well as a mural painter in Venice during the lifetime of Michelangelo. My favorite artist has always been Michelangelo, probably because I saw his work firsthand and strived to emulate it in that existence. In this lifetime, I translated this infinity with clay and carving into figurative clay sculpting.

Yet, despite my abilities, I have no desire to make art my life's work. Proficient in many mediums, I always disliked painting, particularly landscapes. I also always had an aversion to the smell of oil paint. I understood why after I experienced an existence in the 1700s as an artist obsessed with painting only dark brooding abstract landscapes nobody bought. I could have made a living painting portraits like other artists did. As a willful Soul then and even now, in that existence my wife and five children starved to death because of my obsession. Embittered and alone I continued to paint those dreary landscapes until I starved to death myself. Ironically, in this life I just sketched people when I was younger and almost exclusively sculpt people in clay now. An illusionary whiff of oil paint acts like a trigger from that existence. Whenever I get obsessive about writing, sculpting, or anything else for that matter, I catch an illusionary whiff of oil paint to remind me to maintain balance in my life.

Like tuning their consciousness dial to a particular radio station's band wave, a past-life Reader aligns their consciousness to your energy frequency. Their consciousness moves along the rim of your wheel of life and slides down a spoke into your axel Soul-center. From there they tap into the frequency of the existences that resonates the most with your current existence. They can tell you who you were in those historic timeframes and identify the lesson parallels between your various lives. However, their interpretation is somewhat biased by their own perception, as most psychic reading are. Although I have experienced several excellent past-life Readings, I prefer to induce and interpret them myself. What bias exists is my own and can only lead me to a greater understanding of my consciousness. Meditation and relaxation cycles enable you to enter the Alpha state where you can access these existences yourself.

When you have a hypnotic or self-induced regression, your subconscious metaphorically slides down your own current life-spoke to your Soul center, and onto the spoke of another existence. You merge with that consciousness yet experience everything subjectively, as if it is happening to you right now. You respond to the environment and circumstances through your own senses as well as through the perception and feelings you possess in that existence. It is an extraordinary sensation to be an observer as yourself and participant as someone else at the same time. While in the Alpha state, you will often experience flashes of other lives to trigger awareness of something buried in your subconscious that is ready to be resolved now. When your journey is self-induced, you may not know where you may end up but you will always connect with an existence relevant to your current experiences.

Another benefit of connecting with other existences is that you will recognize the present day counterparts of people who shared those existences. Look into their eyes and you will recognize who they are in your life now. This helps clarify issues now that originated within those relationships. You may recognize your only daughter from another life is your husband now and realize your smothering mothering attitude towards him is a residual behavior from that existence. It enables you to change your behavior within your relationship now. The visual and sensory impressions you get when you meet someone new or during your interactions with those you know well are also based on alternate lives and offer insight into the lesson you are learning through each other now. If the thought of experiencing another life through hypnosis or in Alpha is intimidating, then play this make-believe game in your head. There are no rules to this game so you can be as outrageously playful and creative as you want.

Exercise # 7

Think of a geographic location and era in history that interests you. Imagine whom you might be if you lived in that location and era. Make up a story about your life. Were you rich or poor, a man or a woman? What did you do for a living? When and how did you die? Do this once a day for several days and write down these make-believe lives in your notebook or journal. Add to them whenever anything triggers an interest in a particular historic era.

You will be amazed at how closely these make-believe lives mirror your other existences. They may be somewhat embellished by your own unfulfilled desires but they are based on trace memories of real existences. Pretending gives you permission to play like a child and Ego lets you bypass your filters because you all believe children have vivid imaginations. If you want to explore these alternate existences further, pick one from your list and instruct yourself to go to that existence during one of your Alpha cycles or in your dreams. Tell yourself before you sleep that you will awaken, refreshed and revitalized, remembering your dreams of this or another existence. Your own subjective experiences may well provide you surprising evidence. Do not feel disheartened if nothing happens right away. You are just not familiar yet with using these extended senses. If you want to try another approach, you could trigger memories of other existences with the following exercise.

Exercise # 8

Stand in front of a mirror in a small room like your bathroom. Light a candle and place it on the counter in front of you so your face is visible in the mirror by candlelight when you turn off the lights. Relax and take a few deep breaths. Then look into your own eyes in the mirror without blinking. Mentally ask to see who else is reflected through your eyes. It may feel uncomfortable at first because you are not used to looking directly into people's eyes, particularly your own eyes. Continue to hold your gaze until your features appear to blur or shift a little, meaning a change is taking place. If you accept whatever happens without judgment, you will soon see other features superimposed over your own however briefly. Do this several times until you feel more comfortable looking into your own eyes. Don't be surprised if you dream about someone that looks like one of the images you saw briefly. Pay attention to your feelings and what that dream triggers in you and write down any impressions you get in your Dream Journal.

Children often act out their memory of other existences while they play until they are discouraged to do so. As parents, you would glean valuable insight in the greater identities of your children if you watch and listen while they played their make-believe games. They would also willingly share their memories if you asked. With technology's infiltration into the toy industry, too few children are encouraged to play with their own imagination. By observing and mimicking you, they learn to become spectators of virtual entertainment rather than participators by engaging their own imagination to explore their identity.

If you want a playful look at simultaneous lives, may I suggest you read a novel called '*The Education of Oversoul Seven*'. Now available in a trilogy, Jane Roberts, a trance medium from the 1970s, channeled the information and wrote the series from the perspective of her own Oversoul. It is an absolute hoot! In the book, Oversoul Seven, quite the interesting personality, has to interact more intimately with four of his 'physical incarnations' while his competence is being lovingly tested by his own higher frequency Oversoul, Cypress. I consider it an excellent introduction to the concept of how multiple personalities interact with their Oversoul while both expand their own consciousness.

The second part of the trilogy, '*The Further Education of Oversoul Seven*', centers on the main character, a skeptical psychologist in the 70s, who discovers the parallels between himself and one of his ancestors while he battles with his own depression. Resistant to his own subjective experiences because of his psychological training, you discover the ways an Oversoul can influence your thoughts, choices, and actions on a subconscious level when you ask for help. The final segment, '*Oversoul Seven and the Museum of Time*', deals with a different kind of participation by Oversoul Seven. Temporarily inhabiting a real physical body, Oversoul Seven must help connect future personalities with personalities from their distant past in order to ensure their collective history remains intact. This trilogy is a fascinating & humorous read that will definitely alter your perception and view of how we manifest and manipulate energy both within and outside of this reality.

Gender Perception

Your Soul is comprised of both masculine and feminine energy, each of which expresses a different polarity aspect of consciousness. The dictionary defines polarity as, '*the particular state either positive or negative with reference to the two poles or to electrification.*' adding that to polarize is, '*to cause (as light waves) to vibrate in a definite pattern.*' Separately, the male and female polarities possess their own kind of electrical charge and frequency energy pattern. Unified, these opposing charges create a unique power source, defined in the dictionary as '*a different source or means of supplying energy*'.

Much like charging a battery, when you connect the masculine and feminine energy terminals, you create the elemental juice that fuels creation itself. The Soul uses this energy source to, amongst other things, split its own consciousness to experience itself through different genders on many frequencies at the same 'time'. With each birth, you choose either a male or a female body even though the opposite polarity still exists within your body. Children freely express both polarities until their life programming determine appropriate gender behavior within their society. By the time they become young adults, they express themselves entirely through one gender polarity.

Although both genders feel the same physical sensations, your gender determines how you *translate* your experiences. Masculine energy represents action and aspirations – the outward thrusting of mental and physical elements in order to view their immediate effects. Female energy represents receptiveness - pulling experiences inward to be felt subjectively before outward action is determined. Sometimes your Soul has an energy preference and sometimes you pick a gender because you want to learn your lessons through that particular polarity. Often your choice depends on gender availability within the bloodlines that provide the best circumstances for your overall intentions.

The dictionary definition of assimilates is in part, *'to take in as appropriate nourishment: absorb into the system'*. The same event experienced through male and female energy results in a completely different kind of comprehension. If you chose more existences as one gender than the other on a Soul level, your consciousness often develops a predisposition towards and expertise in the use of that kind of energy expression.

All that is about to change now with the insertion of the higher frequency of love, a female energy, into what has predominantly been a male-energy reality. A re-balancing of these two polarities is taking place within each of us. Consciousness on all frequencies is seeking unification of its two energy aspects to realign with the Cosmic Pulse of its origin. We need to unify the alternate polarity in our own consciousness as well as all the different gender personalities on our own wheel of life. This kind of realignment does not happen without disrupting and expanding our existing gender perceptions.

In the more ancient history of humanity, many cultures like Atlantis and Lemuria were androgynous. Androgynous is defined in part as: *'having the characteristics or nature of both male and female.'* The early Lemurians in particular developed and maintained a perfect balance between their male and female energy. They lived to be hundreds of years old because they could direct their biological functions through this powerful unified frequency. In effect, they became completely self-sustaining and interaction with others was essentially unnecessary. The problem was that after thousands of years this kind of individual self-containment created an extremely self-centered society. Self-sufficient on all levels, there was no need to interact with anyone. They eventually became so stratified they lost their ability to express love.

They also used this unified energy to transform themselves biologically when they wanted to reproduce, which they also did singularly. Due to cataclysmic earth changes, there were periods in our very ancient history when humanity needed to self-generate in this way. The second helix within human DNA still contains the codes that enable us to reproduce singularly if the survival of the species were at risk of complete annialation. The Immaculate Conception in the Bible is a metaphor for this androgynous ability. Our consciousness shift to a higher frequency will reactivate a more unified use of your male and female energies.

As a spiritual energy being, you have taken many different gender roles in your various earth lives. Although envisioning yourself in an opposite gender body may be strange, women can more easily imagine themselves as a man because of their intuitive nature. Men are much more resistive to acknowledging their feminine aspect. Consciously, their Ego equates the female principle as weak and inferior to their own masculine strength, a perception fueled by the male polarity that has long dominated this reality. Yet, men's greatest lasting monuments and structural wonders rise from the creative and intuitive elements of their own feminine aspect. Overall, men are terrified of the power of the feminine principle. As the frequency of female energy becomes more prevalent in this reality, the male principle will have difficulty relinquishing its autonomy. Men will have to learn how to embrace their female aspect. Women will have to help them do so if they want this male dominant society to change.

The purpose of exploring other existences is not to escape from your current reality or boast of past-life fame and achievements. The intention is to expand your self-identity by unifying these aspects within yourself. Your identity now is much like the reflection of one shard of glass from a broken mirror that represents your whole consciousness. Although the break lines represent the veils between these identities, as you reassemble these pieces you begin to see the multi-faceted reflection of who you really are. Although each shard represents a separate and unique consciousness, each is an integral aspect of the whole Soul identity as it relates to this physical plane of existence.

You will also begin to realize how illusionary your beliefs are once you re-experience how many different beliefs you have had in your many existences. Whatever you believe to be true now, you have believed the opposite and variations thereof to be true in other existences. As a born-again Christian now you may negate the religious beliefs of Eastern cultures or Spiritualists as vehemently as you negate the religious beliefs of Christians when you possessed other belief systems. Although you are primarily responsible for what you do with this life, integration of your other aspects automatically expands your perception of the expansiveness of your own consciousness. The experience is much like discovering a website on the Internet allowing unlimited free access to your own universal domain; a domain that contains all the frequencies you operate on as well as access to all other consciousness. Your inner consciousness is your personal cursor. The expansion of your awareness is determined by how many windows you are willing to open and explore.

"on learning . . .
"Never judge; pass critique, yes. Never judge, for in the judgment of any learning comes the end of that learning, even though the

judgment be positive, for then the mind is set into the pattern of saying, 'That part is good and that part is bad; therefore, I shall only study the part that is good, I will not study the part that is bad.' Because of that, areas of thought begin to become closed to yourself. Do not judge the learning, do not judge the teacher, and above all do not judge yourself. For learning is never ended; it is only continued to a new form. Do not ever say to yourself, 'I am finished', for then you will be finished."

... *The Evergreens*

The free-will law within the universe and curious nature of your Soul consciousness provides you with delightful opportunities for self-exploration. There are dramas upon dramas created by each of you on many different frequencies. All these dramas provide you with an opportunity to increase your awareness of yourself and validate just how meaningful your existence is.

Relationships

One of the great mysteries and conundrums of human interaction is relationships - particularly love relationships. Outside of procreation, what role do relationships play in your spiritual explorations? Many of you seek to find your Soul Mate or ideal partner. You visualize this person as your perfect counterpart, one possessing all the idealized qualities you desire. You think once you find this person you'll live happily ever after. What you actually seek is something else entirely.

Relationships help you learn about yourself through energy-interchange and mirroring. Everyone in your life, without exception, presents an opportunity to trigger the higher frequency of love within yourself. They reflect back to you different aspects of your existing beliefs and identity. Consequently, they reflect back to you *what you are or what you are not*. On an energy level, you have various kinds of relationships with these Souls.

Some are Soul-buddies, aspects of your own Soul or KINDRED SOULS. You like to incarnate together because

173

you have similar interests based on your aligned intentions and shared consciousness history. TWIN SOULS are a different kind of physical counterpart with whom you have an androgynous polarity resonance. And your SOUL MATE is a spiritual counterpart whose frequency resonates with yours perfectly. When you reunite with your Soul Mate it feels like you have returned to the wholeness of your higher frequency identity. Since this rare resonance is pre-destined through ancient agreements, you continue to yearn for a reunion with your Soul Mate even if you do not share the same existence. Part of discovering your own spiritual identity is to understand the purpose of these different types of celestial relationships.

Kindred Souls

Your higher frequency self, or Oversoul, continues to explore its own consciousness while you are living your life in this reality. Just as you would choose History or Science as your university major because it interests you, Souls align their energy with like-minded Souls who have the same interests. Only they use a wide range of sensory abilities to learn what they can create with their own consciousness on a cosmic scale.

There are those who build worlds or civilizations they may never inhabit and those who are genetic scientists that create species to inhabit these newly created landscapes. Others are explorers who travel through space to discover what they can experience and create in the vast framework of other universes. There are also those Souls, like you and me, who want to experience themselves as human holographs on this little jewel of a planet called Earth. We are all here because we want to experiment within the sensory framework of this reality. Therefore, we seek out other like-minded Souls to fill significant roles in our physical adventures.

When you first begin your cycle of earth lives, you are unfamiliar with how energy works in this reality. As a higher frequency entity, you think you will retain all your senses during this physical experience. You are unaware of how conscious programming quickly limits your perception and shuts down your timeless creative senses. The wonder of your own sensory responses captivates you. Since you forget what you are here to learn, when one life is over, you plan another to reach the understandings you intended for these physical experiments. The Souls who share these existences also send fragments of themselves into your new existences because they get sidetracked just like you do. Together you may replay the same lesson many times by taking on different roles and dramas within different historic periods. The resonance created through these recurring interactions form a certain kinship on a Soul level.

In the earlier cycles of earth lives, there were not as many people on this planet. The same Souls incarnated over again until they learned their lessons, raised their frequency, and left this framework of experience. A Kindred Soul may have played the role of a parent, spouse, sibling, offspring or some other significant person in your life during each of these incarnations. Even when Souls split their consciousness, their various aspects continued to incarnate with other aspects of the same Soul consciousness. Consequently, you shared your existences with a relatively small core group of Souls you knew pretty well. When you make a casting call prior to setting up your next physical experience, you first seek out your kindred Souls to see which of these want to participate in your next adventure.

Such a reunion happened to my mother at the extended care unit of the hospital not long before my father passed away. She had taken an instant liking to Vera, the wife of my father's dying roommate. Vera, who was years younger than my mother, would scold her as a mother would a beloved daughter. She would always reminded her to *'walk straight'* before they parted. This was odd since my mother's posture is excellent. My mother was unusually fond of Vera and told her she thought she was her personal Angel to which Vera firmly replied, *"I'm not an Angel. I'm your mother."* When I finally met Vera, my intuitive impressions supported her statement.

Vera was my mother's mother in another existence. Brisk but loving, she was particularly fond of my mother, her youngest of four daughters and a son. The two had a meaningful relationship in that existence. This was interesting in light of my mother's background in this life. She was also the youngest of four girls and a brother but in this life she was orphaned at 22 months of age and never knew her mother. Although my mother does not believe in reincarnation, when I asked what era she thought that life was, her immediate response was, *"The early 1800s. Posture was very important then."*

Elderly people near the end of their lives begin to slip in and out of the Alpha state. As their mental capability deteriorates, their consciousness loosens its grip on this reality and their perception of 3-D sequential time blurs. They often mix past and present events with memories of other existences when they tell their stories. Alzheimer's patients also recount events from other existences, and when their eyes go vacant, it indicates a portion of their consciousness has left their body, perhaps to plan another existence. Losing your grip on reality at any age can be disturbing and confusing if you do not realize how flexible your consciousness is. An excellent description of what may really be going on in the minds of the aged in our care facilities is portrayed by the personality Tweetie, in *'The Education of Oversoul Seven'*, by Jane Roberts. It certainly helped me be gentler and more understanding during my father's periods of mental confusion. Now that my mother is 90, I can see the same thing beginning to occur with her. As much a control freak as I had previously been, she is very upset when she gets muddled mentally.

Humanity's fear of death has fueled our global desire to prolong life at any cost. This fear traps many of our aged in bodies that are barely functioning. Resuscitative measures extend the natural shutdown of the biological body that occurs prior to death. To me, this reflects a complete disregard and disrespect for the dignity of those who are ready to leave this existence. Many of these lovely Souls are trapped in a cycle of resuscitation, deterioration, and further resuscitation by medical practitioners and the emotional attachments and fears of their family members. We need to allow those that wish to leave to do so respectfully. It is not for those that remain behind, or medical practitioners to decide when they can leave. Once we embrace our own eternal existence, we can help reassure these departing Souls of theirs.

Drug-induced near-death ramblings reveal what may already be occurring on other frequencies. My aunt, in the weeks prior to her death from cancer, was terrified of dying when she was conscious. Yet, after her drug-induced naps, she would tell me she had been dancing with her long deceased mother and yearned to be with her again like in these dreams. Consciously she believed she had to fight death to her last breathe. It took two agonizing weeks before she finally released her pain-racked body. Helping my aunt leave was important to me since she had been my mother in other existences, a mother I loved deeply. This painful experience only reaffirmed my conviction that we need to ease each other's departure with love and grace.

My personal encounters with kindred Souls always results in a deeper understanding of myself. Over a decade ago, I met one on a computer instant messaging venue. My profile contained information about my spiritual interests – Wicca, Self-awareness, Lemuria, Reincarnation, etc. New to instant messaging I was surprised by my attunement with the first person that contacted me. Andy, an older married gentleman who lived in the United States, asked if I could talk to the spirit of his departed son. My answer was no but his question kick-started an online relationship that continues to this day.

Little did I know then that he would help me resolve the recurring memory of an existence we had shared that triggered many disturbing emotions within me. I sensed I had blocked the memory of my traumatic demise in that life and that he knew why. As difficult as it was for both of us to relive my death, after pussy-footing around it for a time, Andy talked me through it. I am grateful for his courage in taking that painful sensory journey with me, particularly since he participated in my demise. The trust established through other shared existences enabled us both to release emotional blocks originating from that experience. As dear to my heart as a beloved brother, which he was in several existences, Andy remains *'mon gentil ami'*, and a beloved Kindred Soul.

I learned even more within 'present' life circumstances from another Kindred Soul, my older brother Max, who passed away in the fall of 2007. Extremely close as children, different belief systems and life directions shattered this closeness. A born again Christian, he was most disapproving of my 'Spiritual New Age' explorations and continued to pray and minister to me in hopes of redeeming my Soul.

Unknown to me and the family, over the past six years he had physically manifested what grew into a 60 lb. neurofibromatosis tumor in his belly and a 15 lb. tumor on his left scrotum. Reconciled several years ago by my disclosure of childhood and teen incest he knew nothing about, he was shocked into looking at his own self-image issues and the physical, mental, and emotional abuses we had shared as children. We began a most difficult but interesting journey of self-healing together. After many years of disapproving silence between us, he contacted me after my Eclipse of the Soul and ensuing suicide attempt. He shared his fear that he had a cancerous tumor that was growing slowly but steadily, one he could no longer hide with heavy sweaters and his welding overalls. He was terrified to go to the doctor and have his suspicions confirmed, choosing instead to pray for a miraculous healing through his unwavering faith in Jesus. We spoke on the phone almost daily as I went through my trauma counseling and shared the difficult journey of healing our toxic shame, guilt, and fear. That is when a real miracle began to happen right under our unsuspecting noses.

Despite the differences in our spiritual beliefs, we gained understanding of our own survival mechanisms, bridged our judgments and differences, and reclaimed the close bond we had as children. His tumor represented the physical manifestation of childhood abuse he had suppressed and never addressed. My suicide attempt had been a more outward thrusting cry for help since I was unaware I had completely detached from the feeling aspects of my abuse. We had actually reversed the gender energy format whereby he internalized, and I externalized. We humorously called his enormous belly our 'family hairball' - manifestation of the convoluted family trauma and abuses that had to be healed.

The miracle healing from Jesus he continued to hope and pray for never materialized and the last few months of his life were horrifically painful, despite the morphine. Yet, the awareness and understandings we reached in working through our issues and practicing 'The Power of Now' were treasured gifts. As difficult as it was for me to allow him his experience and watch his slow death, I was grateful to spend nearly every weekend in Pemberton with him during his last six months of life. Although his faith in God never wavered, I had the honor of sharing the expansion of his limiting beliefs in religious doctrine. His most profound self-awareness was when he said that, 'he had become so heavenly minded, he was no earthly good.' He had completely ignored his own physical body.

Near the end, everything that needed to be shared from our heart was said. It was enough to sit in silence in his dimly lit trailer during those final weekends together so when his eyes opened he wasn't alone. I learned more about him and myself during that year than I could ever have envisioned, despite how heart-wrenchingly painful many aspects of this experience were for me. Despite our different personalities and perception, we had both reached a loving acceptance and understanding between us that would have never occurred without this experience.

I continued to discover new things about him after his 'Celebration of Life' gathering in the valley. A reclusive, shy, and humble man, I was amazed at how well loved he had been both by the turnout and the personal stories people shared with me. Even now, my perception of him changes as I discover new things about myself. Despite his belief that he would be in Heaven with God, where he will be for a while, he lets me know in a very real way that he is around me in spirit. Thank you Max, my kindred *'gentil ami'*.

Someone you dislike immensely or have interactive difficulties with can also be a Kindred Soul. In these roles, they act as valuable teachers who mirror the beliefs and aspects of self-identity you need to address. If someone presses your buttons, you need to explore why as my brother Max and I did when we began our healing journey. Sometimes your feelings about a person are discordant with the circumstances of your current relationship. Trace-memories of a different kind of relationship with this kindred spirit can bleed into your current interactions and influence your instinctive attitude towards each other. Since kindred Souls play a diversity of roles in your life, your children, boss, or friends now could be your partners or adversaries in other existences. You may have been the domineering parent of one of your current parents and still interact with them from that perspective. The variations are endless but the more you know, the more you can learn about yourself within your existing relationships.

The insertion of the higher frequency of love into our reality is dismantling the veils between the many aspects of your higher frequency identity for a specific reason. Your concept of love and relationship needs to change as much as your perception of your identity does. It is necessary to unify these different aspects of your identity in preparation for a more expansive consciousness experience. As you recognize more and more of your Kindred Souls, you realize what a creative and co-operative energy game this physical experience is.

Twin Souls

To reach unification within yourself, you also need to balance the male and female energy polarities of your own consciousness through the unification with your polarity counterpart, or TWIN SOUL. The spiritual affinity between Kindred Souls results from shared interests and experiences within a consciousness collective. The resonance with your Twin Soul is a result of your own polarity-split soul-consciousness. You are each half of the opposite but balancing energy polarity aspect of the same consciousness spark that has begun its own physical expression.

Originally androgynous, this consciousness consists of a positive masculine charge and a balancing feminine negative charge. Imagine for a moment that your Oversoul has decided on such a split. Due to this reality's gender framework, these two polarity halves now exist as individual and separate gender aspects of the same consciousness, making them Twin Souls. Although each possesses both polarity charges within themselves, the predominant polarity in each determines their obvious gender. Consequently, consciousness can experience the two polarity aspects of this one spark of itself through two separate biological bodies and focus in the same or different earth timeframes.

This method of gathering experience and knowledge worked just fine for eons. With the insertion of the higher love frequency into this reality, consciousness began to remember a more ancient and unified version of its identity. It yearned to become complete again and reconnect with its own Divine Source. To do so, it needed to unify all its parts, particularly its twin polarities. It could not move onto a higher frequency until it has done so. Triggered by this desire, you and your Twin Soul arrange to incarnate into the same existences to balance your polarities. However, your beliefs about relationships usually prevented this from occurring since you do not view your relationships from this perspective. Consciously, you translate this yearning into a physical desire for emotional love and sexual pleasure not spiritual unity. Although there is nothing wrong with the former, you need spiritual awareness to recognize your twin soul and achieve the latter.

When you meet your Twin Soul you feel like you have know each other forever. That is because you are immediately attracted to this reflection of yourself. Although your personalities may be different, you are attracted to the existing aspects of your own psyche as well as the *missing* aspects of your psyche this individual possesses. Fascinated by what you continually discover about yourself through each other, your Twin Soul is the person with whom you can share your most intimate fears and aspirations with a trusting candor you would not even share with Kindred Souls. You unconsciously interact through the resonance of your unified identity when you are together. You feel complete when you are together and continue to experience this heightened sense of well-being even when you are apart.

The conscious yearning for your Soul Mate actually represents your desire for spiritual unity with your Twin Soul. Since your original polarity split, you have both taken on many different gender identities. You may not recognize your Twin Soul because they can be the same gender, a child, old person, a relative or in a committed relationship with someone else. They may also be your sibling, boss, co-worker or someone you have yet to meet. Unity with your Twin Soul reunites the two halves of your whole consciousness. This relationship is not designed for a traditional sexual liaison or life-partnership if they are of the right age and gender. Although many do, in effect, they marry themselves. These couples are like two peas in a pod, almost indistinguishable as individuals. Since you love that person deeply, the feeling of unity triggered by this merging is easily confused with sexual love.

Once you have unified these opposing polarities with your Twin Soul your attitude towards relationship subtly changes. You no longer seek a partner to feel complete since you have already balanced these polarities within yourself. You now seek a different kind of love partnership, one you may not yet be able to define. Potential partners become the means through which you can now create a powerful new energy source to help each other fulfill your individual but aligned spiritual intentions.

Soul Mates

Many of you yearn for a Soul Mate and think when you find them life will be perfect. But this pre-destined arrangement is not based on our earthly ideals of love. In fact, it is a relatively rare occurrence. Your Soul Mate is your whole consciousness resonance counterpart whose energy oscillates on the identical frequency as your own. This kind of relationship was pre-arranged by Souls when the earliest cycle of earth lives first began to realize specific pre-destined high frequency intentions. Soul Mates are meant to be together for a specific purpose and carry this desire to reunite into all their existences even if they do not share the same existence. However, such a union is only possible when both have integrated all the other aspects of their own consciousness, their twin polarities, and raised their frequency to match each other's perfectly in the same existence. This happens rarely, even if they do meet in the same lifetime.

Your desire to meet your Soul Mate rises from the memory of self-expression through an ancient kind of masculine and feminine energy interchange. On this high frequency you accept others just as they are, without exception, expectation or judgment. You share and blend your energies freely with no loss of personal empowerment or self-identity. You also have no desire to control or press your beliefs and views on your partner or anyone else. You are each complete within yourself so your partnerships intentions are fueled by what your combined energies can create together, while still remaining intact within yourself. Energized by high frequency love, this is the most powerful energy in the universe; the excelsior of creation itself.

This unique resonance between Soul Mates is a spiritual alignment designed to change the way male and female energy interact with each other when human consciousness needs to expand. Since this reality was predominately experienced within a male energy grid, outside of giving birth to new life, female energy has only held some dominance in sexuality, nurturing, and healing. The periods in earth's history where female energy was predominant were short and happened so long ago they have almost disappeared from memory. Traces of ancient Goddesses remain only in token icons within masculine religious organizations or within mystic tales of the past.

Neither male nor female energy is better or more powerful than the other. Each is its own kind of power source that activates higher frequency aspects of consciousness to influence the nature of self-expression. Inner receptiveness and creativity is as limited without outward expression as outward expression is without intuitive receptiveness. Without a balance of the two, human consciousness was missing an important aspect of its whole identity and could not realize its full potential, until now.

The Australian Aborigines are currently the only existing culture whose society is, and has always been, based on complete male and female equality. They maintained their dream memories of this balanced existence largely because of their long time isolation. Although the influence of western society has diffused much of this unified expression, many are now returning to the old ways. I once had the honor of meeting an Aboriginal Elder whose wife was also an Elder. He said I reminded him of her and told me he respected the power of the feminine principle as being more powerful than masculine energy in one elemental way. He referred to women as *'the givers of life'*, an extension of the female principle of Mother Earth who sustains all life while masculine energy directs the actions of this life. He said male energy did not understand the feminine principle yet envied it. He aligned the feminine principle to the moon cycles that directly influence our physical environment and the ebb and flow of human emotion. That is largly why men fear women and try to suppress them, yet at the same time yearn to possess them. They seek to reclaim that important missing aspect of their own consciousness.

By uniting female receptiveness with outward thrusting male energy, the combined positive and negative charges create a unique energy source that can fuel the manipulation of our reality in unimaginable ways. Such balance existed in the earlier civilizations of Mu and later in early Atlantis and Lemuria where many of these soul-mate reunions were first arranged in reparation for the 'future' eventuality of a gender split They understood the power of unification and able to 'see' into their own high probability futures, prepared for this eventuality. Our consciousness shift presents an opportunity for us to ride the wave of this higher frequency again. Many of these Soul Mates are here now to raise their frequency in preparation for this reunion.

Both the Atlantian and Lemurian culture became highly stratified in their polarities in the latter period of their civilizations. The Lemurians refined the female principle to the point where they could no longer interact with anyone else. The Atlantians amplified the male principle by producing technology and weapons that eventually annihilated both their civilizations. Their energy manipulation experiments set into motion environmental changes that redistributed all the landmasses on this planet and changed the axis rotation of the planet itself. Many of these ancients have reincarnated into this time frequency to re-write their own past. We are those ancients who seek unification of our split energies. We have returned to use this energy to create a new civilization that can co-exist with the natural environment while maintaining our own unified consciousness.

Your beliefs about reality have intentionally diverted you from attuning yourself to your own higher frequency authority. By regaining it, your actions would rise from a self-regulated spiritual integrity. You would not resonate with the frequencies that manipulate you now through laws that empower a select few. The controlling faction of our world would begin to lose its power because you will no longer be energizing its inhumane agenda. Many of you are already beginning to recognize and resist this inhumane agenda. Additionally, a more expansive and flexible androgynous spiritual identity would replace your existing gender and sexual identity. As long as the true nature of your sexual energy remains suppressed, you are unable to use this powerful energy to expand your consciousness. The frequency of love is the key to expanding your ability to do so.

Sexual Energy

It is vital to understand what happens when you exchange bodily fluids during sexual intimacy. Even more important than your body's blood that carries the imprint of your physical genetic ancestry, your sexual secretions are the excelsior of life itself. Your sexual fluids transfer the very essence of who you are as a spiritual being to your partner's consciousness. So with whom are you mixing and exchanging your essence? During the inadvertent ingestion of bodily fluids and orgasm, you absorb more than your sexual partner's energy. You absorb the residual energy of everyone with whom they have been sexually intimate. You in turn, transfer the energy of all your sexual partners to their consciousness. You and your partner/s both absorb and transfer the energy of all your past sexual partners to your current and future partner/s. You can, however, do a 'sexual smudging' to cleanse these energies from your energy field.

Exercise # 9 – Sexual Smudging

Focus all your attention on a candle flame in a quiet darkened room. Breathe deeply to relax and clear your mind. Then bring each of your sexual partners to mind visually, one after the other. Thank them for the experience and ask that they leave your energy field. Then visually release their energy back into the universe - WITH LOVE. Start with your most recent sexual partners and move backwards through time. If you cannot remember their names or forget some of the sexual encounters you have had, do a collective smudging that spans your sexually active years one decade at a time. Ask them to leave your energy field and release them back into the universe - with love. It is that simple, yet that important.

It is difficult to move on to new relationships with a clean slate when your energy field holds the energy of past sexual partners. If there is a lot of low frequency energy attached to them, you still carry it in your energy field. It is essential to ask a potential partner to do a sexual smudging before you are intimate. Also, do a smudging whenever a sexual encounter is over. If you both smudge at the start of a new relationship, you will only be sharing your own essence with each other.

This is not to say you should not have sexual relations and wonderful orgasms. Once you realize your orgasms are more than sexual feel-good sensations you will be more discriminating with whom you share bodily fluids. When you have an orgasm with someone you are fond of or love, this blissful state permeates your whole being. It stimulates your inner senses and triggers your 'feel good' dopamine. Your heart Chakra opens and allows your higher spiritual energy to flow down to your sexual base Chakra. This energy then moves back up through your whole being as a unified spiritual and physically sensual frequency. When such an exchange takes place without love or fondness, your heart Chakra remains closed. Only low frequency energies are stimulated and exchanged during your orgasm. On these low frequencies, you can acquire a whole bunch of negative stuff by absorbing the fears and other low frequency emotions of your partner and their past partners. That is often why you can both love and hate a person. You love the person but dislike all that negative energy 'stuff' attached to them.

Once you understand the energy significance of your orgasms, you may decide to enjoy physical intimacy without sharing an orgasm or bodily fluids with a partner if they refuse to smudge or you are uncertain what kind of energy they carry. Those who practice the satanic arts understand the significance of sexual energy and use it for their own empowerment. They purposely seek the pure and creative energy of children, virgins, and young animals for their important rituals and sacrifices. Untainted by the energy residuals of sexual exchanges, they use this vital and pure energy to empower their own agenda.

As awareness of your identity begins to expand, you will develop a clearer understanding of your own spiritual intentions. Your inner senses will guide you towards nourishing relationships and you will be more discerning with whom you share intimacy. You will actually become more loving toward everyone yet choose not to love some physically.

The current practice of using sex to market both consumer and identity enhancing products keeps your sexual energy resonating at its lowest frequency. This prevents you from using your sexual energy and orgasms as a powerful spiritual tool to expand your consciousness. Love whom you choose, but trust your inner senses to guide these choices. These senses will ensure the partners you choose possess an essence that will nourish not diminish you. The more nourished you are, the more loving you will be towards everyone, which draws an abundance of love into your life.

Like learning how to maneuver in this reality physically since birth, you gain experience in traversing the sensory landscape of your own consciousness through trial and error by first-hand experimentation.

Chapter 8.

The Process of Self Awareness

"Where the mind goes, the energy flows."

WHEN you were a baby you could not just get up off the floor one day, walk into the kitchen, and ask your mother for a glass of milk and cookies. Learning to walk and talk was a process of trial and error. No matter how hard you concentrated on a picture of yourself walking like others did, your body did not automatically respond to this desire. You had to learn how to instruct your body to do what your mind imagined yourself doing. Physically, your body still had to master gravity and balance. Your mind also had to learn how to translate your mental images into physical action, then how to interpret them through your senses. You began by pulling yourself up and falling down. Fueled by your successes and undeterred by your failures, you practiced until you mastered standing. You then practiced moving your legs while upright until you mastered that skill. Your view of your world expanded but you could still only interact with what was within your physical reach.

Then one day you saw something you really wanted, perhaps a set of colorful plastic keys lying on a chair across the room. Your desire to grasp those keys created a new determination in your mind, one of walking to the chair by yourself. In a leap of faith, you let go of whatever support you clung to and took your first solo steps. Propelled by your desire, you took a few shaky steps, fell, pulled yourself upright, fell again, but persisted until you reached your prize. Empowered by the knowledge you could independently fulfill your own desires, the perception of your world changed forever. You learn how to direct your mental processes, consciousness, and energy in the same way.

Self-awareness is a process of trial and error through experimentation. When you embark on the human experience as a new energy spark on the wheel of physical existence or a more experienced soul, you are not born knowing how to maneuver in this reality, let alone how to manipulate it. With each new lifetime, you had to learn how to synchronize your body and mind until physical mobility became an automatic byproduct of mental direction. You moved from dependency to inter-dependency, and finally to relative independence through the same process of trial and error. This occurred quickly if you were validated, encouraged, and nourished, and more slowly if you were not.

Learning spiritual mobility using your inner senses is also a process; a process fueled by trust in your own subjective experiences rather than validation from your outer reality. Although the memory of other existences and a multitude of spiritual resources reside within you, you are the one that has to activate them and explore them. If you do not, instead of making things happen by directing life circumstances, you will just wonder what the hell happened!

The Mistakes of Life

Children learn what they see. A child can be viewed as a sensory survival mechanism in a continual process of learning. A child experiences its environment through its five senses, primarily its visual and feeling senses. Specifically designed to learn during those informative years, a child is curious and interested in all things within their reality. The mind correlates everything associated with the self and learns through the gratification of needs by discovering what causes and enhances its survival and what does not. If what it learns enhances survival, the child forms a trust of self and its environment. If non-learning enhances survival, it does not learn and the child's natural pattern of self-exploration is changed. It begins to quell its genuine qualities and idiosyncrasies, the traits that make each individual unique. A child's stages of growth are like the layers of an onion. Each developmental stage builds on and adds a new layer to what existed previously. Therefore, within the central core of this onion is still the knowledge of what you first learned as a child.

The mistakes you made as a child and continue to make as an adult are a result of *a perception formed by conclusions based on partial information.* Your sensory curiosity and physical need to survive prompted your learning from birth. The whole world revolved around you and your needs, needs that were either met or not met. You were unaware of the consequences of your thought images until faced with the external result and/or reaction to your own actions. The reaction may have been your own responses, the reaction of others, or a combination of both. For example: If you touched something hot as a toddler, your own pain and the fearful reaction of a parent could establish a belief that not only were your actions faulty but that you were faulty. These mistaken conclusions result from a child's limited cognitive ability to reason. In spite of these kinds of mistakes, you continued to experiment.

If your explorations were supported and your curiosity encouraged, you learned to trust both your sensory responses and environment. When you received disapproval for behavior considered inappropriate or inconvenient to others, or if you suffered abuse, you learned to get approval within the limits of your sanctioned parameters. Since you learned 80% of what you now know by the time you were 8-10 years old, your interpretive methods now are still induced by these childhood coping mechanisms.

Information - regardless of source - creates, maintains, and alters your perception of yourself. Mis-takes indicate you need to expand your perception by expanding the beliefs and ideals that diminish your authentic identity. You need to trust your feeling-responses when you interpret your experiences to stop setting into motion the cycle of 'mistakes requiring absolution' that leads to harming of the self. As a child, others decided which of your actions were faulty. As an adult, you still use their criteria to decide if an error occurred and if you need absolution for this perceived error. You make mistakes because you lack information and experience, not because you are faulty. Having said that, there are no mistaken actions. All your experiences and choices present an opportunity to learn more about who you are. *There is nothing wrong with you and there never has been!*

Sensory information is the key to expanding your awareness of yourself within every circumstance. By trusting your inner senses, you gain experience at interpreting their meaning. Your life is not about what actually happens to you but your interpretation of these events. The judgment that an error is made is a perception, either someone else's, or your own, which is generally based on someone else's. Mastery of your mind is acquired by exploring your identity with the same interest and curious exuberance that propelled you here in the first place. Then every conscious mess you create through your mistakes becomes a grand awareness.

When I make a mistake, I say to myself, *"Another grand mess I created. Now let's figure out why?"* I love my aware-messes because they remind me to pay attention to what I am doing. Conscious living means being fully engaged in the moment – in the power of NOW. You allow yourself to jump into a situation when your heart and senses say, *'go for it'* even if your mind and reason screams *'No'*. The moment you hit the ground you begin to learn. Since your experiences enable you to explore your own consciousness, ungluing a dogma, bypassing an automatic reaction or trusting your subjective responses is the icing on the cake. You are the cake

- a cake made from all kinds of wonderful sensory ingredients. Your subconscious turns these ingredients into entrées that reveal different aspects of your own psyche. It is always about *you* not the event, about revealing more about yourself to yourself.

"on obstacles . . .
"The only obstacles are the ones that you create for yourself. Cease to create them, cease to give them energies, cease to see them as major focal points, then will you find the greatest ease that you have ever experienced in your life. Then you will begin to flow more with the abilities, capabilities and understandings of yourself, then will you understand more to yourself and to the clarity of yourself and the uncovering of the abilities that you have. For it is virtually that you have your hand upon the handle of a small door that open into a vast storehouse. The door is yours, the hand is yours, the storeroom is yours, yet the door say 'Push' and you are pulling. It is only a matter of reversing your direction, then will you find the door opens."
. . . The Evergreens

I've done a lot of 'pulling' on doors in my own personal journey of self-awareness. Living in the moment requires acute awareness of your subjective feelings within each experience. It also requires a willingness to examine these feelings, even those you consider negative or bad. Not doing so is what led to my eventual 'eclipse of the soul', despite my many spiritual resources. I had deftly sidestepped that part because, frankly, it was horrific and I did not want to deal with the feeling aspect of my traumatic childhood experiences.

It also requires trust that this and every moment you experience fits into the tapestry of your greater identity and intentions. Surrendering to sensory exploration with the enthusiasm of a child may seem inappropriate as an adult. Yet, it is by bypassing reason and engaging your inner child's curiosity that you will reclaim your genuine identity. When your senses prompt a change of direction or the waves of change wash away the sandcastles you have built, you can joyfully build another.

Your energy is always 100% for you so *where the mind goes, the energy flows.* When you gauge your progress through self-judgment, each perceived failure dims the light of your authentic identity instead of illuminating its expansion. Find something beneficial in every experience. If your energy is not invested in judging Self or your actions it can go to nourishing your mind, body and Soul. Nothing pushes open the door to your spiritual storehouse like love. So love yourself within all your experiences. Awareness cannot be forced or controlled through conscious will. It is a byproduct of self-love and self-exploration.

What methodologies you use are as unique as your genuine personality and Soul essence. Your subjective explorations will reveal all kinds of extra-sensory skills. Like opening Pandora's Box, at first you will not know what is going to pop out of the box. You may not be able to see or speak to ghosts like some people can. Unless you intend to help lost Souls cross over you do not need this skill. You may not be able to heal people. Some people can only get self-validation, love or attention through the manifestation of pain and illness. When you maintain your own well-being, you always transmit loving energy to those in need. If you cannot bend spoons it is also no biggie either. Many of these extra-sensory abilities just provide subjective proof that you *can* influence and manipulate reality.

I chuckle as I remember when my children went to a self-development workshop with me in the 1980s. One of the things we learned was how to bend spoons with our minds. It became evident my eight year-old son Brian was naturally gifted in this area. For weeks afterwards, my cutlery drawer contained a bizarre assortment of twisted forks and spoons. Fortunately, he got bored with the game before we ran out of useable utensils. My fourteen year-old daughter Jackie barely managed to bend one spoon yet was nonchalant about being able to link empathetically with the participants in the workshop. She did not think this intuitive ability was a big deal since it was a natural extension of her empathy to other people's feelings and kept whining about not being able to bend spoons like her little brother.

You will all discover your own kind of extrasensory abilities. They are part of your unique identity and have nothing to do with anybody else's abilities. Acquired in other existences many of these abilities are an aspect of your consciousness heritage. Although you may use these tools to aid others, they exist to enhance your own experiences, which is why we ALL have these abilities.

If you want to measure your awareness and expertise, compare what you now know and can do to what you knew or could do a week ago, a month ago, or a year ago. When you act as your own point of reference, your mind is not influenced by social ideals. It is free to follow your own personal curiosities. If a methodology someone suggests or one you have read in a book inspires or interests you, try it and see if it works for you. Application is the only true test of effectiveness. Give yourself permission to explore and experiment without judging the process or outcome.

Assessing Your Personal Resources

Before you can script new possibilities and intentions for yourself, you need to identify your existing resources. Find yourself a lovely workbook that represents your Journal of Self-Discovery and name it whatever you wish. This will be your personal diary of self-assessment and self-exploration. Since this exercise is for your eyes only, be completely honest in order to discover what your resources truly are. If you lie, or omit truths, you are only lying to yourself and prolonging the process expanding your awareness. I suggest you dedicate a week to this identity evaluation but you can take as long as you wish. You will be surprised at how much you will discover about yourself.

Exercise 10-1.   PERSONALITY

1. Title a page in your workbook <u>MY PERSONALITY</u>. Divide the page in three columns. In the first column write the heading, '<u>What I Like About Me</u>'. Then list everything you like about your personality – qualities

like kindness, droll sense of humor, interested in what others have to say, etc. Include everything you like about your personality no matter how insignificant. This is not the time to be modest or shy. Write down everything you consider wonderful about yourself. If you fill a page, continue on the next page, and the next. Add to this list throughout the week.

2. In the second column, write the heading, 'What I Don't Like About Me', and list all the things about your personality you consider negative, faults or weaknesses, qualities like impatience, easily bored, judgmental, easily angered, defensive, etc. Pay attention to your behavior during the week and add any other weaknesses you notice about yourself. Leave the third column blank for now and go onto the next phase of the exercise.

Exercise 10-2.   SKILLS

1. At the top of a new page, write the heading MY SKILLS. Draw a line down the center of the page and title the left column 'Can Do'. Divide each column into three equal horizontal parts. Write the headings, PHYSICAL, MENTAL, and EMOTIONAL at the top of each of the three blocks of space in each column. Keep in mind that these are skills not goals. List everything you can do relating to physical action under the three headings in the left column. Your physical skills will include things like riding a bike, driving, mowing a lawn, ironing, cooking, etc. Be as spontaneous as you can and include all the small things you may think are self-evident like reading or writing. Your mental skills may include things like a good memory, learns new things quickly, organized, efficient, etc. Your emotional skills may include things like being a good listener, a supportive friend, tactful, etc. If you need a second or third page, continue until you run out

of things you can do. Put a star beside any items you add to this list during the week.

2. Title the second column 'Can't Do' and list all the things you would like to be able to do but feel you can't do for whatever reason. Your emotional 'can't do' may include things like trusting others, not taking everything personally etc. Your mental 'can't 'do' may include items like a good memory or organizational skills. The majority of these skills may relate to physical activities like dancing, singing, designing a website, etc. since you don't often assess what mental or emotional abilities you wish to develop. Put a star beside any items you add during the week.

Exercise 10-3.   ACHIEVEMENTS

1. Begin a new page and title this section 'MY ACHIEVEMENTS'. Write the heading 'Past Achievements', and list everything you have already done or achieved until now. List both the big and small achievement, like writing poetry, learning to cook, filing your nails just the way you like them, etc. Take as many pages as you need. Write down everything you have actually done and watch the list grow as you remember more throughout the week.

2. On a new page write the heading 'Present Achievements' and list all the things you are currently doing in your life. Include what you consider both big and little things. You can add to these lists throughout the week as you remember other things.

3. On a new page, write the heading 'Future Achievements'. Divide the page in half horizontally. In the top half write the heading 'Short-term – 6 month Goals', and list all your short-term goals or what you wish to achieve within

the next 6 months based on what you have already set in motion. Add to this list during the week.

4. In the bottom half of the page write the heading 'Long Term - three-year Goals', and list all the goals you want to achieve within the next three years. Add to this list during the week as well.

Exercise 10-4.   ESP – Extended Sensory Perceptive Abilities

1. Title a new page in your workbook, 'MY EXTENDED SENSES'. This section assess your ESP or extended sensory abilities. Draw three vertical columns on your page and divide the whole page into four horizontal sections. Each column should have four squares in it.

2. Write the heading 'What I Have Now' at the top of the first column. Then write the headings AUDITORY (hear), VISUAL (see), SENSORY (feel), and INTUITIVE (know) on the first line of each square in this column.

3. Under each heading list the kind of sensory experiences you have had that are outside your concept of normal reality. Write them down without judging their validity. For example, under Auditory, you may have heard a voice speak your name in your head, or under Visual, received picture images during your daily activities or meditations you cannot explain rationally. Under the heading Sensory, you may have received an insight about someone during an interaction or knew something would happen that has not occurred yet. Under Intuition you may just know something that later proves to be accurate. Add to this list during the week.

4. At the top of the second column write the heading, 'What I Want to Have' and under each of the four headings list what kind of extended senses you think you would like to have no matter how silly they seem.

5. At the top of the third column write the heading, 'Why' and list what you would like to do with each of the skills you would like to have under each of the four headings.

We tend to overlook the obvious aspects of our personality so pay attention to your thoughts, actions, and feelings during the week. Add anything that comes to mind to your lists but put a star beside these add-ons.

EVALUATING YOUR RESOURCES

Exercise # 10-1.

A. Whatever you have listed under PERSONALITY represents your general attitude and perception of how you see yourself. The items listed in the 'What I Like About Me' column are your *primary tools*. You can stop focusing on these characteristics since you already possess and express them.

B. The items listed in the 'What I Don't Like About Me' column represent your *secondary tools*. They are strengths you also possess but have not yet energized or integrated into your primary tools.

C. Go and Title the blank third column 'Flip Side' and turn around everything you dislike about yourself from the second column. For example: impatience is the flip side of patience. Everything you listed in your Dislikes has dedicated energy attached to it. To release this energy, focus on the flip side of these characteristics and view them as strengths you are still developing.

D. Objectively compare the first two columns to see if you are putting more energy into what you like or dislike about yourself. This is not good or bad. It is an assessment of your identity and focus right now, the foundation upon which you will build the changes you desire.

E. Then ask yourself which of these likes and dislikes reflect other people's perception of you. Cross these items off your list and highlight what remains. This is what you actually dislike about yourself. What others think of you is none of your business – what YOU think of yourself IS.

Exercise #10-2.

A. Look at your Skills list. Everything on your list represents your *primary skills*. There was a time you could do none of these things. Reflect a moment on just how much you have learned since birth.

B. The second column represents things you only think you cannot do because there is currently a perceived *benefit* to not being able to do them. The benefit may be subconscious or something you consciously observed or learned.

C. Evaluate each skill to identity what this benefit might be.

D. The items you added to your list during the week are your *secondary skills*. Although not part of your primary resource of skills you use consistently, these skills come in handy occasionally.

Exercise # 10-3

A. Review your Achievement page. Your achievements reveal if you need to expand your perception of the value of achieving small goals or big goals. If you have primarily listed big accomplishments, your perception leans towards gauging value by *big effects*. Perhaps you can begin to look at the value in all things – no matter how small or insignificant they may be.

B. If you primarily listed small accomplishments, you see all things being valuable or you are playing it safe by limiting the possibility of failure at attempting to achieve bigger things. Expand your concept of what is possible for yourself. Begin to see the value in every experience and accomplishment, both large and small.

Exercise 10-4.

A. Everything listed on your ESP page reflects senses you already possess as extensions of your conscious five senses.

B. The first column represents the extended senses you consciously accept as valid and already use to varying degrees. Begin to trust their validity by using them more.

C. The second column represents the senses you want to explore but do not trust as being valid or credible. Begin to experiment with these potential abilities.

D. The third column represents sensory skills you have an innate talent for but the opportunity to exercise them has not arisen. For Example: I was unaware of my ability to connect with other people's past-lives until presented with the opportunity to assist in the regression workshop.

CONNECTIONS

The exercise profile you have just completed provides an overview of your personality and skills right now, which you can now modify and enhance as desired. Focused more on what you are not and cannot do, many of you overlook the vast resource of personality traits and skills already at your disposal. You cannot change what you do not know so this profile provides the resource for the last two exercises.

Exercise #11.

1. Label a new page in your workbook 'CONNECTIONS'. Divide the page into two columns. Title the first column 'Past Achievements', and list the characteristics and skills you used for what you have already achieved on your Action page.
2. Then divide the second column in half horizontally. Title the top half 'Strengths', and list which of your existing strengths you can use to achieve your short and long-term goals.
3. Label the square below 'Weaknesses', and list the existing weaknesses you think may prevent you from achieving each of your short and long-term goals. The conclusions you reach while reviewing your profile will reveal a great deal about your current attitude and perception. These you can change.

ENHANCEMENT PROJECT

Exercise # 12.

1. Title your next page 'ENHANCEMENT PROJECT'. Divide the page into three columns. Write the heading 'Weaknesses' in the first column and transfer all your weaknesses to this column. Everything you do has a perceived benefit to it or you would not do it. These weaknesses provide coping mechanisms that supported your self-image at various development stages of your life.
2. Title the second column 'Benefits'. Determine what has been the perceived benefit of possessing each of these weaknesses. For example: by following someone else's advice when you have to make a decision, you can blame them when the outcome of this decision is not desirable.

3. Title the third column 'Flip Side'. Write down how you can now turn each weakness into a strength that can help you achieve both your short and long-term goals. Just as the solution is the flip side of a problem, a weakness is the flip side of a strength.

Half your weaknesses are a result of fears associated with change and self-accountability. The other half result from what others told you about yourself. When you understand the source or what you protect yourself against, you can begin to energize the flip side of these weaknesses and transform them into strengths.

Manipulation and Control

Control is a paradox. What do you think you do have control of? You do not have *any* control over others, period. All you can control in this reality is your own thoughts, actions, and responses. You just learned how to manipulate others by triggering their fears and guilt through your life programming to create the illusion of control. Control of others is a result of their compliance based on their own self-image and self-interest. It is how you are manipulated into accepting an edited version of reality. If others do not comply with your intentions, there's not a darn thing you can do about it.

How much control do you have over your problems? More than you think. A problem represents an event where time, space and circumstance are not in proper alignment to realize your intentions. If you put your problems on the back burner for a time, or pop them into a 'Worry Jar', many will resolve themselves. It is all energy in transformation. When you attempt to force an immediate resolution to everything, your interference with e-motion often creates new problems that will also have to be resolved. Cease to see these energy misalignments as problems and they will no longer be problematic. The solution will generally reveal itself as soon as you ask for spiritual help or focus on something else.

When you do not get the results you want, change something about what you are doing. Often the solution is as simple as not reacting. Allow your inner senses and feelings to indicate when action is required, and when no action is required. An effective trick in these circumstances is to visualize a traffic light in your mind. Green means GO, Red means no or STOP, and Amber means PAUSE. Amber indicates the need to assess the situation further on a sensory level. This technique is particularly useful when you want to know if an emotion you are feeling is yours or belongs to the other person during an interaction. Amber also indicates you are about to act on an automatic reaction rather than a real feeling. You are here to gain experience in how to direct your energy and mental systems by using as many intuitive sensory skills as possible, so begin to do so.

Nothing exists by itself. Nothing that comes through any of your senses is processed by your mind in that pure form. It is always influenced by the data that is already in your mental storage files. Learn to use the Alice in Wonderland Rule: YOU HAVE TO TELL YOUR SUBCONSCOUS WHAT YOU WANT. Then listen to the sensory triggers that ensure you are receptive to opportunities that lead to the manifestation of these desires.

Conscious Living

Everything you do is a process of trial and error wherein attitude determines the nature of the experience. Your attitude is one of your greatest tools, particularly when you are in the middle of a grand aware-mess. There is a saying I have learned to appreciate, *'You can't save your ass and face at the same time'*. When you get into a pickle, pick one, salvage what you can, remember the lesson, let it go, and focus on something else.

Like learning to walk as a child, you gain experience in directing both energy and your mental systems through practice. Since early childhood beliefs still fuel your automatic reactions, sometimes your methods will work and sometimes not. If you do not judge these experiments, you will not get disheartened or perceive them as failures as I did so often in my past.

My first official 'healing' of a woman's severe migraine headache in the 1980s was an awesome disaster. I had previously done well at relieving minor physical ailments and headaches in particular, until I started taking myself too seriously. My Ego preened from verbal affirmation of my powerful healing energy. I believed I was the only one who could heal this woman. This illusion was confirmed when her migraine disappeared after my healing. I thought I had finally found my calling and envisioned myself healing the multitudes. The lineup to my door was long and winding – in my Ego-driven mind. With one phone call a few days later, my Ego got run over by my Karma. I had put this poor woman into such a deep Alpha state she was unable to function at all. Her speech was slurred and she could barely talk and staggered around like in a drunken stupor. A Tarot Card Reader, she was furious that she had to cancel her appointments for the week. I was mortified as she screamed at me on the telephone!

In response to my silent plea for help, an experienced healer dropped by the New Age Center where this had occurred. Since I had obviously already lost face, I decided to salvage what I could of my ass and blurted out what had happened. He laughed then explained that I had continued to pour energy into that poor woman long after her migraine was gone. Doing so had put her into a deep state of Alpha for days. Unaware I had this ability I did not bring her back out of Alpha when I was finished. I also did not understand her migraines were the ongoing manifestation of mental blocks she was unwilling to address. My preconceptions about healing changed that day. Over time I learned how to direct my energy more subtly, by transferring healing energy to others through a hug without pre-deciding where that energy is needed. I understood the Tarot Card Reader participated in this experiment for her own reasons. I had done nothing *to* her that was not a learning opportunity *for* her.

Money

Desires based on 'not having' will perpetuate more of the same. For Example: if you envision yourself winning the lottery, you may well be disappointed if your desire is motivated by the absence of poverty instead of the acceptance of abundance. Your mind will energize 'not having' if the fear of poverty is greater. And if you want money for the sake of security, it may elude you. What you seek is the feel-good sensations you think being financially secure will give you. Money does give you a certain freedom within our current economic framework. However, fluctuations and sudden drops in the stock market and other investment venues are an example of how the illusion of financial security exists only as long as the economic structure that supports it is sound. Basing your security on external sources leaves you vulnerable to external change. Enron and our current credit crunch is a good example of this.

Your needs will always be met when you change your attitude towards money. You may not have as much as you want, but you will have everything you need. You can attract many of the things you want without needing money to buy them as long as you don't attach expectations to *how* these things can come to you. Abundance springs from the knowledge that the universe supports your well-being if you do. Those of you who have always been prosperous may have scripted this condition into your existence to learn something from the perspective of 'having'. Those who are not may have scripted this condition into their existence to learn from the perspective of 'not having'. Both conditions are illusions designed to expand your understanding of spiritual abundance. What you do or do not have in the way of money or the material props it buys has little to do with who you are and why you are here. It is all creative play. As your sense of inner spiritual security grows, you need less and less of these exterior trappings to ensure happiness, yet more and more of the material things you do desire materialize.

You can change these external aspects of your life by visualizing a more abundant existence. Nevertheless, when you begin to direct your energy towards abundance, you can't just visualize prosperity, sit on your buttocks, and wait for it all to fall into your lap. You need to participate in the process of energy in motion. Once a desire is energized and released, focus on something else but pay attention to promptings to take the required actions as they present themselves. Money is a 3-D by-product of giving service and doing what you love to do. If you want more abundance, give more service. Find new creative ways of marketing the skills you have. You each set the parameters of how much prosperity you believe you need or want. When you release your attachment to money and do what you love to do your needs will all be met.

Managing the Discomforts of Change

How you initiate your own process of change is as individual to you as the changes you wish to make. Although you cannot change everything overnight, small adjustments in your thinking trigger a domino effect that reaps great change over time. Begin with one small adjustment here and one there until you are comfortable with these new patterns of thought and behavior. If you want to experience more feel-good sensations try a random act of kindness to a stranger once a day without expecting anything in return. Allow yourself one mistake a day without beating yourself up or perpetuating self-devaluing thoughts. Examine one fear or guilt a week. You do not have to solve it, just own it, feel it, and explore it. Change one thing about your daily rituals.

For example: instead of showering before you have your morning coffee or tea, have it after your morning cuppa. You can also change the procedure of how you dress by putting your socks or hose on before your underwear. Instead of coming home after work and checking your phone messages or email, do something else first. Hug your partner, children, dog or cat. The more you mix up your daily rituals the more you interrupt your programmed habits. Your life will begin to change as soon as you make even small adjustments to these daily behaviors. Conscious living is choosing *every* action in your life, moment by moment.

Confusion is a result of the comparison of opposing or contradictory beliefs while you reshape your attitude and patterns of thinking. Change disrupts existing patterns, so expect confusion while new behaviors and old patterns butt up against each other. It is important to nurture yourself physically and emotionally to prevent fatigue, stress, and anxiety while changing your patterns. They trigger your automatic reactions and affect the brain's electromagnetic receptors that transmit information to the different aspects of yourself. Fatigue slows down this messaging system so your desired responses elude you. Stress scatters your focus so your synaptic nerves fire contradicting messages to and from the brain, and anxiety triggers your self-image survival mechanisms – the very programs you are trying to change. When body, mind, and spirit are in alignment, you immediately know when you are falling back on old patterns of thinking and can make appropriate adjustments.

The 'failed' experiments are as much a part of the process as those that succeed. Despite your new intentions, your desires may not always manifest the way you want or expect. You may only get part of what you wanted because your beliefs and spiritual agenda are not in alignment. In a 'Dreams' workbook, briefly write down your daily intentions on the left side of the page along with the main events of that day. Remember to date your daily notes. On the right side of the page write what you remember about your dreams each morning to help you compare what you asked for to what you get. Any discrepancy between the two will reveal the beliefs that are holding you back. When you are attuned to your higher frequencies, your thoughts align themselves more closely to your Soul intentions. The more you trust your senses the quicker your real desires will surface to conscious awareness. You may find you no longer want many of the things you previously thought you wanted.

Thoughts you energized in the past do not just disappear because you have designed yourself a new life script. They will still manifest but your attitude towards what you get can change. You can acknowledge them without emotion, find something beneficial in them, let them go, and re-focus on your desired intentions. If you still do not get the desired result, it is still not a *'failed'* experiment. This intention may not be for your higher good or you may still have core beliefs of unworthiness preventing you from realizing these particular desires.

Failed experiments make you an expert at what does not work; an expertise you can share to aid those who face similar roadblocks in their journey. You will *all-ways* be a work-in-progress no matter what level of understanding, spiritual awareness or mastery you reach. As you become more empowered, you may still not know what you will manifest with your thoughts but you will appreciate ALL your experiences for revealing more about your consciousness.

Although your reality is unique, you all have a common agenda – to feel what it is like when you get or do not get what you image with your thoughts. Experiencing the sensation of having or not-having reveals a great deal about your identity. Since your conscious mind operates from the partial perception of your beliefs, realizing perceived desires generally only gives you a temporary feeling of satisfaction. You soon hunger for more because your real desires are still not satisfied. Instruct the subconscious to reveal your real desires and you will begin to feel a more permanent sense of satisfaction as they are realized.

Pat yourself on the back when you make mistakes for it means you are in the process of learning. If you are unwilling to take risks and move into uncharted waters, your perception and self-identity will never change. Every action has an effect, even inaction. Playing it safe through in-action IS action, allowing others to manipulate you in order to promote their own agenda. However, the effects of inaction are rarely to your benefit. So change something, anything about what you do.

> *"Change...*
> *If I always think the way I have always thought*
> *I will always feel the way I have always felt.*
> *If I always feel the way I have always felt,*
> *I will always do what I've always done.*
> *If I always do what I've always done,*
> *I will always get what I've always got.*

> *If I always get what I've always got,*
> *There is no change.*
> *If there is no change, there is no change.*
> Anonymous"

Expanding Your Resources

The first time Mozart sat down at a piano at the age of 3 or 4 was most certainly not the first time his consciousness had ever played the piano or other musical instruments. This intuitive skill was developed in other existences and genetic ancestry within this reality. From a conscious perspective Mozart's personal life was not viewed a success. Although admired for his composing skills, he was both envied and resented for challenging the musical limitations of his day. Society considered him rude, crude and insane for living an unconventional life with such self-absorbed passion. Despite his immense talent, he died a pauper. The trailblazers of any era rarely conform to the conventional standards of their day, yet the impact of their creative expression survives.

Your own passions, interests and curiosities are neither insignificant or without effect. They not only enrich your experience but also infuse human consciousness with a new variation of self-expression - yours. You can access skills you acquired in other existences or those inherent in your genetic ancestry while in the Alpha or dream state. Due to life programming, many of your innate skills just never had a chance to surface. During your meditations, ask that your dreams and impulses reveal these skills. As a time traveler in this vast universal thought-resource, you can acquire whatever information you may need or desire to enhance your own creative expression within this reality.

Information, *regardless of source*, expands your mind. In order to grow, you need to let go of your automatic reactions, everyone's expectations including your own, and limiting pre-conceptions about what is possible for yourself. When new information enters your data banks previously unrelated data begins to hook up to expand your conscious perception.

Your Soul will fill its need for stimulation even if you consciously refuse to provide it. Spirit will press you into doing something dramatic or traumatic to get you unstuck and back onto your intended path. There is nothing better than a grand disaster to shake you out of your mental ruts. If you stay stuck in replaying and analyzing these disasters, you are not dedicating energy to discovering the limiting thinking they might reveal. As soon as you realize you are stuck, you are learning about perception, so it is not a mistake either.

For Example: If you keep a spoon in your cup while you drink your coffee, it may poke you in the eye every time you take a sip. Although you may find many creative ways to shield your eye and hold the spoon, you can simply remove the spoon from your cup. As silly as this example may seem, many of you create just such repetitive situations in your life. Pay attention when you notice yourself think or say, *"Every time I . . .* (do this or that) *. . . this or that happens."* Just stop doing what you are doing when you say or think *'every time'* and you'll eliminate many of your problematic habits. Your modus operandi, *(a method or procedure)* can be changed to a 'Modus Vivendi', *(a manner of living)* to bypass these automatic programmed behaviors.

Scripting Your Reality

Your reality mirrors your beliefs 100%. If you believe everything in your life is destined and that you are powerless to influence events – you are right. If you believe your life is designed to comply with the dictates of a higher power – you are right. If you believe your life is a series of random events you cannot control – you are right. And, if you believe that as a self-actualizing aspect of all consciousness you can create your own reality by directing your thoughts – you are also right.

If you do not care for your life script, change it by expanding your beliefs about yourself and your reality. There are so many ways you can expand your awareness that it matters not which one you pick. Your attitude determines whether this will be a comfortable or uncomfortable journey. Attitude is a choice. It will not eliminate sorrow, pain, fear or loss during your life, but it will determine how you experience them and what understandings you reach through them.

Although others are quick to point out your mistakes, it is only you who guilt yourself for making them. If someone says you made a mistake, agree with them and ask what they think you can do to fix it. Listen to what they have to say and thank them for their input. Then use your own senses to determine if the information they share is helpful. Even if you disagree with their suggestions, this approach changes the dynamics of your interactions and your attitude within them.

You will begin to see how many beliefs and habits are perpetuated when you engage your wonder-full curiosity. I heard a story about a woman who always cut a small piece of meat off the ends of her roast before she put it in the roasting pan. Having watched her do this for years, her husband finally asked her why. She said she didn't know but assumed there was a good reason because her mother always did it. The next time they had dinner at her mother's house the husband asked her why she did this. After a moment's puzzlement, the mother laughed and said, *"Oh, it's silly really. I only had one small roasting pan when I was first married so I cut the ends off so the roast would fit into the pan. I guess it's just a habit now."* Her solution was appropriate to the initial problem but continuing this behavior for two generations without question was not. Personally, I am more curious about what she did with the pieces she always cut off. You will never cease to amuse yourself once you begin to question the origins of your own and the habits other people perpetuate.

Changing Patterns of Behavior

Participating in your own mental processes means learning to pay attention to everything you do all the time. Created by your mental systems to increase processing efficiency, these patterns determine the kind of circumstances you manifest and your reactions to them. The more aware you are of these reactionary patterns, the greater your ability to short-circuit them if they are not beneficial. You will begin to identify themes that present themselves repeatedly because you have not resolved these issues. You will also recognize when you are expanding your understanding of a particular theme. If your problem-solving methods do not work the first time, they will not work the tenth time. Call on your system-busters, the spiritual artillery of your inner senses. The more you use these senses the quicker you can identify your blocks.

You also need to be aware of the physiological patterns that mirror your state of being. The next exercise will help you become familiar with your body language, tone of voice, and choice of wording.

Exercise # 13.

1. Title a new page in your workbook, 'BODY LANGUAGE'.
2. Record your body language, tone of voice, and choice of words when you are happy, confident ,and feeling good. How do you stand? What words do you use? What does the tone of your voice sound like?
3. What kinds of circumstances or individuals trigger a change in this pattern? How has your body language, tone of voice or choice of words changed when you're triggered?
4. Record who or what has triggered this change and what the circumstances are.
5. Then write down what you think you may be defending yourself against. Once you discover what kind of triggers diminish you, you can nourish yourself by expanding your beliefs about yourself within these circumstances.

Others respond to the frequency you broadcast and treat you accordingly. If they treat you badly, it is because you think poorly of yourself and allow it. Yet, despite how others treat you, it is not they who needs to change - it's always you. Change how you view yourself. It does not matter a hoot how many diplomas you have, what your net assets are, or how beautiful you are physically. If you do not feel worthy inside, you will not broadcast worthiness despite your achievements, assets or appearance. Fortunately, you can always determine the state of your self-image by what others mirror back to you. If you forget you are a valuable and worthy individual a situation will present itself to remind you. If you ignore these prompts you will always be reminded by a 2x4, 4x8, or a honker of a tree may fall on you. One of the first metaphysical jokes I ever heard was 'My karma just ran over my dogma'. I had many such hit-and-runs before I finally addressed and changed my own poor self-image and resulting survival patterns of behavior.

Relationship is the arena wherein you can learn the most about yourself and what love really is. Be it with your family, partner, or friends, nothing reflects your own identity more clearly than how you express love. If you have conditions and expectations attached to either giving or receiving love, you still have work to do. When you feel unworthy and unloved, your relationships will mirror these feelings. Your relationships will as clearly reflect when you operate from a position of self-love and self-worth. Love is not about compromising or transforming yourself to appease others or meet the ideals of what you think you should be. Until you understand this, you may continually find yourself feeling dissatisfied and disappointed in your relationships. This elemental lesson will repeat itself until you learn to love and nourish yourself for the precious gem you are.

Years ago in Edmonton I orchestrated a grand problem for myself to learn a lesson I had cleverly side stepped. It involved a friend's offer to help edit a creative project dear to my heart. Flattered by her enthusiasm for my project *(Ego)*, and thinking her much more experienced than myself *(giving my power away)*

I ignored my own feelings and sensory signals. I continued to let her help which encouraged her to believe we were now a team *(in-action creating its own effect)*. I also said nothing when she referred to her participation as co-creator wherein I was the rough diamond and she the expert that would refine and polish the project to perfection *(fear of confrontation and loss)*. Not knowing how to respond, I played along; allowing myself to envision future projects we would do together after this project was completed. When the project was completed and she stated it should bear her name as co-creator, I knew I had a serious problem *(honker of a tree falling on me!)*. I realized my lack of action created the mess but did not know how to resolve it without losing a friend. Tormented, I asked Spirit for help.

The answer came two days later during an evening walk with another friend. The brisk evening wind had lifted several sheets of paper off the boulevard and sent them fluttering around us. Impulsively I picked one up and read it. On one side was an underlined heading in bold type. It read, *"MUSE WORKS - Turning Potential into Reality"*. On the other side was one sentence at the top of a blank page that said, *"What's here for me to learn about myself and others that isn't immediately apparent?"* Coincidence? I think not. The Muse Works message prompted me to look beneath the surface of the problem to identify the real issues it represented. I realized there were many things I needed to look at beneath the surface, foremost being my lack of confidence and the Modus Operendi I habitually used to avoid any kind of confrontation. When it came to fight or flight, I was a master at in-action and flight. By deferring to my friend's expertise, I affirmed she could realize her own aspirations through my project instead of initiating her own.

Just when I thought I had confronted the worst in me an unpleasant memory resurfaced. Several years prior I was the one who had sought personal fulfillment by claiming and trying to transform someone else's dream into my own. Being at the other end of the stick gave me a different perspective on the current mess. The memory of how badly that situation turned out did little to encourage me to confront this one. Aware the lesson was about my own patterns of behavior, after a short pity-party I was finally ready to change them. Although addressing the situation did not go well, I am eternally grateful to Muse Works and my dear friend in helping me change those patterns. As a result, I lost both face and a friend. I also had to redo my project to reclaim it. Had impulse not propelled me to pick up this powerful message carried by the wind, I would have learned this lesson some other way later, but perhaps more painfully and with greater loss. Whatever the flyer was for, I still have it tacked on my bulletin board beside my computer. It reminds me to pay attention to my senses and deal with issues when they surface not to wait until they explode in my face.

When you ask yourself, *"What's here for me to learn about myself and others that isn't immediately apparent"*, you will be surprised at how quickly your senses will respond. Whether you believe in God, Krishna, Buddha, Earth Spirits or nothing at all, you are never alone. You are ALL-WAYS supported in your desire to expand your consciousness by the source of your own greater identity. When only your conscious Ego directs your actions you think you must resolve everything yourself. You cannot. The circumstances of your conscious life are only the tip of the iceberg of what is really going on in this physical experience. It's much like having a universal library at your disposal yet referring only to the one reference book you parents passed on to you. The perceptions of the author limit what the reference book contains. Your inner resources reveal what is really going on beneath the surface of your conscious activities. If you are stuck resolving a problem, ask for help and be willing to explore the data your inner senses provide.

Lessons can be obvious or subtle, self-contained in one issue, or linked to several related themes. Many lessons appear to go away when you ignore them. You may not recognize a new problem as the same old problem because it underwent a costume change. Until you resolve these recurring issues, you will deny yourself much of what you desire. You are deserving of everything you want to experience but will continue to sabotage yourself until you realize you *are* worthy of what you desire. Life is a self-fulfilling prophecy that gives you exactly what you believe you deserve. If you give your power away, don't be surprised someone will take it and use it against you. If you find yourself defending or qualifying yourself to others, you need to examine your fears and vulnerabilities. If others continually disappoint you, you need to examine your expectations not their behavior.

Once your love-of-self broadcasts this sense of inner worthiness, others treat you differently. If not everyone treats you well, you will not take it personally. Life is not a popularity contest but about making personal choices for individual self-expression through your mind and heart. Pay attention to your thoughts, feelings, words, and actions. They reflect the state of your identity. If you are unwilling to participate in the process, you will just get more of what you have right now. Some key thoughts and phrases that help identifying recurring patterns are: *"this is just like when . . .not this again . . .every time I . . .every time he or she . . .I just knew this would happen . . ."*

All your experiences are about you. Nothing happens to you since everything happens through you and *for you* as an opportunity for self-awareness. The word self-awareness is bantered about with little understanding of its true meaning: *"To be aware of Self in all situations"*. Instead of feeling diminished by your life challenges and obstacles, empower yourself by investigating your own identity. The confusion and upheaval you may experience when you begin to change your patterns is a GOODY. It is a sign of energy in motion. It is often when you throw your hands up in the air and say, *'What a mess! I give up. I don't know what to do'*, that you surrender Ego and allow yourself to access your spiritual resources. When you are so frustrated you say, *"I just don't care anymore"*, you are actually saying you no longer care to operate through your automatic programs and responses and are ready to change your habits.

217

Chapter 9

LIVING IN THE PRESENT

"'There is no time like now, for now is all there ever is."

YOU do not have to do anything to become spiritual. You already ARE a Spiritual Being. When you understand how your mental systems work you can begin to diffuse the reactive conditioning that diminishes your awareness of this and consciously nourish your genuine identity and intentions. Some who consider themselves spiritual think there will be no more obstacles or challenges if they keep all negativity at bay, meditate or pray for hours or isolate themselves from interactive life experiences. They become so 'heavenly-minded, they're no earthly good' as my brother had said. The intention of this life is not to rise above this physical experience. You are here to achieve mastery *within it*. You cannot do so unless you are willing to explore and direct your own consciousness.

"on personal growth . . .
You have found a small part of yourself. Therefore, seek another part,
seek another part, seek another part and seek another part. Do not
say that you have found self, for you have but found a part of this, you
see. If you have found self, then would you be totally complete."
. . . The Evergreens

Self-exploration is a do-it-yourself project. You become an expert at this physical game through practice. There is no other way to gain skill at using your extended senses. You operate in a wondrous free-will universe where you can experience yourself how you choose. Although you drafted some specific lessons for this life, you determine your ongoing destiny by the thoughts you choose to energize. If your script has been ponderous and boring, you can transform it into a de-light-full journey of self-discovery. Knowing how your mind creates what you have in your life now enables you to use these same mental systems to change what you wish. Based on your beliefs, some things may change immediately while others may take more time. Leaps of faith can take you beyond the edges of your existing perception but continuous participation in your mental processes keeps you there. You can establish new patterns of thinking and behavior whenever you choose, but there is no time like the present, for now is all there ever is.

Trusting the Process

It does not matter how you intend to play this joyous game of experimentation through thought-projection and sensory feedback. You are so good at the game already you have tricked yourself into believing life is happening to you rather than created by you.

If you want to fix a bicycle, the job is easier with a bicycle repair kit or if you want to bake a yummy cake, you need the right ingredients and a recipe to follow. Expanding your consciousness also requires tools - tools that are already inside you. Once you have mastered the basic techniques of how to bypass your existing mental programs, you can dip into other aspects of this vast universal resource to see what you can discover. Your library of self-knowledge contains your own life experiences, your bloodline's genetic history, as well as your Soul's ancestry on this and on other frequencies. This library also contains all existing knowledge within the universe as well as the planet's own earth consciousness. With this vast resource, you can access anything you need to broaden your sensory perception within this physical experience.

So how do you tap into this resource? Your primary keys are belief and trust. Believe this resource exists and trust it will provide what you need or desire. Be willing to suspend judgment and examine your programmed beliefs to push open the doorway to this sensory storehouse. Begin with one small adjustment here, one there, and trust the process while you continue your sensory experiments.

The cornerstone of freedom is responsibility - the '*ability to respond*', which means making the choice to take risks. How can you be an expert at something you have never done before? You cannot. You do not blame or punish a child when they try to walk and stumble or fall because you realize they are learning something new. You even encourage them to continue no matter how often they fail. You might argue the mistakes you may make as an adult are more serious. To a toddler, falling on its face when everyone around them is walking with ease is just as serious. However, they pick themselves up and try again. Mastery of any skill requires trust in yourself, and perseverance. Honor all your efforts and cease to judge yourself or compare your level of skill to others. You will do no harm to those on whom you practice for they are willing participants, despite how they may react consciously to your mistakes.

How you feel about what you do is a choice. You decide when you awaken each morning if you will have a good day filled with opportunity, or a repetition of yesterday's humdrum or disappointing existence. Your life can be an adventure of self-discovery wherein you evaluate this, view that, and explore whatever sensations arise through the sensory dramas you manifest for yourself.

"on choice . . .
"The choice is yours. The force within you will be expressed no matter what. Now is the time for this force to be expressed. The choice is yours in how it is used; to harm or to help, to aid or to hinder, to remove ill or to establish illness. Can be done for good; can be done for not so good. Is your choice, and we do say choose, choose, choose, joy; and seek within yourself the God within yourself. It will not lead you astray, not one footfall off our Golden Road, not one hair's breadth from the path of joy"
. . . The Evergreens

You cannot see air but trust this invisible substance to keep you alive. You trust that when you wake up in the morning your body has not undergone some horrendous mutation during the night. In fact, you do not give it a second thought even though on other frequencies you can change your physical appearance with just a thought. If you can trust this continuous re-manifestation of your physical form, you can also trust the inner consciousness that makes all this possible. Your inner consciousness is the reason your body replicates itself so effortlessly you are not even aware it is doing so.

There is nothing 'out there' that did not emerge from what is 'in there' - inside you. Yet, you ignore the evidence of your own sensory perception. You allow others to define your experiences and blame them if you do not care for the results. You believe a strangers opinion of you to be true and often change your persona to align yourself with it. Although you are here to fulfill your own creative intentions, you allow others to define and alter these intentions. You even borrow their words, mimic their actions, and expect to get back an enhanced version of your own ideals. You are a grand magician, fooling even yourself with your creative illusions. That is how powerful you are.

Everything you need is contained within your own consciousness. Your own senses are like library cards that connect you with these spiritual resources. You do not have to understand how everything works. You only have to trust that it does, for it already does. How many coincidences does it take before you accept a synchronicity of timing and circumstance exists in your life? How many times must your gut feeling prove to be right before you trust your own feelings? How many miracles within the natural environment must you view before you acknowledge the magical aspects of creation? And how many extra-ordinary first-hand subjective experiences must you have before you trust their validity? When you suspend your judgments, the evidence you seek will be apparent. It is not proof you need, it is trust. Proof is self-evident once you begin to trust your own senses.

Where do some of your skills and talents come from if you did not learn them in this life? From where do your inspirations and ideas spring? Meditation, and time spent in nature help still the noise of your programmed mental babble so you can be receptive to the sensory evidence you seek. Gift yourself with small pockets of quiet time each day to clear your mind and feel your own inner senses. If you are visual, images may flash through your mind and if you are sensory or tactile, you will begin to experience different physiological sensations. A cerebral person may receive new kinds of mental data while others will just know something or impulsively pick up a sheet of paper the wind blew their way. These are all miracles of your own sensory energy-in-motion.

To your higher frequency self, the shortest route from point A to point B may be via point G. Consciously you believe you are in the wrong place but your spiritual aspect knows from its broader perspective that point G will directly catapult you to point B. Hindsight provides evidence that following a gut feeling got you where you needed to be to seize an opportunity you desired. There are no limits to how your desires and intentions can manifest, providing you do not try to orchestrate the details.

Universal energy takes care of that. However, your task is to set the universe in motion with your thought intentions and the propulsion of your desires.

Trust is a decision. Trust in the power of your own senses increases with each success. Eventually trust becomes as natural as the limiting mental processes through which you now operate. Everything happens for a reason, even if you do not know what that reason is consciously. *You are always in the right place, at the right time, for the right reason, for your higher good.* You are a Divine Spiritual Being who has chosen this physical existence in order to experience your own creative consciousness in this unique way. Many of you seek an ultimate truth to this existence when there is none other than energy in creative action. Truth is belief and reality is perception. Both are based on choice – your choice.

on trust . . .

"Truth is an ephemeral. The true test of truth is the paradox of truth. If it is paradoxical, you will also find that it is true. Beware of one-sided truths."

"What starts a car? A key being turned. Indeed. What keeps it running? The gasoline that's in it. There are several small children that believe what makes the car run is a small piece of flat plastic that is carried upon the person of their father in his wallet for if that not be given to the gasoline attendant, then there be no gasoline, you see.

Which is the truth? The truth is depending on which perspective you perceive it as. The child perceives the credit card as the thing that makes the car go; the driver sees it as the key; the engineer sees it as an interaction of electrical and mechanical forces. And the engineers may be broken down into different divisions such as power engineers and vaporization engineers and oil engineers, and it becomes a whole host of perceptions. And each one of them is truth."
The Evergreens

Gather your information from whatever source you wish but process it though all your senses to see if it resonates with you. No matter how valid it appears or how well it works for others, external data is influenced by the perceptions of its source to varying degrees. Use the traffic light technique to see if this information is for you. Green means GO, red means STOP, and yellow means PAUSE. Yellow can be neutral, either/or, to proceed with caution, or to gather more information before you proceed. If you get the green or red light, act on it even if it makes no conscious sense to do so. This technique also helps identify if a sensation you experience is an authentic feeling or a programmed emotional reaction.

When you live in the NOW, all your sensory experiences are meaningful. You no longer need to create trauma or participate in the dramas others create for sensory stimulation. Your inner security rises from trust in your own consciousness and its connection to a universe that supports all your explorations. Attuned to your patterns you also become more sensitive to the patterns of others and can choose to participate in their processes without manipulation on either side. You may not love everyone but you can learn to feel loving towards everyone. Forgive them for the pain they may cause you to release the pain you carry within yourself. Allow others their own experiences without judgment.

Be prepared to run into roadblock while changing your patterns of thinking. Hindsight is always 20/20 since you can see the effects of your past actions. It is OK to look back but not to get stuck there by reliving the emotions attached to these experiences. Foresight is hindsight turned around. It can be a feeling of hesitation, a cold knot in your stomach, the ringing in your ears or other physiological changes in your body. These sensations warn that what you are about to do may have adverse affects you are not consciously aware of. Within this rapidly changing reality, you will need all your sensory finesse to maintain your existing identity let alone expand it.

This physical experience is one of flux so remain open to the inevitability of change. Your physical experience consists of continuous change and re-alignment. Just when you think you have it all together, up pops something new to throw you off-balance. You may even feel a sense of loss at leaving behind your old survival mechanisms and habits. Letting go of your previous comfort zones can feel painful. That is from where the expression 'no pain, no gain' originated. Your attitude determines the ease with which you accept the ebbs and flows of energy in motion. When you can say something like, *'Oh my, did that ever press my buttons. I wonder why?'* you approach your lessons with the loving awareness that every change in your life is *for you*.

Goals are short or long-term agreements you make with yourself to focus your energy on a specific intention. When you reach this goal, this block of dedicated energy is released and you immediately focus on another intention or goal. Therefore, your goals are *directed thought-projections* in action. However, achieving goals will not ensure self-worth or happiness if you lack it right now.

Everywhere else always appears better than now if you are not happy with your now. After an initial period of euphoria when you are 'there', you will feel just the way you did before, when you projected your intentions through your existing thoughts and feelings. If you feel insecure and set a goal to change this feeling you will still feel insecure after you reach your goal. A good question to ask when you set your goals is, *'Will reaching this goal change how I feel about myself right now?'* If the answer is yes, change your thoughts and feelings 'now'.

There is no better 'there' than your now, in spite of what you envision in the future. When you get there and it becomes your now, you will simply envision another there that will look better than that now. Your memories reach into the past to evaluate your identity from your thoughts and feelings now, and your desires reach into the future from your thoughts and feeling now. If you are dissatisfied with your now, you will not feel satisfied with your future achievements either. So change how you feel NOW.

The curiosity prompting you to reach for a 'there' is the same curiosity that propels you to design new aspirations once you reach your goals. What holds you back from a natural flow of new creative experiences is emotional attachment to the security of existing circumstance or the material by-products of your achievements. For example: Many of you think you have to stay in your current job particularly if you've invested time and money into getting there. You label yourself a Computer Technician, an Artist, a Nurse, a Manager or other specialist and think this persona defines who you are. You are more than what you do to earn the money you need to live. Continue to do it if it brings you joy and satisfaction but don't get so attached to a career persona that you're unwilling to try something else when it no longer feels meaningful.

Now is all there ever is. If you do not like it, change your perception by finding something beneficial in it. If you do not believe how swiftly this can occur, here is an example many women can relate to:

"As you move through your house with your morning coffee in hand you remember you have company coming for dinner. You think "Crap" as your heart sinks. The house is a mess! Depressed, you walk into the living room and see a layer of dust on the shabby furniture you have had forever. You envision what your guests will think. You notice the cat's scratch marks on the side of the couch, the brittle dry leaves on your tropical plant, and the lack of luster on glass ornaments that look like cheap bric-a-bracs. You see several spots on the carpet, smudges on the windows, and a new heat ring on your coffee table. Now you feel both crappy and depressed. How can you invite people into this dump?

Embarrassed by what they will think, you want to cancel the evening. The phone rings. It is a friend who immediately begins to gush about the wonderful dry flower arrangement you dropped off at her house a few evenings ago. She tells you not only how creative and clever you are, but how everyone who has seen it admired it. You start to feel a little better. She then says what a wonderful time they had at your home last week and that your candle lit living room was so cozy, she did not want to leave. You begin to feel better, pleased by the ambiance you create for your guests. She goes on to praise the wonderful appetizers you served, and asks for the recipe for the delicious carrot/curry soup. She finishes by saying she looks forward to coming over tonight, for you always serve delicious meals at your dinner parties, a skill she envies.

Suddenly your world looks brighter. Your mind on the evening's menu, you walk into your living room with your cleaning products. Before long you pause and notice the sun dancing off the lovely glass and brass ornaments you just polished. Your plant looks lush again after you pulled off the dead leaves and watered it. You stop to enjoy the shadows play on the wall behind it for a moment and chuckle as you notice how artistically your throw blanket hides the cat scratches on the couch. You polish the tabletops, pleased with how the cluster of candles you arranged on your glass cake tray hides the heat ring.

When you are finished and the three small stains on the vacuumed rug have vanished, you view your living room through new eyes. Your nose tingles from the orange-scented furniture polish and the breeze from the open window fans your plant fronds as it wafts fresh air through the room. With candlelight and soft music that evening, you envision the room inviting and comfortable, the ambiance you intended to project. You are now humming to yourself as you dash out the door to buy your groceries for dinner."

Perception created and changed the experience. All it took was a simple shift in focus: same material props - different attitude. You may not always have a friend call just when you need a perception boost, but you can give yourself these boosts. Your feelings are your responsibility. You determine the nature of ALL your feelings, perceptions, and resulting experiences. When you feel dissatisfied with your now, give yourself an internal *checkup from the neck up*. Now is as good as you decide it is, and tomorrow will be wonderful, awful, or anything else you decide it will be. Reality is not a result of events, but your perception of these events.

Exercise # 14.

Write down your thoughts and feelings about everything that happens for one full day. Objectively record what circumstances trigger a change your mood and perception. It could be someone pointing out a mistake or complimenting you. In the evening, review what you wrote and identify what words or circumstances triggered these changes. Before you go to sleep at night, relax and tell yourself, *"This day, I have always felt secure and content within all my experiences - effortlessly"*.

The next day record your thoughts and feelings again, but administer your own affirmation boosts whenever your perception turns negative. Jot down the key words or thoughts that changed your perception. If you do this once a week for several weeks you will begin to see a pattern emerge in what kind of triggers change your perception of yourself. Identify what diminishes you and affirm what validates you.

You experience your whole life through your perception in the moment. You cannot experience a memory of when you were ten as a ten year-old since you no longer have the thoughts and feelings of when you were ten years old. You re-live your past through your thoughts and feelings when you remember these events right now because time is simultaneous. You continually edit the past through your perception right now. You can remember an event as an error that reinforces your perceived failings or in a way that nourishes your expanding awareness of yourself. For Example: Think of something uncomfortable or embarrassing that happened this past week while you are feeling good about yourself. Write it down from this perception. Think about that same event when you are feeling cranky, tired, or angry and record it down from that perception. When you are finished, compare the two.

Your circumstances now are a result of the 'there' you projected at some point in your past, based on how you thought and felt then. When you spend your time reliving the past or imagining idealized future events, you are not choosing your thoughts in the moment. Wherever your mind goes is where you take 100% of yourself. By changing your mind now you change your past, present, and future. Use your memories as the point of reference where you might say, *"I am more flexible about new ideas now than*

I was before" or *"Yippee! I used to pout for a week over what was said to me, but now I only pout for an hour."*

Your memories, intentions, and conscious view are only the tip of the iceberg of what is actually going on around you. Your other-frequency experiences still exist in the X-Files of your data banks. This resource supports your self-worth in a way you do not on a conscious level since it represents your more expansive identity. It affirms that you are a precious aspect of the God Source no matter what you do. When you have an open dialogue with your Spiritual Self, higher-frequency thoughts provide the nourishment you need. However, you cannot just sit back and expect Spirit or God to run your life. You are the director of and responsible for your own physical experience.

If you were to leave this physical life one minute from now, the totality of who you are is WHAT YOU ARE RIGHT NOW, not who you were last week or intend to become tomorrow. Just as the quality of your here is determined by your attitude now, the quality of your there is determined by your attitude now. The sooner you direct your thoughts and choose your feelings, the sooner you will move through the events you energized in the past. *'Every event in your life, whether you view it as good or bad is divine grace in action'.* If you have a need to check your progress, compare yourself only to yourself. This develops a pattern of thinking that affirms the value of all your experiences.

Nothing is interesting until you become interested in it, so become interested in yourself. Comparing yourself to others or social concepts of success is as crippling as guilt and fear. No matter what you have done or what you know, there will always be others ahead of you, those who parallel you, and others behind you who perceive you as possessing all the characteristics they desire. We are ALL Unique Divine Beings of equally extraordinary value. Learn to reach one hand forward for assistance from those who know more, and one hand back towards those who perceive you as knowing more.

Everyone in your life is there to trigger you, support you, challenge you, and mirror your progress. There are no accidents or meaningless encounters, for all exist by design - your design. Although you are in the driver's seat, they act as your windshield, side, and rear-view mirrors to reflect your identity back to you while on this journey. If you doubt the loving support of your spiritual self, look at the variety of irritating and problematic people who push your buttons to help you change.

There are no shortcuts to any place worth going. You cannot just pop an awareness pill once a month and acquire enlightenment. You need to integrate all your sensory resources into your conscious interpretive processes and use them all the time. The euphoria from self-awareness seminars or motivational books quickly fades. You soon find yourself back in your old patterns of thinking if you do not nurture and maintain these new thought patterns. If you do not direct your own mind – all the time - someone else will.

Changing Personal Interactions

You may continue to be triggered by those who judge and criticize you. Your irritation with some people is an unwillingness to accept their truth to be as valid as your truth. You do not have to choose this truth for yourself but you need to recognize it is also valid. Beliefs are perceptions that do not require agreement in order to interact with respect. All things are true to the believer and perceiver.

As you release your own judgments you will recognize these characteristics as the defense mechanisms they are and stop taking them personally. You may not love everybody, but you can feel loving towards everyone. The frequency of love creates energy bubbles that surge through your bloodstream and energy nerve systems to dissolve blockages throughout your whole being. To feel loving towards the people who challenge you may not change them, but it will change you. When you catch yourself judging, defending, criticizing or reacting in anger you need to ask yourself what perceived harm you are protecting.

This was a tough lesson I learned fairly recently, while sitting on the toilet of all things. After a frustrating telephone conversation with my mother, I dashed to the bathroom. Sitting there, I suddenly realized how angry I was feeling. In fact, I realized I always felt anger after speaking with her. I knew the anger was because she had not protected me from physical and sexual abuse as a child. I still felt she had not protected me like a mother was supposed to do. Although I had forgiven her years ago during my trauma healing, in my innermost core I continued to carry a smoldering seed of anger and resentment. However, now I was finally tired of feeling anger. It had not occurred to me that I triggered and energized anger within myself whenever I heard her voice or was around her. Sitting there, slightly awed by this discovery, I finally release this anger. It was a simple decision that stuck to this day.

Angels can fly because they take themselves lightly. The worst nightmare for a serious-minded individual is a light-hearted person. Light-hearted people are wonderful mirrors to help loosen rigid minds. A light heart does not lack responsibility. They just allow others their own experiences. Half of what irritates you about others evaporates when you allow them to be who they are.

Sympathy is a learned emotion whereas empathy rises from your Soul. Empathy holds no judgments and requires no first-hand knowledge of what an experience may feel like. You did not have to be abused yourself to validate the feelings of those who are. Empathy rises from a loving compassion towards any suffering while knowing these painful experiences are opportunities to learn.

Sometimes, what others mirror back at you, is a wonderful reminder of unprofitable patterns you once expressed and have already successfully changed. Pat yourself on the back if you can relate to a broad spectrum of characteristics for they reflect all the understandings your consciousness has acquired. If you get triggered by fear, guilt or shame, look at your own expectations and beliefs. If it is in your life, it's for you, and your TASK is to discover why by utilizing both thought and sensation.

Although energy is neutral, you attract both the same and opposite polarities to you. Although the dark attracts dark, it also seeks out the light in order to reclaim its origins. Light also requires the dark to integrate its dark aspects and define its own integrity and radiance. Both are polarities of each other that represent different aspects of your divine origins. All your relationships and experiences help you achieve your understandings of both the light and dark. I like the following exercise as a check-up from the neck-up every six months or so, to evaluate existing relationships.

Exercise # 15-A.

Write down the names of all the significant people in your life on separate pages in your book. This includes the people you work with on a daily basis.

2. List what characteristics you like about each of them on the top half of each page and draw a horizontal line below your list.
3. Go back and circle the one characteristic you like the most about each.
4. Below the line, list what you currently dislike about each of them.
5. Write one or two words to describe how each of these negative characteristics makes you feel and put a star beside these feeling words.
6. Go back to the previous pages and write #1 beside the characteristics you think you usually project yourself.
7. Write #2 beside characteristics you project sometimes.
8. Write #3 beside the characteristics you only occasionally or never display.
9. Then write your name on the top of a new page. Divide the page into two columns and list the characteristics you circled in the first column. List the remaining characteristics in the second column.
10. Draw a line below these two columns. Now list all the dislikes you have numbered under #1, #2, and #3 in the

first column. If a characteristic appears more than once only list it once.

11. Read the list of characteristics you like from column A aloud. You possess and express all these characteristics yourself. Pat yourself on the back for you are looking at a reflection of yourself.

12. Your B list mirrors what you want to achieve or strengthen in yourself with the help of your existing mirrors (the individuals you have listed).

13. Look at the column of characteristics you dislike and cross out the #3 list. The items under #2 are what you are currently working on and the items under #1 represent characteristics that still trigger you.

14 Copy the words you wrote describing how these #1 characteristic made you feel onto your #2 list. These are the feelings you need to explore within yourself.

It is important to recognize who impedes as well as who aids you. People who do things for 'your own good' as they say are doing it for *their* good. You always have the choice to choose your choice, and the right to change your mind. Those who do not uplift you, support, validate and nourish you, are not *for* you, no matter how much they may profess to love you. However, what they mirror to you IS for you, if only to recognize you no longer resonate with this kind of manipulation.

Exercise 15-B.

Over a period of a week, ask yourself how you feel after each interaction with your family, friends, and co-workers. Write down their names on a sheet in your workbook after an interaction with them. Pay attention to your feelings during your interaction with these individuals. At the end of the week write yes or no to each of the questions below for each person you have listed.

1. Do they stimulate you mentally?

2. Do you feel better after than you did before your interaction with them?
3. Do they share information that makes you think?
4. Do they put themselves down during the conversation?
5. Do they criticize you or others?
6. Do they talk about what they lack in their lives?

Those who primarily scored yes for the first three questions support and nourish you even if you do not agree with what they say. If the answer to the last three questions was yes, they are using you as a sounding board for their own self-dialogue programs. The following week pay attention to what *you* say during your interactions and ask the same questions about your own conversational behavior. How did you rate? The answers will reveal much about the energy frequency you currently broadcast and attract. If you do not like the results of this self-evaluation, begin to change how you interact with others.

All negativity reflects an absence of love. You can send a negative person love and change your position during your interaction with them, you can send them love and limit your interactions with them or you can send them love and stop interacting with them altogether. It is your choice. Pay attention to how much of your energy goes to counteracting negativity in your existing relationships. Decide how much energy you wish to invest in balancing this negativity within those relationships. Allow negative people their experience, send them love, stop participating in their dramas, and pat yourself on the back when they lose interest in you. It means you no longer fuel their low frequency emotions.

When you reclaim the use of your spiritual eyes, you'll be shocked to see nearly everything in this reality is designed to promote materialistic consumption, separation, and interactive discord through fear and guilt. *Goody!* Acknowledge the overwhelming sadness you may feel, for it IS a sad state of affairs. Once you can recognize manipulation you can stop allowing it to trigger you. Information creates choice, choice allows for independent thought, and independent thought enhances a sensory clarity whereby you choose all your thoughts and responses.

Say *'Yippee!'* every time you recognize control or manipulation is taking place. There are no shortcuts to expanding your consciousness for the experience is entirely subjective. You need to do the work to reap the rewards. You create, develop, and maintain self-awareness through curiosity, intention, and application. The prize is experiencing each day fully while you dream, share, and connect with all aspects of consciousness in this reality.

Life programming perpetuates the illusion of security through a belief in 'forever'. The only thing that lasts forever is your Soul consciousness. Everything else is an illusion. Because of your belief in forever you stay in circumstances long after they served their purpose. Half your relationships have already served their purpose. They would cease to be problematic if you just walked away. The relationships left represent lessons that persist because you resist. Joyfully learn these lessons and you will have an abundance of energy to realize your unfulfilled desires.

Although relationships are difficult to release because of emotional attachments, on an intuitive level you always know when they are over. Yet you feel guilty and devastated when a friendship or meaningful relationship fizzles away or ends. Longevity does not necessarily equate to quality. In fact, many relationships endure simply out of habit not because they are interactively fulfilling. Some people are partners or befriend each other for life. Some are short interludes, and some are brief but meaningful encounters. It is not how long it lasts but how fully you experience it and what understandings you reach through it. Learn to release others graciously. Holding others as emotional hostages diminishes you both. Love is an ever-changing expression of inner feelings, not a certificate of ownership endorsed by longevity. Many of your existing relationships will naturally dissolve or transform when you change your attitude within them, leaving room for new individuals to enter your life.

Commitment and a certain permanency in parenting partners are beneficial but not essential to children in their early years. What is essential is love and nourishment so they can move through their developmental stages in a supportive and validating environment. Many parents try to control and direct their children's experiences. This very attitude imprinted you with your own parent's beliefs, many of which have prevented you from developing your own identities and following your own desires. You are temporary caretakers of these lovely Souls. Despite what you say to them, *children learn what they see* and pattern themselves after what you do, not what you say. Teach them to trust and nurture their own sensory resources. Keep them safe but encourage self-exploration and curiosity. The concept of *'It takes a village to raise a child'* is based on providing a diversity of information to nourish and validate a child's consciousness. They learn acceptance and allowance through exposure to many different kinds of people with many different kinds of beliefs. This encourages acceptance of differences and enhances their ability to express love towards themselves and others.

Patterns of Growth

Cracks will begin to appear in the façade of your conscious identity once you begin to shift your perception. You may begin to examine your values and feelings more closely by questioning past actions and reviewing future intentions. Aware of inexplicable yearnings within yourself, you may seek a more meaningful purpose for your existence. From your Soul's point of view, the process of development up to this point in your life represents the pre-school years of physical experience.

Your real education begins when you begin your own sensory explorations. Genuine intelligence lies between education and experience. You are now ready to explore the mind-body-spirit trilogy of your greater identity. This process is not time-specific and there are endless variations of 'time' spent within each phase. However, once this process begins, you can no longer plead ignorance and view the world as you did before. If you do, your experiences will begin to become more problematic than before. With the injection of a new frequency into this reality, the resulting polarization of energy will either keep you stuck or catapult you into the unknown. The frequencies upon which light and dark operate each seek to promote their own agenda. One seeks to prevent you from raising your frequency and the other to nourish the frequency of love that opens the doorway to your spiritual potentials. Where it took the baby-boomers thirty years to expand their awareness since the 70s, many can now do so in one-tenth the time. Regardless of your age, if you are willing to ride this new wave of consciousness you can 'get it' so quickly you will amaze yourselves.

Where you are right now is the springboard from where you begin your consciousness education. Since you are always in the process of becoming, you are never finished, and neither is anyone else. Sometimes others are temporarily stuck in their beliefs, and sometimes you are. You may think your life or theirs is a mess. Celebrate this state of confusion for it represents the dismantling of existing beliefs. If you remember that love allows not enslaves, and evaluates but does not judge, you can learn much from observing the challenges experienced by others. You may also have been judged as you muddled through your upheavals, and I will wager, you didn't much like it. Learn to be gentle with yourself and others.

Changing Relationships

Many of your relationships will change as you begin to direct your mental processes. The greatest change will be in your relationship with yourself. Self-nourishment is contrary to what you learned. You will find many people in your life now less interesting than before. They may also find you less interesting since you no longer feed their low frequency needs. They may attempt to sabotage your efforts not because they are nasty, but because what you now reflect to them threatens their perception of themselves. When these frequency changes make it too difficult to maintain a relationship, walk away - with love.

It is neither good nor bad. It just is. If you insist on hanging on, Spirit will orchestrate circumstances that will justify severing the relationship.

You learn about love through its presence *and* absence in your life. Mothers smother their children, families and friends manipulate each other with self-serving expectations, business associates compete for control on a win-lose basis, and when it comes to Eros love, what the dictionary defines as *"the aggregate of pleasure-directed life instincts, whose energy is derived from libido"*, partners or life-mates often consider each other trophies or possessions from whom they have a right to demand the kind of behavior that fills their own ideal expectations.

Ironically, the dictionary also defines Eros as *"Love directed towards self-realization"*, the authentic intention of expressing love. When you actualize this self-love, you 'act-u-all-eyes', or act through the many unique sensory eyes of your greater spiritual identity. Relationships provide an opportunity to understand that love grows through allowance & acceptance and self-validating nourishment. The people around you continually mirror the presence or absence of your own state of self-love. They are the means through which you know yourself. A key to understanding the dynamics of your relationships and your love of self is to ask yourself these questions:

1. Is love given freely or are expectations attached to each kindness and helping hand given or received?
2. Is the relationship based on who is in control or acceptance of each other's beliefs, feelings, and genuine needs?
3. Does the relationship allow for self-exploration, self-expression, and change?

Learning your lessons does not always result in what you may consider a satisfying resolution to problems or differences. Resolution and healing is always about you. You have no control over another person's agenda or even if they desire the same resolution as you. If they do, that is a bonus – for them. This era's fascination with public disclosure of traumatic experiences, addictions, and dysfunctions, results from the belief that those who do harm must be accountable for their actions. When you seek vindication, vengeance or remorse from the perpetrator rather than self-healing, you generally get none of the above.

As much as you want those that do harm to show remorse, most will not and many cannot. Damaged by their own childhood abuses, sadly many do not know how. It doesn't matter. You are not responsible for making the person who caused you pain or harm to see the error of their ways or to rehabilitate them. It is your responsibility to let them know how their actions affected you if you need this for your own self-healing. The purpose of disclosure and confrontation is to change *your* perception in order to release the emotional blocks attached to your experiences. Examine your issues of pain, abuse, loss, guilt, shame, and fear, and confront whomever you feel you must for your own healing. Allow those that do harm their lessons and get on with yours.

Just as you are a student in the universal schoolroom of physical life, you are also a teacher who aids in ways you do not realize. Some of this aid may be evident as a parent, friend, volunteer or by sharing your time, knowledge, and expertise with others. However, you often have the greatest impact without even being aware of it. When you transmit love by following your own bliss, you influence everyone with whom you interact. I have fond memories of receiving a gift for doing something unawares that had helped a participant in one of my evening classes. She would not tell me what when I asked and surprisingly I did not care what it was for. For me, the beautiful green stained-glass door with its three large white peace lilies was always an uplifting reminder of energy-in-motion when my own self-image needed a boost.

This physical experience enables you to create your reality as you each envision it. What often prevent you from doing so are your own self-sabotaging beliefs. So how do you stop self-sabotage? You use your sensory tools. Ask yourself these questions whenever something you desire eludes you:

1. What is the benefit of NOT getting it?
2. What problems, fears or guilt will getting it create for me?
3. What do I have to give up to get it and what am I unwilling to give up?

Once you have determined the answers create a one-time exception to expand the beliefs that hold you back. Then, visualize yourself having what you desire. See it, desire it, fully experience the sensations of having it and let it go. If you still do not get it, envision something else you want. You often get what you want when you stop consciously wanting it.

Embrace whatever your mirrors reflect and turn around the images that do not enhance or nourish you. When you are filled with love, you see all your manifestations with wonder of what they reveal about yourself. Hindsight reflects how all the individuals and circumstance in your past led you to where you are right now. There will be times when your mirrors reflect the light shining from within you and times when they do not. Draw any dark reflections into the light and own them. Love and light illuminates and thus allows you to transform these low frequency energies. Denying the dark will not negate its influence over you. You cannot ride the higher frequency of love without owning, understanding, and integrating the darker aspects of yourself. You do not have to energize them but you do have to own them.

Giving Service

Part of your physical experience is to give service while engaged in creative play on this jewel of a Planet. The service you give represents your energy-infusion of appreciation for the planetary resources you consume. Whether you are rich or poor, you all rely on Mother Earth's resources to sustain your physical bodies and to provide the raw materials to create the form constructs for your earthly games. You have the response-ability to nurture an environment severally compromised by your very existence. The energy you contribute to planetary consciousness both nourishes and damages it. Honor what Mother Earth provides and care for the little piece of earth you currently inhabit.

Your energy transmissions affect all things. Trust your impulses and desires to do what you feel needs to be done. Only do it because you genuinely want to not because you think you should. Then giving service becomes a natural byproduct of expressing the passions that bring you joy. You may seek a specific purpose for your life and miss the truth that following your own bliss uplifts and nourishes all human and environmental consciousness. Nevertheless, you cannot give what you do not possess. Every time you express love towards self, you send a ripple of higher frequency energy through both human and earth consciousness. Changing one unprofitable habit can fuel another to do the same. You have no idea what they will do with their energy once they are empowered by your actions. Your influence on one individual can literally impel them to change the world.

The church calls giving service tithing, the giving of 1/10th of what you reap. Unfortunately despite this mandate many religious coffers primarily fuel their own self-promotion, the beautification of their churches, and conversion initiatives instead of nourishing the hearts, minds, and bellies of those in need within their own communities. Call it volunteer work, charity, or tithing. Service is the energy you return to planetary and human consciousness in exchange for playing, learning, and manifesting within this framework of reality.

I find it appalling that The United States, the richest and most powerful democratic country in the world commits less than1% of its entire Economic Budget to poverty within its own borders and overseas aid combined. I am embarrassed to say the Canadian government dedicates only a fraction more. Other countries with a much smaller economic infrastructure do much more for their own people as well as providing global aid that actually reaches its destination. Most Katrina and other natural disaster victims have received none of the aid promised to-date.

On top of this indignity, America's largest insurance company has done everything it can to stall payment of legitimate insurance claims. Much of America's overseas aid commitments have also not been forthcoming and in many cases were downsized after the fact, and still go unpaid. However, they have endless funds to finance their endless wars. Most citizens of these two prosperous countries are unaware of this gross economic imbalance unless affected by this imbalance.

What will change the world is re-activating our hearts and changing our minds, one heart and mind at a time. Your individual impact on this reality is highly significant. When each human being is valued as being precious, then all humanity is nourished.

It takes courage to reclaim your identity as the grand Energy-being you are within a conscious reality constructed to hide and diminish this identity. You seek freedom and mastery of your own destiny yet fear change and reprisal from your peers. You have learned to be afraid of taking risks and making mistakes. These fears are paper dragons you can de-energize one after the other. Embrace who you are now, decide what you wish to be now, and act as if you already are that now.

> *"All truth passes through 3 stages:*
> *First, it is ridiculed,*
> *Second, it is violently opposed,*
> *Third, it is accepted as being self-evident."*
> … Arthur Schopenhauer

Shifting Your Perception

Your perception of this world also needs to change. In the Western World most of you no longer struggle for physical survival like your ancestors did and many still do in 2/3 of the rest of the world. You may think you are struggling in your quest for money and stuff, but most of you have everything you need and more. If you live in North America, consider this statistical information, forwarded in an email:

"*If you have food in the refrigerator, clothes on your back, a roof overhead, and a place to sleep … you are **richer than 75% of this world.** If you have money in the bank, in your wallet, and spare change in a dish, you are **among the top 8% of the worlds' wealthy.***

*If you get this on your own computer, you are **part of the 1% in the world who has that opportunity.***

*If you woke up this morning with more health than illness, you are **more blessed than the many who will not even survive this day.***

*If you have never experienced the fear of battle, the loneliness of imprisonment, the agony of torture, or the pangs of starvation … you are **ahead of 700 million people in the world.***

*If you can attend a church meeting without fear of harassment, arrest, torture or death … you are envied by, and **more blessed than 3 billion people in the world.***

*If your parents are still alive and still married, you are **very rare.***

*If you can hold your head up and smile, you are not the norm … **you are unique** to all those in doubt and despair.*"

You stimulate human consciousness with your leaps of faith, and diminish it with your fears and guilt. When you resist triggered manipulation or control by others you loosen the bonds of human enslavement. The more energy directed towards your own self-empowerment, the more others take heart and find the courage to change their own minds. You are never alone in your journey of self-discovery. Your feel-good surges and inspirations may be a love-infusion from someone else's leap of faith. The people you attract into your life are there because of your thoughts, not because your body is the right shape or you have enviable material possessions. They are in your life because they resonate with your energy; an energy that mirrors your own frequency of love or one you need to explore and change within yourself. All else are the illusions created with this energy.

If you want peace, stop hating war and love peace more. If you want to change the world, activate your heart to help change your mind. Many of you operate on the premise of "I'll believe it when I see it". Turn it around and you have an elemental key to life - *"When I believe it, I'll see it"*. If you want more love in your life, fill yourself so full of love there is no room for anything else. Then all you will see is the love within all things and you will begin to allow all things to be what they are.

The Soul's curiosity and need for stimulation plunged humanity into the dark ages then pulled it out again into the era of enlightenment. Now it facilitates a potential leap in consciousness that can propel human consciousness onto a new and higher frequency of existence. Each moment is a clean canvas on which you can paint new thoughts to alter your existing circumstances. You can't rest on your past achievements. You may have had a day in 1998, a Tuesday perhaps, when you felt the love and the joy of creating something wonderful. The event is not relevant now, but the thoughts and feelings that fueled it are. Recapture those feelings. Your life is a self-fulfilling prophecy based on your thoughts. You determine the kind of experiences you have by the feelings that fuel those thoughts.

'Energy flows where the mind goes'. You get more of the 'more of' all the time. For Example: Energy dedicated to resentment against a person fuels those feelings every time you bring that individual to mind, like I did with my Mother most of my life. Mentally you scan every wrong they ever did you in the blink of any eye and re-experience these events emotionally as if they were occurring now. That individual feels nothing. You feel it all! To interrupt this pattern, pause when these memories arise and choose to view them as opportunities to explore your own feeling reactions.

'The art of Wisdom is knowing what to overlook'. Begin to overlook what you do not want in your life or what is not important. If you maintain a position of judgment, anger or

resistance it is because you perceive a benefit in doing so. If your energy is directed towards what you do want for yourself, the things you do not want will wither on the vine because you no longer fuel them. Focus on what you DO want and overlook the rest.

You all know what your issues and triggers are. You can itemize them, dissect them, embellish and justify them from endless perspectives. Most of these stem from an elemental belief in your own unworthiness and lack of information about how to change it. Begin to love and cherish all the foibles, quirks, weaknesses, strengths, and biases that make you so interesting, unique, and precious. Then change what is not working for you.

You did everything you ever did for a reason, based on what you knew then in order to survive then. When you recognize a flaw in your past attitudes, methodologies or behaviors now, you have reached a wondrous realization. Addressing and validating the painful experiences that established these survival mechanisms are an important step in the process of self-healing. Pout, feel sorry for yourself or get angry. Disclose, share, and confront if need be. Weep in someone's arms or replay the events in your mind to understand them. Mourn your pain, sorrow, and disappointment passionately and fully. Then forgive those involved, forgive yourself, and move on. Integrate new information into your operating data banks that enables you to make choices that validate and empower you.

When your child comes home from school hungry and asks to be fed, do you say, *"Oh for heaven sake, you ate yesterday. How can you be hungry again?"* Many of you approach self-awareness in the same way. You have an inspirational fix here and a consciousness snack now and then and think it will do the trick. When the temporary high from these experiences wears off, you are back to your old habits. If you do not continue to choose all your responses, your mind will automatically revert to your programmed reactions.

Practice leads to mastery. New information is only as good as its application and self-awareness techniques are useless if not used. If you want to ride a bike, you need two wheels on it all the time, not just sometimes. As the director of your own physical experiences, you need both your conscious and subconscious resources to explore and expand your consciousness.

Your body, mind, and spirit all require your participation and nourishment in order to function at optimum efficiency. How you feed your spiritual needs is up to you. You can read books, listen to tapes, study a particular philosophy, take seminars and workshops, or create your own self-nourishment regime of meditation, prayer or interaction with Mother Earth. Regardless of methodology, you need to *think and feel yourself into being what you choose and decide to be.* It is what you already do so you already know how to do it. You just have to change the kind of thoughts you project and energize.

You will find useful information within every philosophy. However, just because you like the taste of chocolate covered cherries does not mean you like all the flavors in a box of chocolates. Choose what resonates with you. If you do not feel something will work for you, it will not unless you expand your belief or suspend your judgment long enough to test the process and results. You are not in contradiction of yourself if you utilize a portion of Jesus' teachings, Buddha's, a self-help guideline, even something shared by a person you briefly met on the street. If you feel you must chant 99 affirmations for 99 minutes every day for 99 days in order to feel spiritually nourished, do it. Your beliefs create your changing truths. It does not mean other information is faulty. It just means that information is not for you right now. Living well is the craft of exercising choice as you explore and express your every-changing beliefs and identity.

Energy requires thought-focus to transform itself into physical events. Therefore, thought is pro-active. You cannot stop your thoughts, but you can direct them. Attitude is a habit, and changing a habit requires vigilance and perseverance. You may not be able to control the mystery of many aspects of this physical experience, but you can learn to direct your own energy within it. This free-will universe mirrors back to you exactly what you project. How you feel about these experiences is a choice. Your mental systems will continue to run the show unless you explore the origins of your thoughts and beliefs. Humanity has become lazy because the efficiency of these mental processes makes it easy to be lazy. You give your power away when you do not choose your position within all circumstances. You accept unworthiness, disease, and hopelessness because the alternative, mastery of self, takes commitment and on-going participation.

on mastery of self . . .
"If you do not decide who you are by yourself, you will find many that will make up your mind for you, despite your protestations towards independence."
The Evergreens

This journey of self-discovery is the most lucrative investment you will ever make. No retirement or investment fund will secure your future like establishing inner security through the expansion of your own consciousness. By nourishing your mind, body, and spirit, you can stand naked without any material possessions and feel secure in knowing the manifestation of your needs and desires is only a thought away. Realize you have been living a dream others script for you. Now is the time to wake up, remember who you are, and begin to take charge of your life.

"on power of thought . . .
If you would wish to have good things in your life, then have them within yourself first. If you wish to have joy about you, then be joyful, be joyous, be happy. Remind yourself continually that you are in charge of your life. You do run your own house, for that is what has been said in Biblical scriptures; 'What is in your house?' - and that is to the meaning of yourself. If there are dark spots within yourself, eliminate them, bid them leave, for you are the master of your own destiny; and as your mind dictates, so then does your mental and physical self respond."
The Evergreens

You can begin a new Modus Vivendi right now. Life is a pro-active adventure, not a spectator sport. You now know the framework of how this 3-D reality works, how your mind works, and the diversity of sensory tools at your disposal. Use these tools to change your reality to what you envision. Some of you wait for verifiable proof before you take the plunge without realizing you will not have proof until you take the plunge. Some of you also seek the ultimate philosophy to define physical existence. Much like with computer technology, you get caught up in finding new programs to upgrade your computer and never fully use the extensive programs you already have. Trust that your needs will always be met. You already have everything you need inside you.

A few words about philosophy . . .
"First, in that 'philos' itself as a means to an end, is exactly that; it is a means to an end. It is a tool, and as a tool, must be viewed for that which it do, not for what It is.
And here we come to a definition of philosophy.
"Anything that divide the individual, negate certain parts within the individual, cause the individual to feel harm within themselves for the choices they have made and the possible choices they could make in the future, that is not a philosophy. That is but a regimen that is bounded by certain individuals' objectives in the manipulation of others."
"A philosophy must be practical. It must aid. Many philosophies fall flat because they do not wish to get their hands dirty. And that is what a philosophy need to do; plunge itself wholeheartedly into clearing the basin."
"Philosophy, in order to be philosophy, must not only present a new way, additionally it must take the energies that exist in the older systems and alter them so that they may power the new Philosophy."
The Evergreens

Changing Planetary Energies

Why is it so important to remember your spiritual identity now? We are on the threshold of the transformation of all consciousness. We all feel the effects of many dramas at play in this universe. We are running out of time because time itself is speeding up. We have forgotten our humanity and earthly connections in our fascination with technologies that already control us. We are racing through our physical experience in a state of stressful activity, forgetting where we're going, or why. Without spiritual integrity, we are playing with life, death, and weapons of destruction whose power can affect more than we can even comprehend. We are at the point of consciousness where, taking a line from the movie *Powder*, "Our humanity has not yet caught up with our technology."

Consciousness must evolve for that is the nature of what it is. We each contribute to what the results will be. Do we become spiritual creators and activate the dormant portions of our consciousness? Are we willing to create a new world of individual integrity or will apathy result in a continuation of low-frequency existence for humanity? The answer is in your heart and mind. It is your thoughts, my thoughts, and our collective thoughts that will determine our future. A polarity of consciousness is already taking place. Two major energies are vying for control of both this planet and our known universe. The outcome of this energy battle draws the attention of life forms from all corners of the cosmos. The potential to raise all consciousness to a higher frequency is observed with great interest, for our choices will affect all consciousness.

Many will continue to live as they have always done even if it becomes more difficult to do so. Then there are people like you; the brave Souls with the courage to risk changing your minds to help create a loving, peaceful, and spiritually conscious world. You are a trailblazer already if you are reading this book, meaning you already have the intention and ability to affect changes that will release humanity from its bondage. Just as the planet itself is purging itself of toxins, many of you are releasing their own toxic beliefs, attitudes, and reactions. If you do not learn to operate on this changing frequency your challenges will become greater and their effects more devastating.

In the first chapter I referred to the energy grid around the planet, and the love frequency that helps create form and substance within this reality. Operating on this higher frequency is much like plugging into a universal satellite dish with unlimited channels versus accessing only a few channels that promote low frequency expression. If you are not plugged in, you will miss the sensory data you need to evolve to this higher frequency. You are already being pressed to look at your beliefs even if you resist consciously. The energy behind this new frequency is providing the impetus to activate and stimulate your DNA and the unused 9/10th of the brain. The magical aspects of our ancient fables and myths will also begin to resurface to reinforce the wonders of what you can create with this high frequency energy.

As a species of hunters and gatherers, where we once hunted meat and gathered berries, we now seek to reclaim our greater identity. You have chosen to participate in this exploration or you would not be here. A transition in the 'time continuum' within this reality has already begun and your thoughts manifest more quickly than they did before. In spite of the prophecies and predictions of an impending doomsday, the future can be whatever you envision. It can be a wondrous new beginning or a terrible ending. It is your choice, and mine. You cannot stop the process, but you can influence the results.

A dishonored and polluted planet is beginning to re-establish its own balance. You already feel the effects of a realignment that will escalate in the coming years. Loving thoughts, self-empowerment, and personal conservation efforts to consume only what you need will also directly affect the emerging global consciousness.

When others cease to fuel your victim-based dramatizations, you will stop being a victim because there's no benefit to it. When no one aids you, you will begin to use your own resources to change your circumstances or die. When you try to control others and they do not allow it, you will cease and begin to control your own mind. As you heal yourself, your love ripples outward like an enveloping balm to those who need healing. When you love yourself, you inspire others to do the same. The point is not to stop doing things because they are 'bad' or 'wrong', but to stop energizing them because they lack integrity and do not nourish you or others.

When you live through spiritual integrity, you fulfill your own desires without harm to others. Of all the experiments played throughout history, humanity has not exercised self-regulating spiritual integrity since the early days of Atlantis and Lemuria. Your spiritual integrity lies beneath the conscious belief that you would turn into an irresponsible force of destruction if there were no rules to dictate what you can or cannot do. Spiritually, you know your consciousness is connected to all other consciousness so harming another is the same as harming yourself. You do not wake up in the morning with the intention of doing harm. You wake up with the intention of experiencing a satisfying day.

You have chosen to participate in this most exhilarating time of change. You need to affirm you are already a spiritual being until you actually believe it. All your experiences contain opportunities to affirm your higher frequency identity. When you live through love of self, you walk with your heart in the clouds - in Spirit. When you walk in Spirit, your feet tread lightly on the ground. Your inner light illuminates the path before you and serves as a beacon for those who have temporarily lost their way. You are all-ways loved by your Creator and supported by its energy.

Imagine yourself for a moment as if huddled in a small dark box created by the perception of your own unworthiness. Within this illusionary box you feel alone and disconnected, unloved and unlovable; not even worthy of the comfort of your own arms. Then imagine a small glimmer of light flickering off to one side, a spark that flickers on and off, a spark soon joined by others until a circle of pulsing light forms around you. Each mote within that circle of light is a spark of the God-energy of your own spiritual identity. Imagine this circle of light expanding around your body, slowly filling the room, and surrounding you with a glowing warmth; the illumination of your own greater consciousness. It surrounds you even while you feel the despair of your perceived unworthiness, unaware of its existence. This light patiently awaits acknowledgement, your acknowledgement, to validate you with the expansive and loving support system within which you operate. The light waits to infuse you with awareness of the true nature of your identity. You have never been alone for this light that shines around you is the radiance of who you really are.'

Your purpose for being is simple yet grander than anything you can envision. You are an Eternal Light Being experimenting with thought projection in this self-manifesting reality. The body you reside in will perish eventually, but who you really are continues as the light-energy being you always were, are, and will continue to be. You are worthy of love as a precious spiritual gem of self-actualization like no other. You are worthy of love because you are created from Love, through love, with the frequency of Love. The answers you seek and the keys to the wonder of yourself are already within you and love unlocks the doorway to your heart and mind to reveal the treasure lying within.

Prologue

An Alternate Creation Story

IN the beginning there is a creative energy called **All That Is** that was so eternal, it does not even remember its own origin. This Original Creator is a loving and curious consciousness of pure light-energy experiencing and exploring its own thoughts. In the infinite space of timelessness, the Creator thought into being galaxies, universes and planets. Wanting to learn even more about itself, the Creator thought into existence a grand plan. It would split its own consciousness and send these separate energy pulses of itself into space on various frequencies to see how they would evolve on their own within the cosmic template it has created. Since each energy aspect was a part its own consciousness, All That Is would learn more of itself as these sparks experienced their own thought-creations. All That Is also knew these sparks of consciousness would eventually find their way back to their origin - itself. Thus, All That Is would become more. Knowing more, All That Is would again split its consciousness, repeating the process with an expanded storehouse of knowledge and experience because of what these sparks of consciousness experienced.

Over time, within the void of 'no time', some of these independent sparks became grand Entities in their own right. They eventually evolved into such high frequency Light Beings that they discovered the formula for the creation of life within their own origins. They began to experiment as All That Is did. They split their own consciousness into separate aspects, mixing and mingling the required elements in order to create a diversity of species and life forms to inhabit the many worlds thought into existence. Over time, they perceived themselves as Creator Gods. Although there is no time, some of them even became so enraptured by the diversity of their creations they believed themselves to be the Original Creators of the Universe.

In one corner of this universe our planet, affectionately known as Terra, was a favored playground for these Creator Gods and their offspring. Terra was rich in mineral resources and its three dimensional reality provided a unique kind of sensory experience. Several of these Gods came to like the power and adulation the low frequency humans they had created accorded them on Terra. Although they vaguely remembered their own origin, they did not want to merge back with the thought-energy of All That Is. They preferred to maintain sovereignty within this sensory and resource-rich dimension and wielded their Godly powers over the planet's various low frequency species for their own intentions. Some of these Creator Gods eventually left to evolve on different frequencies and lost interest in Terra for long periods in this planet's timeframe. Others just popped in every few thousand years or so, to see what the lowly humans were up to.

Several of these Creator Gods came to love their creations like their children and pampered pets. Curious about the limited sensory focus of these single-gender humans they even mated and merged with them to experience the density of physical form for themselves. Fascinated by the sensations these physical bodies provide, and unrestrained by the limitations of sequential time as the humans were, they often inserted themselves into humanity's consciousness to play their own Godly games or to influence human evolution. Through the infusion of their knowledge, great civilizations flourished on Terra, civilizations all too often destroyed by their own Celestial war games.

Many Gods completely forgot the love frequency of their own origin. They began to bicker over ownership of Terra's valuable mineral resources and easily manipulated low frequency humans. They sent their children there to play so they could practice manifestation in this reality and indulgently ignored the destruction of the planet wrought by their childish games. While the ownership of Terra often changed Godly hands, its life-forms helpless pawns in these celestial squabbles and battles, other Creator Gods were busy with a grand secret experiment.

They wondered what would happen if the consciousness of this lowly species could evolve. Some of these Creator Gods were specialists in genetic manipulation and had seeded many life forms on many other dimensions. Awed by the resilient and adaptable nature of Terra's primitive humans, they gathered genetic material from different species throughout the universe and combined these components with human genes in various ways. Although some combinations failed to flourish, one in particular endured. The Godly Geneticists secretly encoded their own DNA into their human consciousness to ensure the species would survive, a DNA containing the memory of their own divine ancestry. They knew the ownership of this planet would go back to Gods that are more benevolent eventually. Although rendered dormant by the existing fourth-dimensional owners of the planet, they hid these genetic keys in the second strand of the human double helix. They also encoded strands the frequency of love would stimulate when needed.

By splitting the consciousness of humans into the two polarities of masculine and feminine energy, the Scientist Gods ensured the physical survival of the species. Biologically attuned to the moon cycles within this reality reproduction was somewhat regulated but guaranteed. This experiment created a unique opportunity for these Gods to learn more about their own unified polarities through the expression of its separate aspects. To ensure success they also encoded the formula for polarity unification into human consciousness, an important component for its possible ascension to higher frequencies in one of many probable futures of the species. These Creator Gods knew the potential of their beloved humans could be realized when this coding was triggered by the frequency of love.

Thus, constructed from a vast gene pool comprised of many different species, humanity was secretly programmed with the potential to reach their own Godly fourth dimensional frequency of consciousness. Many within the Cosmos anticipated this event, needed it in fact, for its effects would ripple through all consciousness and propel these Creator Gods themselves to higher frequencies. Since many had forgotten their own origins, only such a monumental consciousness shift would trigger the reunion with All That Is many longed for.

Mind you, not all the Creator Gods were thrilled over this possibility. Who would adore them if these lowly humans also became Godly? Tremendous battles of intention raged on many dimensional levels over an experiment that was no longer a secret. Every million years or so these battles resulted in unimaginable destruction of the planet Terra and its inhabitants. Every time this occurred, the Geneticist Gods again secretly encoded the humans with their own DNA. After these destructive battles, as ownership of Terra changed hands, the planet's consciousness - a living entity empowered by the loving frequency of All That Is - rejuvenated itself to support the new biological life forms seeded by these Creator Gods.

Eventually the consciousness of these Creator Gods split into two primary frequencies of intention. One was the dark low frequency energy of dominance and enslavement. The other was the light frequency of love that promotes free will and creative expression. As a frequency of love, All That Is allowed this fluctuation of planetary ownership. It could learn even more of itself through these polarized Creator Gods. All That Is has plans unknown to these Creator Gods, plans wherein Terra's precious encoded humans could through their own awakening re-balance the predominant masculine polarity of this universe through its own infusion of feminine energy. A merging of the two would propel all consciousness and itself to an even higher frequency of expression.

Ruling from their fourth-dimensional reality the existing God Owners of Terra did not want their lowly humans to gain their abilities and knowledge. They selected a few bloodlines with which they mated to ensure their DNA remained in these bloodlines. The enticement of unimaginable power and wealth guaranteed these ruling families continued to promote their own controlling agenda. These earthly rulers created systems, laws, and other restrictions to keep humanity on a frequency low enough to prevent it from realizing it was being controlled and manipulated. To ensure success, these Ruling Gods surrounded the planet with powerful energy grids to contain their systems of bondage. This grid kept the planet screened from galactic interference or penetration by other more benevolent Creator Gods. These grids were so strong, even the Love Frequency could only penetrate their electromagnetic shield to a small degree.

Some of the Creator Gods that inhabited this planet before these Ruling Gods claimed Terra had another bag of tricks up their own Godly sleeves. They had implanted other powerful codes into the human gene pool. If the humans accessed these codes through their subconscious, the existing electromagnetic grids would weaken. Once the encoded humans collectively reached higher frequency consciousness, the shield constructed by the planet's existing Rulers would weaken and simply fall away. In reclaiming the loving frequency of their own higher consciousness, humanity would be able to transmit the Love Frequency throughout the galaxy. Other Creator Gods could then enter this dimension and help shift the existing balance of power.

While this plan plays out in timelessness, All That Is continues to beam the pulse of its own Love Frequency at this planet through the Milky Way. There are multitudes of others species awaiting this consciousness shift in order to expand their own consciousness. As more and more humans awaken from their conscious dream-state and allow the frequency of love to trigger the knowledge encoded in their physical bodies, the grids designed to keep Earth in bondage are slowly dissolving. Within this free-will Universe none of the Gods can interfere directly. Despite their long-time complaisant arrogance, ruling Gods on the fourth dimension scramble to contain this contamination of self-awareness that has already taken root on our lovely planet. Benevolent Creator Gods cheer humans on and lovingly offer assistance when asked. Both can only watch and wait to see what humans will do with this opportunity to expand their consciousness. What will they create with this frequency of Love?

Your greatest service to yourself is to nourish yourself and *love* is the key to kick-start this process. As you expand your awareness of yourself, all else expands. Your victories uplift all humanity, your understandings nourish all consciousness and love towards yourself the key that enables the manipulation of energy and manifestation of your spiritual intentions and desires. To love your Self is to love all else, to honor your Self is to honor all else. Mass consciousness is the energy transmitted by every human being on this planet - a reflection of our collective state of mind and heart. So what is this world reflecting back to you about who you are?

Those who now Rule the planet rule only because humanity unknowingly complied with their low frequency agenda. The Geneticist-Gods expel celestial chuckles as their secret plans begin to unfold. They are not entirely sure where this awakening will lead human consciousness, and in turn, their own. As the eternal frequency of love emitted by All That Is grows stronger, what has been set into motion will play out - through the minds and hearts of humans. If we are willing to participate, a new creation story is about to begin again – on a frequency of love.

References

1. The Evergreens Gentle Book of Practical Living Pointers – by Michael Blake Reid & Philippa M. Lee
   (a) Quotes by the Evergreens used by permission.
   (b) Models developed for the New Age Centre by the Evergreens, used by permission.

2. *Page 10* – Gregorian Calendar – World Calendar Years, Lunar, Jewish, Solar, Julian & Gregorian Calendars – www:limemits.com/wcp/World_Calendar_proposal.htm

3. *Page 11* – French experiments with Energetics (1960-1970) by Antoine Priore – Reversing Diseased Cells (a) http://www.explorepub.com/articles/energetics,html
   (b) http://www.cheniere.org/techpapers/Visions%20 2000%20paper.doc
   (c) Kaznacheyev in Solviet Union Confirms Priore's Results Using his Electromagnetic Phase Conjunction Machine.
   (d) CIA MK-ULTRA Experiments on Mind Controlled Children – based on various articles on

U.S. & Russian experiments, declassified from 1954 onward.

4. Scalar Energy – Scalar Wars (The Brave New World of Scalar Electromagnetics by Bill Morgan) re: Nikolas Tesla – http://www.davidicke.net/mysteries/reports/scalar.html, http://twm.co.nz/Beard_scalem.html,

5. Free Energy – http://depalma.pair.com/Absurdity/Absurdity07/ProblemOfFreeEnergy.html

6. *Page 41* – Flea experiments – (a) Article by Desert Animal Adaptation of Desert Agriculture, Jacob Blaustein Institute for Desert Research, Ben Gurion University of the Negave
(b) Jump performance of seven desert fleas – Journal of Insect Psychology, (c) Article in 1970s issue of Psychology Today.

7. *Page 83* – (a) Lemuria, A Home – translated from The ancient records of the Rosucrucian Order. The Rosicrucian Fellowship publishes & sells books on Esoteric Christianity and Philosophy, Spiritual Astrology, and Bible Interpretation. Max Heindel, an Initiate of the Rosicrucian Order, founded the Rosicrucian Fellowship & wrote his many books based on firsthand knowledge of occult facts.
(b) The Lost Continent of Mu by Col. James Churchward, first published in 1959

8. *Page 129* – Russian Food Studies Experiments (children choosing their own foods), (a) Psychology Today article (1970)

9. The New Age Centre (1970-1980) – Alpha & Insight Training, Advanced Insight Training